★

"Tell me what happened, Julia," Nick whispered.

"I don't know what happened. He was fine, talking about how good breakfast was and then he went into the bathroom. He didn't look good when he came out."

"Look," he said. "They're moving him, taking him to the hospital. It'll be all right, Julia. He'll be okay."

I glanced over at Nick. He stared down at his empty hands, and his eyes were filled with profound helplessness. I knew he didn't believe what he was saying.

★

SO DEAR TO WICKED MEN

Takis & Judy Iakovou

WORLDWIDE.

TORONTO • NEW YORK • LONDON
AMSTERDAM • PARIS • SYDNEY • HAMBURG
STOCKHOLM • ATHENS • TOKYO • MILAN
MADRID • WARSAW • BUDAPEST • AUCKLAND

To our daughters, Angie and Mari
who have had faith in us throughout...
no parents have ever been more blessed.

SO DEAR TO WICKED MEN

A Worldwide Mystery/June 1998

First published by St. Martin's Press, Incorporated.

ISBN 0-373-26277-9

Printed in U.S.A.

ACKNOWLEDGMENTS

The authors would like to gratefully acknowledge the following individuals for their assistance in matters pertaining to the law, investigation and immigration: Attorneys Stanley Durden, of Athens, Georgia, and Lance Tunick, of Golden, Colorado; and Captain Clinton Spear, formerly of the Atlanta Police Department and currently Captain of Security at DeKalb Peachtree Airport in Atlanta.

In addition, we would like to express our appreciation to all the friends and fellow writers who gave of their time and talents to help make this book a reality: our agent, Joan Brandt, and editor, Elisabeth Story; Beverly and Charles Connor, Jim Howell, Diane Trap, Alice Gay, Dannie Prather, Larry McDougald and especially Harriette Austin and all the members of her Writer's Workshop.

And finally, thank you to our family: the Kerleys, Conahans and Iakovous. Just knowing you were behind us helped.

...for from enemies' devising our much-adored city is afflicted
   before long by conspiracies so dear to wicked men.
Such evils are churning in the home country, but, of the impoverished,
   many have made their way abroad on to alien soil,
sold away, and shamefully going in chains of slavery...

—Solon of Athens
c. 630-c. 550 B.C.

ONE

GLENN BOHANNON'S breakfast was served on a gleaming white platter edged in a geometric pattern of deep, Mediterranean blue. Nick had garnished it with an artfully twisted slice of Valencia orange and a sprig of fresh mint. I set it in front of Glenn, on a blue tablecloth that matched the trim on the platter, and added a side order of homemade biscuits. Murder à la carte.

IF, AS THE ANCIENTS believed, all men are accompanied by *daimones,* agents of the gods to act out their will in our lives, then surely our *daimon* must be Epimetheus. Unlike his brother, Prometheus, whose name means foresight, Epimetheus, "Hindsight," has never been celebrated for his good judgment. Witness his disastrous marriage to Pandora, who unleashed all evil upon the world.

It seems to me, now, that we were players on a stage, manipulated by Zeus from a great director's chair. Perhaps he was flanked by the lesser gods, who paused in their feasting and infighting to watch us in amusement. They have a cruel streak, these gods, often choosing the most battered and vulnerable of humans to play out their conflicts. Darkly bruised clouds must have rumbled and tumbled under the divine fingertips, gathering finally over our little college town of Delphi. And there, two hapless mortals, clinging to each other and struggling to right our lives, innocently stepped onto the proscenium. But there would be no deus ex machina ending to this drama. The mortals would have to find their own way out.

Had a great tragedian written the script, there might have been dark skies and an ominous roll of foreshadowing thunder. But there was not. In its place, a crackling October sunrise sliced the horizon, and a light wind shook the last crimson leaves from their branches. The crisp air stung my nose. It was a day so fresh and clean, so promising, as to bear the heart away.

There should have been dramatic dialogue, high passion and melodrama, but these elements are difficult to sustain at breakfast, in a crowded cafe, when sunlight splashes through the windows and sparkles on the glassware and cutlery. The dialogue was mundane, and the only passion was a fruit served on the "Tropical Breakfast" plate. Melodrama arrived later in a gray Pontiac.

The playwright's stylus would also have fashioned a chorus to chant the history and predict the downfall of the heroes. They would have intoned the details of a tragic accident on a twisted mountain road four months earlier, and told of the comings and goings of strangers in the shadows of night. They might have sung of wolves and coyotes and helpless sheep.

But Euripides did not pen the script. In fact, when it had all been played out, from the opening ruse to the final bow, Aristophanes might have enjoyed our antics very much. And only now, in the company of Hindsight, have Nick and I begun to understand our own fatal flaw. Naïveté, thy name is Lambros.

Ironically, we did have a chorus—a cluster of coffee-drinking cronies, not unlike the groups that plague most restaurants. We called them the Buffaloes, and they were seated on A deck when I arrived.

They huddled around the tables, grazing on the fodder of local gossip. Tammy stood among them, coffeepot in hand, snacking on one of the doughnuts they'd brought in from Dinah's, while Rhonda scurried over B deck. I dropped my purse and the deposit bag at the register. A Tammy Wynette oldies tape throbbed through the sound system. Nick wouldn't like it. He's very particular about that system, claiming it's too delicate to be handled by the crew. I took it down a couple of notches before he could discover it.

To the right of the register was an ever-growing stack of bills. Most of them were making encore appearances but there, on top, was a new one. The return address read Delphi General Hospital. I opened it and staggered against the counter as the Total Due figure leapt off the page. It fluttered out of my hands as I hastily made for the Bunn-o-matic in the wait station, pouring my first cup of coffee with shaky hands and dumping in a couple of creams.

"Come on, maybe we ought to clear out of here and let him cook. Nick, we'll see you at seven. We're at Norm's this week." Read herded several of the Buffaloes out of the kitchen.

"Hey, Julia. Where've you been?" Lee shot Norm a sharp crack in the ribs and turned to me, embarrassed.

"Nice to have you back, Julia." He glanced only briefly at me before turning away. I understood his awkwardness and knew that I would have to deal with it for a while. It was one of the reasons I had stayed away from the cafe for almost a month. I had to come to terms with the loss myself, knowing it would be incumbent upon me to make the others more comfortable with it. They moved on out, shuffling and whispering, glancing back at me from time to time. I peeked through the wait-station door into the kitchen.

Nothing had changed. Steam spiraled over the stove from a pan of bubbling grits. A pair of eggs crackled in the skillet and the oven fan droned, exhaling the dry smell of baking biscuits. A double clump of hash browns sizzled on the grill. Over it all, the radio above the stove blared Gloria Estefan.

Nick was there, his black hair poached into ringlets around the band of his Greek sailor's cap. He had formed a conga line of one, swiveling his hips between the grill and steel tables, lithe and disciplined as a flamenco dancer. I ducked into the kitchen to watch him, conscious, as always, of the buzz that ran down my midline and straight to my knees at the very sight of him. In the six years we'd been married, that hadn't changed, except possibly to grow stronger. He thrust his arms left and right, swirling the pancake shaker to the beat of the music. As the song reached its crescendo, he spun on his toes, poured wide circles of batter onto the sizzling grill and with a trill of his tongue cried, *"Arriba! Arriba!"* Nick is a morning person. I love him anyway.

I waited until the performance ended, then topped off my coffee and poured him a cup. "It's getting busy out there. What do you need?"

He danced to the stove, flipped the eggs and lined up a platoon of bacon strips in formation. Gloria Estefan had been replaced by

Billy Joel. Nick grabbed my waist and cha-chaed me out of the grill into the main kitchen. His breath smelled of mint when he tickled my earlobe with the tip of his tongue.

"You! I need you!" He spun me until my toes scarcely touched the tile floor.

"You're in a good mood this morning."

"I'm just glad you're back." He stopped, looked closely at me. "Are you sure you're okay? Ready to come back to work?"

I nodded. I didn't want him to know how tight my throat was, how hard it was for me to breathe. The last time I had stood in this kitchen, I was almost five months pregnant. Just starting to show. How empty my clothes seemed now.

Still, it was not my own grief that concerned me, but Nick's. It had taken all that we had, my obstetrician, his associate, the nurse and me, to convince Nick that my losing the baby was not his fault. It had nothing whatever to do with the cafe, with the hours on my feet. It was, at the least, an act of nature. More likely, an act of God.

Whatever Nick had felt about the loss itself, he never said. But the image stayed with me, the luminous joy on his face when I announced my pregnancy. He had danced then, too. During the busy lunch rush, he had taken to the floor between the decks, moving in the slow, graceful steps of the *zembekiko* which represent, to all Greeks, the heart and soul of the man. And that was what he had lost. But he never talked about it—only about me.

I had returned to work resolved to put the best face on it, for both our sakes. We would recover from the hurt and disappointment, and maybe, in a year or so, we would try again. Meanwhile, we still had our other baby—the business. It, too, was the fruit of our partnership, an obscurely comforting thought during an otherwise bitter time.

"In fact, I'm really glad to be back." I picked up the dance step, swaying dramatically. Nick pulled me close and brushed my hair with his lips.

"But if you start to get tired, or it gets too hard..."

"I'll be fine. Besides, it's Monday. We probably won't be that busy."

"Oh, we're going to be busy, all right. Have you looked outside? The weather's porfect."

"*Per.* Perfect."

"That's what I said. We're going to be packed today."

We continued our dance, back past the dish machine, toward the freezer, cooler, and dry storage. "Oh no!" I stumbled over Nick's feet.

"Step-step, step-step-step," he whispered in my ear.

"I know. Nick, what's Foxy doing here?" I gestured to a stocky, gray-haired man who stood outside the cooler. He was holding a large motor in his hands and shaking his head slowly from side to side.

"Whole compressor's got to be replaced, Nick."

Nick's step flagged and I felt a little droop in his shoulders. "How much?"

Foxy shrugged. "I'll see if I can find you a used one first. If not, I'll call you with the bad news."

"Have you got something on the grill?"

Nick twirled me around and headed me back into the kitchen. "Just Glenn's order. Oh, and pancakes!" We picked up the pace.

"Well, there are probably six tickets in the window by now."

Our hesitation step carried us back into the grill. "Up-ton girl," he sang tunelessly. "That's you." He left me at the worktable and two-stepped on to the grill.

"Mmm. More like midtown, I think. What do you need?"

"Biscuits," he said, flipping a stack of pancakes onto a plate. "I'm gonna need biscuits."

I floured my hands and the rolling pin, mechanically rolling and cutting the biscuits. In a way it was true. Before I met him, I was living in a "white-bread world"—quiet, orderly, focused on my own career. Marrying Nick certainly changed all that. But it was okay. I liked the frenzy of restaurant life—the tension of the unpredictable. I liked the customers and the vendors. Most of the time I even liked the Buffaloes.

And if I liked the business, Nick lived for it—nursed it, coddled it, guided, and occasionally rebuked it like a spoiled child. The Oracle Cafe ranked in his top three, occasionally interchangeable with soccer and me. Until the miscarriage, which propelled me indisputably to the top.

He tapped the bell and Rhonda swooped in to pick up her order. "Have you got a game tonight?"

Nick nodded. "At Norm's, at seven."

"I don't know what you see in them, Nick."

He shrugged, turned the hash browns a couple of times, scooped them up and tossed them onto a plate with eggs and bacon. "I like to play poker. Besides, they're harmless. Just a bunch of rednecks." He twisted an orange slice, planted a mint leaf on top and slid the plate through the window, giving the bell a perfunctory tap.

"That's *red*necks, Nick. Red necks. And it would be nice if, just once in a while, they'd buy breakfast."

"Well, Glenn does, anyway." He scraped the grill and pushed the crumbs into the grease trap. "Biscuits ready?"

I pulled the pan and tossed him a couple of hot ones while he checked over the tickets. He gave the bell a good smack. "Your order's up here, Tammy. Where is she?"

"Probably doing her hair. Nick," I hesitated. "The hospital bill came yesterday. I saw you hadn't opened it. I'm afraid I did."

"Let's talk about it later. No point spoiling the day just yet." He called through the window. "Tammy, pick up this order! It's getting cold!"

"I'll take it, Nick. We're going to have to do something about her."

"I'll talk to her after the rush. That's Glenn's order. Go ahead and take it. I've got things under control now."

I tugged off my apron and grabbed the plate, snagging the side of biscuits, on my way to deliver death.

TWO

Norm reached over Glenn's head, grabbed his cup and held it out to me. "You're in my seat, Mitch," he growled. Mitch went on as though he hadn't heard him.

"You got to accommodate the handicapped. Gotta be ramps. Doors on the stalls gotta be wide enough. Life was a helluva lot easier before we started making concessions to all these minorities. And I'll tell you when it started, too. Right out there in Montgomery in the fifties. Beginning of the end." Having finished his speech, Mitch got up and lumbered around to the end of the table. He pointed an accusing finger at Glenn. "You better be thinking about that when we go over your plans." Read moved in to take Mitch's seat, the game of musical chairs in full swing.

"Where the hell is Morgan this morning?"

"Planning-commission meeting at seven," Lee said.

"Well, I wish he'd hurry up and find out where that highway's going in. Land values are going to roller-coaster as soon as they make that announcement."

"Man, these are really good!" Glenn scraped up the last of his hash browns and grinned at the other Buffaloes. "I'd offer you fellas a bite," he drawled, "if there were any left!" He turned to me as I refilled his coffee.

"I don't know how anyone can start the day on a doughnut, do you, Julia? I mean, they say breakfast is the most important meal of the day."

"So I've heard."

He turned back to the others. "A man just can't do business on an empty stomach!"

Sonny gazed down into the cup I had just refilled. "Oh well," he said, "I usually eat before I come down here."

I turned away, resisting the temptation to pour coffee down his shirt collar. Glenn winked at me. "We've got to keep these people in business, though, Sonny. It's hardly worth the time they spend serving us for a couple of cups of coffee.''

That was one of the many reasons I liked Glenn Bohannon. A big, broad man with a west Texas drawl and a heart to match his home state, Glenn was considerate and generous.

I moved around the tables to splash coffee into their waiting cups, smiling as though my lips had been starched. It was no wonder their wives sent them out for breakfast. The tabletop was littered with sugar cascading from half-opened packets, crumpled napkins, banana peels, and puddles of creamy coffee. Both salt and pepper shakers lay on their sides, spilling their contents all over the blue cloth. I righted them with an elaborate flourish.

Sonny thrust his mug—that is, his own personal mug that says ''Sonny Weaver Insurance—Fire Life Casualty—Insure and Feel Secure''—at me. He was wearing a turquoise baseball cap that matched the clasp of his bolo tie. White, fuzzy letters advertised Lee Blaine's company, Blaine Diversified, across the crown. Sonny is very fond of baseball caps, especially the ones that promote his customers. It's a Buffalo quid pro quo.

''Oh, Julia doesn't mind. Now, about the insurance on that place, Glenn. I need you to come by sometime today and give me a rough estimate of what you're gonna need....''

''All right. Look, I'll be back in a minute.'' Glenn excused himself and headed for the rest room.

''Now, what time are you figuring to have him come in, Sonny? We're supposed to go look at another lot today. If I've shown him one, I've shown him twenty-five.'' Read reached for a creamer, found the bowl empty and held it up. He raised an eyebrow at me.

''Julia?''

I swallowed hard, nodded, and stalked off the deck. Glenn was returning from the men's room, weaving slightly across the floor. His normally florid complexion had turned the color of cream gravy and a wisp of strawberry blond hair hung over his brow. Before I could intercept, he collided with Rhonda, who was hauling a tray off C deck. It flew up over her shoulder, dishes and syrup pitchers smashing to the floor.

"Oh damn, I'm sorry." He stooped to help her, staggered, and leaned heavily against the wall.

I was at their side in a second. Sweat poured off his brow and a stream of pinkish saliva dripped from the corner of his mouth. He wiped it on his sleeve. "Glenn? Are you all right?"

He nodded. "Think I'll just go up there and sit down for a minute, if you don't mind. I'll...I'll give her a little something for cleaning it up." He reached into his jacket pocket and pulled out a money clip.

"No, it's okay. We'll take care of it. Why don't you just sit down?"

Glenn agreed, waved my hand away, and staggered toward the deck. I turned back to the mess on the floor.

"I thought he saw me coming, Julia. I'm really sorry." Rhonda grimaced at the food scraps and pools of syrup on the floor.

"I thought he did too. He must have lost his balance. Listen, go get the mop and bucket, will you? I'll start picking this up."

I had half of the broken dishes back on the tray when the first cry went up from A deck. The Buffaloes were clustered around Glenn.

"He's choking!"

Lee stood behind him, his hands laced over Glenn's stomach in a Heimlich maneuver. Glenn's arms were flailing, his eyes wide and round, face flushed purple. I flew to the order window.

"Nick, get out here! Now!"

He threw down his spatula, met me as I rounded the corner of the wait station. "What's the matter?"

Words failing, I pointed mutely toward the deck.

"Get his jacket off. Lay him down, gotta get him flat!"

"He's choking, you idiot. Can't lay him flat. Pull him up, try to get behind him—"

"Leave him in the chair, get his head between his knees. That always works for Pat's mother—"

"Tried a Heimlich. Not food. Let's get him on the table." Lee yanked off Glenn's jacket and tossed it to Tammy, who slung it over her arm.

Nick was already across the room, punching numbers into the phone. I reached A deck in a couple leaps, found Glenn stretched on the table, Lee's head pressed against his chest. Morgan had arrived and was watching it all from the doorway.

"A doctor! Is anyone here a doctor? A nurse?"

The breakfast crowd swam in front of me, faces starkly solemn. No one came forward.

Glenn's color had faded to a waxy white. His body shuddered a couple of times before becoming very still. Nick leaped over the railing, tipped Glenn's face sideways, stuck his fingers into his mouth.

"No food." He pressed his cheek against Glenn's mouth. "He's breathing."

Relief flooded through me with the warbling of sirens in the distance. Blue lights were heading down Broadway. The Buffaloes saw them, too. They crowded around the windows, their breath fogging the glass. The sheriff's tires squealed into our entrance, throwing gravel so hard it clattered against the windows. An ambulance descended the hill from the opposite direction, cornered on two wheels, and screamed to a stop at the front door.

Two deputies reached the dining room first, pushing us all back off the deck and away from Glenn's still body. The EMTs moved into action, jerking open Glenn's shirt, taking vital signs, working in an efficient, experienced partnership.

Tammy hovered nervously beneath the deck railing. A deputy pulled her back from the deck, took Glenn's jacket out of her arms and hung it over the railing. Rhonda dropped into a chair at the family table, the limp string mop still in her hands. Her face was as pasty as Glenn's.

Nick put his arm around my shoulder to steady me. I hadn't realized I was shaking. "Tell me what happened, Julia," he whispered.

"I don't know! I don't know what happened. He was fine, talking about how good breakfast was and then he went into the bathroom. He didn't look good when he came out. Then he ran into Rhonda, and they spilled this tray and, oh Nick, it's the biggest mess..." I could hear my voice rising, could feel my control slipping away. "...and there's syrup all over the floor, and eggs and...oh, poor Glenn! I wonder if it's his heart?"

Nick pointed to the deck. The EMTs were moving Glenn to a

stretcher. They had inserted an IV in his hand and began carefully negotiating the steps of the deck.

"Look," he said. "They're moving him, taking him to the hospital. It'll be all right, Julia. He'll be okay."

I watched their slow progress, listened to Glenn's strained breathing under an oxygen mask. They had covered him on the stretcher, but the pointed toes of his cowboy boots stuck out, feet splayed in Chaplinesque fashion.

I glanced over at Nick. He stared down at his empty hands, and his eyes were filled with profound helplessness. I knew he didn't believe what he was saying.

And in the background, the husky voice of Tammy Wynette droned over the speakers. *"Stand by your man..."*

SAM LAWLESS arrived as the ambulance was pulling out, parking his unmarked car in a distant corner of the lot. I was glad to see him, a valued and trusted friend. He was also an investigator for the Sheriff's Department.

"Heard the 10-46 on my radio. What happened?"

Nick told him about Glenn's attack. The deputies had moved everyone over to B and C decks, one interviewing the Buffaloes while the other took statements from the other customers. As they were released, they came to the register with their tickets. I couldn't bring myself to charge them, but waved them out the door with a weak smile. "Our treat today, just don't forget about us tomorrow," I mumbled, embarrassed.

The Buffaloes were the last to leave. One deputy, whose name I learned was Jimmy, scratched his head, took notes, admonished them to tell it one at a time. Rhonda quietly finished picking up the broken glass, while Tammy looked on, shifting from one foot to the other. Rhonda tried to work around her, but finally threw her hands up.

"If you're not gonna help me, you could at least move out of my way!"

"Oh. Okay. Whatcha want me to do?"

Rhonda pushed her hair back out of her eyes. "Start mopping this up while I get started over there." She pointed at A deck, where the remnants of the chaotic morning were spread from the windows to the door.

Tammy pulled the mop out of the bucket and listlessly swiped at the syrup pools. "Well, I didn't spill it, after all," she muttered. Rhonda ignored her, grabbed a bus tub from the wait station and picked her way over the mess to A deck.

"So he just keeled over at the table? Without any warning?"

I put a cup of coffee down in front of Sam and dropped into a seat at the family table. "No, not exactly. He went to the men's room, and when he came out he didn't look like he felt well. He was really pale and kind of...dizzy, or disoriented."

"What should I do with this, Sam?"

Rhonda held out Glenn's jacket, a lightweight navy blue blazer. A red-and-blue paisley tie stuck its tongue out of one of the pockets.

"I'll take it." He patted the jacket pockets.

I glanced over at Tammy. She had stopped mopping, stood biting her lower lip and staring at Sam. When she caught me watching her, she tossed back her hair and went to work. I turned back to Sam. He was sitting oddly still.

He held a small leather wallet close to his chest, summarily snapped it shut, slipped it into his back pocket, and hastily excused himself. At the register, he jabbed a number into the phone and stared grimly out into the parking lot.

"Nick, stop Rhonda! Don't let her touch anything else. Yeah, it's Lawless. Listen, I want you to check on something for me. Right away."

I followed Nick over to A deck. "What's going on, Nick? Did you see Sam's face?"

"I don't know. Rhonda, you can leave that for now. No, it's okay, really. Just leave it all there and go see if Tammy needs some help. She's not doing much of a job there."

"Mmm," she said. "Go figure."

I stooped to pick up a broken cup, remembered Sam's instructions, and left it on the floor below the deck railing. "Why won't he let us clean up?"

"I don't know, Julia. Something's really wrong here." We

walked back to the family table. Sam dropped the phone into the cradle and came around the register counter.

"How is he? Any word?"

"Not yet."

"Damn," Nick said. "I feel really awful about this. Glenn's a nice guy." He glanced at his watch. "Listen, Sam, I don't want to be callous or anything, but I've got to get started on lunch. Julia saw more than I did anyway."

Sam shook his head grimly, looked away from Nick to A deck. "Can't do it, Nick. I'm sorry, but I'm going to have to shut you down for the day."

"Shut us down?" My stomach somersaulted. "Why?"

"I don't want to alarm you, Julia, but I've got a crime-scene team on the way." He held up his hand to Nick's silent question. "It's just routine, and I asked them to park around back. Out of sight of the street. That's the best I can do, I'm afraid."

"Wait, Sam. I don't understand. A crime-scene team?"

Sam fumbled with a napkin, rolling the corners into paper strings. He didn't meet my eyes. "Like I said, Julia. Just routine. Bohannon was a pretty young man. What would you say? Thirty? Thirty-five?"

"Probably."

"Well, at that age...Department policy. Don't take anything at face value. You know."

Nick watched him with quiet skepticism scrawled across his dark features. "You don't think it was his heart?"

"Don't know. Probably was." Sam dropped little paper balls into an ashtray. He pushed himself back from the table. "Tell you what. Let's get the rest of these guys," he nodded toward the remaining Buffaloes, "and move them on out of here so my people can do their work."

Nick and I watched silently as Sam lumbered across the dining room to Rhonda, took her hand and drew her aside. They had been dating, I knew, for more than a year, although they kept it quiet. He was probably canceling plans for the evening, a fact which, I felt, did not bode well for us.

The crime-scene team entered through the back door, as Sam

had promised, just as Nick ushered Lee and Mitch, the last remaining Buffaloes, out the front and turned the Closed sign over. We watched them set up, believing all the while that it was, as Sam claimed, strictly routine. And then the phone rang again.

THREE

NICK AND I sat at the family table in the dining room holding hands, feet planted hard on the floor to remind ourselves that the bottom had not dropped out of our world. It just felt like it had. The feeling was all too familiar, a sick sense of loss that catapulted me straight back to my hospital room and the first lonely hours when I realized that the baby was not to be. Only Nick had been able to see me through that terrible time, silently sharing the grief with me. And now, he must have felt it, too, because he squeezed my fingers tightly.

Sam had set up three tables on the tile floor between the decks. We mutely watched as a team of three officers in plain clothes unpacked their gear.

A photographer snapped close-up and distance shots of the tables, broken bits of crockery, sugar packets, and Buffalo droppings on A deck. Sam consulted with the slender, mustached young deputy, Jimmy. Jimmy had recorded each customer's name, address, and statement in a notebook and was describing his own movements from the time of his arrival until Sam made the scene. His partner, a short, heavyset man with pumpkin-colored hair, sorted through his notes. Rhonda sat on C deck chain-smoking, while Tammy brushed her hair and toyed with her press-on fingernails.

A second crime-scene officer carefully arranged envelopes, tags, pens, boxes, bottles on one table; scalpels, wooden tongue depressors, tweezers, and the like were laid out on a second. The third officer loaded a video camera, panned the room logging in date, time, and place through the attached microphone, stopping to consult with the stationary photographer.

When the phone shrilled at the register, Nick grabbed it, calling Sam as he held out the receiver. Sam's conversation was brief, taut, and his expression turned wooden. He set the phone down, called his men to the center of the floor and spoke quietly. Hard as I tried, I couldn't make out what he was saying. They listened attentively, turned to study us, turned back to Sam. Nick gripped my hand and squeezed it. Hard.

"Glenn Bohannon is dead." Sam stood over us, gazing down with the detached, businesslike air of the professional. Gone, the kind, sympathetic Sam Lawless who had been our friend and steady customer since we opened the Oracle. Five years we'd known him, but the officer standing in front of us was a stranger.

"Dead?" The word lodged in my throat like a piece of half-chewed liver. Sam went on as though he hadn't heard me.

"This is an official investigation of a crime scene. Do not touch anything. Do not go near that deck or those tables. Do not enter the kitchen or the men's room."

"But..." Nick stopped. A glance from Sam was all it took. "Okay, Sam. Whatever you say." With a curt nod Sam turned back to his men.

Click, click. Click, click. I knew before I turned to him that Nick had his worry beads out. They were spinning faster than a propeller, clattering like cards clipped in the spokes of a bicycle wheel.

"What are we going to do, Nick? Glenn's dead. And Sam's acting like it's—"

Nick threw himself out of his chair and slammed into the wait station. I gave him a minute, then followed him. He stood with his back to me, his shoulders rigid, tense arms at his sides ending in clenched fists. I came up behind him quietly and laid my hand on his back. It felt warm and hard, but it trembled in silent sobs. I slid my hands under his arms, wrapping them around his chest and laying my head against his shoulder.

"Why?" His words were choked. "Why did this have to happen to us? Haven't we been through enough? We've worked so hard. This is bad, Julia. Real bad. We could lose everything now. *Kai, to moro...*"

It was the first time he'd said it, since the miscarriage. The baby. How deep his hurt went I could never know. At least as deep as mine. And now Glenn's death, and Sam, threatened to rob us of the one thing we had left. It was all collapsing in on us—the days and nights of bone-weary work, the small, hard-won triumphs that, over five years, were just beginning to add up to success. In a few minutes it would all be gone.

"Nick," I said. "We will get through this. We will!" I hugged him tightly.

"You'll have to move back into the dining room." Jimmy stood at the wait-station door. His face was hard.

"Why? We're just talking in here. Can't we have a little privacy?"

"No, ma'am. You got to stay where I can see you."

Jimmy stretched his arm out, herding us out of the wait station. "You just ask me next time, before you go off, you hear?"

We sat back down at the family table, silent, each consumed with his own thoughts. How, I asked myself, had this happened? Why was Sam treating us so coldly? All we had done was cook Glenn's breakfast. And served it....

WE CRAWLED INTO BED that night pummeled and bruised of spirit. Long after the students at Parnassus had deserted their books for the local watering holes and the rest of Delphi had drawn their drapes and brushed their teeth, Nick and I lay in each other's arms, restlessly wakeful. Our fears and phantoms were real, and the escape of sleep would have been a pleasure.

"You're right," Nick said, without preamble, knowing I was wide-awake. "We can't just give up. But I can't cook anymore either, Julia."

"Nick, you're not responsible for what happened to Glenn!"

"What if I am? What if I did something terrible and maybe I don't even know it?"

"You didn't. Besides, I'm all right as a backup, but I can't cook short order. I'm not fast enough. I get nervous when we get busy."

"We may never be busy again. But don't worry. I'll find someone else."

"Don't say that! We didn't have anything to do with..." I trailed off, feeling helpless to explain, or believe myself, that we would not be held responsible. "And anyway, where are you going to find another experienced cook this fast?"

"I don't know. But I've got to find one. People won't trust

me. I don't trust me." He switched on the light and went to his briefcase, pulling out a two-inch stack of business cards. After thumbing through them for a moment, he plucked one out and went to the phone.

"Nick, it's after midnight. Who are you calling?"

"It's all right. He won't mind."

"But who...?"

Nick silenced me with a finger as he listened to the ringing at the other end.

I closed my eyes, wishing again it was just a dream, wishing I hadn't drunk nine cups of coffee in the long, intervening hours. My temples were pulsating, throbbing as though the blood was moving through my veins in waves. No wonder I couldn't sleep.

"Neh? Manoli? Niko! Neh, neh."

My eyes shot open. The Greek was flowing fast and thick. I don't speak it—well, *ligaki,* a little bit. But I understand more than Nick knows, and I like to keep it that way. He disconnected, redialed, and began again. A mounting fear was rising in me.

"Enthoxi, agori mou. Evharisto!" Click. The deed was done.

"We got a cook."

"Oh, Nick, I don't think—" His hand shot up.

"No, it's okay. He's Manoli's cousin, Spiro. He's good, Julia."

"Yeah, but Nick, he's a Greek cook! And you've never even met him. What if he's terrible? What if he's—I don't know—crazy or something?"

Nick's hand circled in the air. "A cook's a cook. What's the difference? Food's food all over the world."

"Well, I suppose.... But I don't know."

"He'll probably get here day after tomorrow. At night. He has to drive up from Mobile. What's that, six hours?"

"Eight, maybe more."

"See? He'll be here for dinner!"

"We don't serve dinner."

"That's good. It'll give me time to show him around."

A prudent wife knows that some battles can't be won. Nick wanted another Greek around, someone to play *tavli* with and share a glass of ouzo. He needed a connection with home, and just the anticipation of such companionship seemed to cheer him. Scylla to the left of me, Charybdis to the right.

"Okay," I said, and sighed. "If you really think so...."

I THINK SAM tried to be circumspect, but the size of the cafe, the myriad sinks and drains, pots, skillets, ovens, and equipment to be examined, scraped, sampled, required calling in a larger force than his original three men. And it meant closing not for one day, but two.

We returned to the Oracle the next day only to sit by helplessly, miserably, while the crime team completed their work. The photographer had finished taking his pictures. He then drew a grid on a large piece of paper and systematically collected shards of plates and cups, bagging them and tagging them according to his grid. I tried to remember what a normal day at the Oracle was really like, to believe that the insanity would end.

I stepped to the wait-station door, stared back through the kitchen, through the open back door at the officers crowded around the Dumpster. Garbage was carefully laid out on the parking lot, like new clothes on a bed, as Sam and the three others picked through it. Jimmy, left inside the cafe to watch over us, stood at my elbow.

"Sit back down, Miz Lambros. They just got to do their work and there ain't nothing you can do but wait." And that, exactly, summarized it all for me. All we could do was wait.

WE REOPENED to a larger crowd than either Nick or I had expected. The Buffaloes were there, of course, holding their own postmortem and filling Morgan in on all the details he had missed.

"I tried a Heimlich, you know."

"Well, Heimlichs don't do much for heart attacks, Lee." Morgan steepled his fingers and leaned back in his chair.

Sonny saw his opportunity and pounced. "Is that the, um, final diagnosis, Julia? Heart attack?"

I weighed the question, loath to tell them that I didn't really know the answer. Thanks to Sam, the newspapers had treated Glenn's death as an accident. But if they were casual, Sonny was not. Besides being our insurance agent, thereby having a personal stake in matters at the Oracle, he was a shameless gossip. I looked at the brightly expectant eyes under the bill of his Delphi Sun baseball cap, and found my tongue sticking in my throat.

"It usually takes a couple of days to get the autopsy report, Sonny. And there's next of kin to notify, too. Julia probably hasn't heard yet. Have you, Julia?"

I shot Lee a grateful smile. "No, not yet," I said, and excused myself before they could put any other questions to me.

Besides the Buffaloes, there were other customers, too—students and professors, regular three-and four-times-a- week customers. Some came out of curiosity, some because they seemed to enjoy the idea that they were tempting fate by eating our food—a kind of epicurean bungee-jumping. Some were there in a demonstration of loyalty and trust. But they lingered long over their menus, settling on packaged cereals and orders of dry toast. They were coming to the Oracle for all the wrong reasons. It hurt.

They grilled Rhonda and Tammy. What had happened to Glenn? Who was cooking this morning? What had Glenn eaten that day? Rhonda fielded their questions adeptly. Tammy spent as much time as she could in the rest room.

Nick and I had agreed that I would work the floor, talking to customers, allaying their fears. But they didn't ask me questions. They turned away, embarrassed and refusing to meet my eyes when I inquired whether everything was all right. "Oh yes," they said. "Just fine." I returned despondently to the kitchen.

"Everything all right out there?" Nick scraped down the grill and dropped an order of hash browns on it.

"Yeah, fine," I lied. I couldn't tell Nick that I felt that some of these people had put in their final appearance, a last gesture of confidence in us, a confidence they didn't really feel. They wouldn't be back. They would satisfy themselves that they had done what they could, then move on to safer pastures.

"Julia, you'd better come out here. Now!" Rhonda stood in the wait-station door. Her face was that same pasty white as the morning Glenn died. My stomach churned as I rushed into the station.

"I can cost you your job, young lady! Now let me have it!" Tammy was frantically twisting and pulling away from someone behind her. "Let me go! Son of a bitch, it's not yours!" She yanked her arm and staggered back toward me, revealing the man who'd had such a powerful grip on her wrist. I blinked, watching openmouthed as Morgan Fox, president of SafeBank and male caryatid of Delphi society, tried to recover his composure.

"What's going on, Tammy?"

Morgan smoothed his vest over his chest and checked his hair. His face was flushed to the tips of his ears, making his copper hair appear redder. Tammy was breathing hard, rubbing her left wrist with her right hand.

"He...he attacked—"

"Now just a minute, young lady! I didn't attack you at all. I simply asked you to return what belongs to me." He turned his anger on me. "Julia, it's very unwise to employ thieves."

"Thieves? I'm sorry, Morgan, but I don't have a clue as to what you're talking about. Furthermore, I think Nick should hear this." I stuck my head through the kitchen door and called him into the wait station. Tammy had eased around behind me, and Morgan glared at her over my shoulder.

"Morgan seems to have a complaint about Tammy. Apparently, he thinks she's stolen something from him."

"I'd like to discuss this with you privately," Morgan said, looking pointedly at Tammy.

"All right. Let's go into the office." Nick led us through the kitchen, turning to Tammy as we reached the office door. "Wait out here a minute, will you, Tammy?"

She nodded sullenly, still rubbing her wrist. I patted her shoulder and followed the two men into the little office. Morgan looked around the room distastefully and refused a seat.

"This won't take long. I've got a little problem with your waitress, but I think we can clear it up quickly."

Nick studied him intently. "Go ahead."

"Well, you see, a couple of days ago, I lost a bracelet. It's Dina's. I had it in my pocket because I was going to take it to Roger's shop to be engraved with her initials. Anyway, apparently it fell out of my pocket, and I haven't been able to find it." He stopped, went on hesitantly. "Your waitress is wearing it."

I looked over at Nick, who raised an eyebrow. "How do you know it's the same bracelet?"

"Because it's one of a kind. Roger carries a line in his shop of handmade, one-of-a-kind jewelry. I bought the bracelet for Dina as an anniversary gift. Roger's holding a matching barrette and earrings for me for Christmas."

"Why didn't you come to one of us in the first place, Morgan? I don't think there was any reason to attack her in the wait station."

He clasped his hands behind him, rocked back and forth on his toes, and drilled his tawny eyes into me. An embarrassed smile flickered across his mouth. "I didn't attack her, Julia. I simply asked her to give it back to me. She overreacted to the whole thing. If I became a little overwrought, well, I'm sorry. You can imagine my anger at seeing someone else wearing my own wife's anniversary gift!

"And I didn't come to you first because..." He flashed a second smile at me, malicious in its baring of even, white teeth. "I thought you all had enough to worry about, what with one of your customers dying at your breakfast table, so to speak."

Nick's jaw muscles flexed as he ground his teeth. I could feel the heat of my temper rising, but he shot me a warning glance and moved in quickly. "Julia, will you call Tammy in here?"

She stood in front of us all, picking nervously at the edges of her apron, tilting her chin up in sulky defiance. We were walking a fine line here, accusing an employee of theft. We had to be careful.

"That's a beautiful bracelet, Tammy. Can I see it?"

She pulled it off her arm and passed it to me, uncovering the angry scarlet circle of a growing bruise on her wrist. Nick noticed it, too, glanced up at me and shook his head. I turned my attention back to the bracelet.

It was exquisite—a 14K cuff, about an inch and a half wide, ornately engraved and inlaid with rosettes and leaves of red and green gold. Must have set someone back four figures. I had the sinking feeling that someone was Morgan.

"Where did you get this, do you mind my asking?"

She twisted a brittle lock of hair around her finger. Her eyes were wary. "I found it, in the dining room. A couple of days ago."

"And you didn't turn it in to us? Don't you think you should have?"

She lifted her pointed chin, eyes blazing. "I was going to. Today. It's just so pretty. I wanted to wear it for a while. That's all. Then I was going to give it to you."

"Well, it belongs to me." Morgan turned to me. "If I have to, I can produce the sales receipt. I'll go home right now and get it."

"No," Nick said. "I'm sure that won't be necessary. We'll take your word that it's yours." I stared at Nick and reluctantly passed the bracelet to Morgan.

"You can go now, Tammy. We'll talk later."

She opened her mouth as though to argue, thought better of it, and slammed the office door behind her. When she was gone, I turned back to Morgan. "Dina's a lucky woman. That's just about the most beautiful thing I've ever seen."

"Well," he said, pocketing the bracelet. "She deserves it. She's a good wife, and a wonderful mother. I'm planning to keep her."

Nick and I smiled politely, watched him as he passed through the kitchen and out the wait-station door. I dropped down onto the cot we keep for emergency fatigue, surprised to find a grin spreading across my face.

"Well, what's left? We've had miscarriage, death, theft... How about a tornado? Hurricane?" A wave of hysterical laughter was sweeping up my throat. "It needs to be something really big. Something guaranteed to provide the end of life as we know it. I've got it! How about a tidal wave?"

"Stop it, Julia."

"Earthquake?"

"Julia, stop!" Nick pulled me off the cot and held me, tightly. "We're hanging on, remember?" I took a deep breath, nodded and clung to him with all my strength, finally relaxing in the warmth and security of his arms.

"Besides," he said. "This isn't that big a deal. This kind of thing happens in a business where you serve the public. It's inevitable.''

I dropped back onto the cot. "I suppose. But this one had all the makings of an ugly little incident. What are we going to do about Tammy? She's sloppy and lazy, but I've never known her to steal. Do you think she really planned to turn the bracelet in?"

Nick sat down at the desk with a weary sigh. "I don't know. She's such an arrowhead—"

"That's airhead, Nick."

"That's what I said. Anyway, I hope—"

"Bastard! He's lying!" Tammy stood in the office door. Her hands were planted on her hips. "He didn't lose that bracelet. It belonged to Mr. Bohannon."

FOUR

"SIT DOWN, Tammy. I think we'd better talk about this." Nick rose, gave her his seat at the desk, and stood leaning against the tall file cabinet. "Go ahead."

"He's lying about the bracelet. I don't know why he made that up, but he did."

"How do you know?"

"Because I know he didn't lose it."

"Go on."

Tammy slumped in her chair. She looked away, at the office wall, and bit her knuckle.

"Tammy?"

She dragged herself upright. "Okay. Well, you remember when Mr. Bohannon got sick?" Indeed we did.

"Well, when the others were trying to help him, they pulled off his jacket, you know? And one of them, I think it was Mr. Blaine, he threw it to me. I caught it, but it was kind of sideways, upside down, you know. And that's when the bracelet fell out of his pocket." Nick and I stared at her.

"I was going to give it back to him. I was! But then he died, and I knew he didn't have a wife or anything so I just figured... Well, when Sam finds out about next of kin, if there's, like, a woman in the picture, then I'd have to give it to her. I know that. But I was just waiting. And it's so pretty, I thought why shouldn't I wear it? I mean, what good's it doing sitting in lost-and-found?"

"It wouldn't be lost-and-found, Tammy. Sam would have it—should have it. But, now... Why didn't you speak up when Morgan was here?"

"Well, first I was just kind of surprised, you know? That he was saying he lost it, when I knew he didn't. Then, I thought if he's lying, there's some reason for it and since...well, since the sheriff's been around so much and Mr. Bohannon is dead...I guess I was afraid."

"But what makes you think there's anything to be afraid of?"

"Well, because, well, there's something else. I put the bracelet in my apron pocket. My hands were full, and I was trying to move those dishes off the rail before they got knocked off. Well, anyway, the jacket was all heavy and lumpy, and it slipped off my arm. When I picked it up, something else was sticking out of his pocket. The inside one, you know?"

"Yeah. Well, what was it?"

"I didn't take it out, but I saw the handle and I could just feel it through the jacket lining. Julia, he was carrying a gun. One of those little ones, you know? But it was heavy, not like a toy or nothing. It was real."

"Did you tell Sam?"

She shook her head slowly. "Rhonda gave him the jacket, so I knew he'd find it anyway."

Nick, who had been silent through this exchange, stepped into the conversation. "You can go now, Tammy. Thanks for telling us the truth. But you'd better think about how you should have handled this. You don't keep things you find. No matter what."

"But I told you..." She stood up, smoothed her skirt over her hips and shrugged. "Yeah, okay. I'll remember." I listened to her heels click across the kitchen floor. Nick dropped back into his chair.

"Well, what do you make of that?"

Nick shrugged. "I have no idea. Is the bracelet really Morgan's?—that is, Dina's? Or is he lying? And why would Glenn have it, if it's Dina's?"

"You think Tammy's telling the truth."

"Yeah, I do. I can't really think of a good reason for her to make this one up. She doesn't have anything to gain from it."

"No. I suppose not."

"The first thing is to find out whether the bracelet really belongs to Dina Fox."

"Does it matter?"

"A man carrying a gun died in our restaurant. He had a very valuable bracelet that belongs to another man's wife, or so the man says. Yes. I think it matters."

I stood up, glanced at my watch and pulled off my apron. "Can you handle things here alone for a while? I'll be back before the lunch rush."

"Where are you going?"

"To find out about the bracelet."

ROGER MUMBORD and his mother, Eleanor, live in Musewood, our neighborhood. Roger runs the jewelry store, but it's widely known that Eleanor keeps a firm grip on the checkbook and a taut hand on the reins of the business. At eighty years of age, she's quite a remarkable woman, active in Junior League, a variety of local charities, and the Musewood Garden Club, of which I am a reluctant member and officer.

Roger is a Buffalo. His regular order consists of ice water, which he could probably just extract from his veins. He drinks it with his morning paper before the rest arrive. He doesn't like me, barely tolerates Rhonda, and loathes Tammy. He is a bachelor, a probable misogynist who, at fifty years of age or thereabouts, still lives with his mother. Roger is always grouchy.

He was waiting on a customer when I arrived. I drooled over tennis bracelets and sapphire earrings, fine watches and gold bracelets. Whatever else might be said about Roger, I thought, he has exquisite taste.

"Something I can do for you, Julia?"

Roger's dry voice snapped me out of my daydream. "Yes. Listen, the Garden Club is having its installation of new officers the day after tomorrow. I'm not sure I can be there for it, but your mother's taking my place as treasurer, and since I was coming downtown anyway, I just figured I'd drop the books off here. Maybe you can give them to her when you go home."

He pointed to the stack I'd placed on the counter. "These them?"

"Yeah. Here's the checkbook, and she'll find all this year's receipts in this folder." I pulled out one and showed it to him. "See, I've written on each one what the money was spent for, and dated it. This was for marigolds to put around the entrance of the subdivision. Of course, it's also written on the check stub."

I set the folder aside and was reaching for the checkbook, when something in the showcase caught my eye. It was an oval barrette, about an inch and a half wide at the center. The price tag was carefully arranged so I couldn't read it. But I couldn't resist asking to see it.

Roger seemed reluctant, but he pulled it out anyway. "I've sorta been saving it for someone," he said.

"I just want to look at it, Roger." I turned it over in my palm, held it out to the light to admire it. It was engraved, delicate swirls and flowers around a center rose.

"Is that red gold?"

"Yup." He pointed to the leaves. "And that's green. Pretty rare. Everything in this cabinet is handmade. Mother knows an artist in Atlanta..."

It matched the bracelet, without question. And there, in the showcase, were the matching earrings. They were an inverted heart shape, engraved like the bracelet and barrette, and dangling from thin golden wires. Nothing else in the case was exactly like these two pieces of jewelry.

"...so it's all one-of-a-kind."

"Excuse me?"

Roger rolled his eyes. "I said, Mother knows an artist in Atlanta. She commissions him to do unusual work like this." He swept his hand over the countertop. "It's all one-of-a-kind."

"And the barrette is already sold?"

Roger hesitated. "Well, not exactly. But it's part of a set. The buyer already bought the bracelet, and he's planning on the barrette and earrings for a Christmas gift. I just keep them in the cabinet because it makes such a pretty display."

"But what if I wanted it?"

"Well, I'd have to talk to Morgan about it, but I'm pretty sure he's already planning on it."

"Morgan Fox?"

"Now don't you go telling Dina about it. He's planning to surprise her with it for Christmas."

I reluctantly handed the barrette back to him. "No. I wouldn't think of spoiling his surprise."

THE OPTIMISTIC Mr. Murphy must have been in the restaurant business. That the rush will hit just when you are understaffed, short of equipment or food, or in the throes of general crisis is axiomatic. That one of the above problems is almost always on-going is no less true.

But restaurants are a service business. It's what customers expect. They come for lunch, with only an hour, and regardless of what may be going on in the kitchen, they expect that a tempting, sumptuous, and satisfying meal will be set before them in record time. And we strive to do our best, no matter what storm may hang ominously over our lives. After all, if you don't please them today, they won't be back tomorrow.

By the time I returned from Roger's shop, the Oracle was in an uproar. Tammy had begged off work for the rest of the day, claiming that she was too upset by the incident with Morgan to go on working. Sometimes Tammy's behavior makes it difficult to defend her.

Rhonda was juggling the lunch rush alone and Nick was stretched thin in the kitchen. Otis, our dishwasher, had appeared for work somewhat the worse for sampling his brother-in-law's white lightning. I filled in where I could, with little opportunity to speak to Nick alone. When the rush cleared out, there was still the cleanup and closing to be dealt with.

"We haven't had a chance to talk, Julia. Are you okay?" Rhonda asked.

"You mean besides having a customer die after eating our food, being closed down for two days while Sam and his crew poked into every corner of the restaurant and reopening without the help of Tammy and Otis?" I smiled thinly at her. "Yeah, I'm okay, I guess."

"So what were they looking for?" Rhonda snapped open a fresh white tablecloth, smoothed it over the four-top and dropped a blue service cloth on top.

"That's just it. We don't know. Sam's not talking much. Just said it was a precaution." I set four places, returned the bud vase, salt and pepper shakers to the table, and followed her to the next one. Nick, who was in the wait station restacking cups and glasses, emerged to answer the phone.

"Two days is a long time to spend on a precaution. You know Sam pretty well, don't you, Rhonda?"

She blushed and fumbled with the tight folds of the cloth. "We date now and then, yeah."

"Well, is he the cautious type?"

"I don't know, Julia. He doesn't talk much about his work."

"He takes his job seriously. I mean, he's been different the last two days. Kind of distant, cool. Nice enough, under the circumstances, but not really himself. I don't understand it."

Rhonda looked away from me and said nothing. We'd finished A deck and were moving on to B. The first glass to crash on the tile got our attention, but when the whole rack smashed to the floor Nick flung himself through the wait-station door, spitting Greek expletives under his breath.

"I gotta go," Rhonda said abruptly as she gathered up her purse.

I watched her cross the floor and called a quick thanks to her retreating back. "See you in the morning?" She nodded and waved.

Otis was fumbling with a dustpan and broom when I made the kitchen. He straightened up and smiled ingratiatingly at me, flashing yawning gaps between his teeth. He always looks as though someone's been jerking his hair out by the roots. Nick was standing over him.

"Seven glasses and a coffeepot! I don't pay you to break glasses. Take them out of his paycheck, Julia. Two dollars apiece and fifteen for the pot."

"But Nick..."

"No, it's okay, Miss Julia. Mr. Nick's right. I broke 'em, I pay for 'em. We all got to pay for our mistakes." He looked sadly down at his feet, where gray, stained tennis shoes gaped open around his big toe. "Them shoes'll still be at K-Mart next week. Yes ma'am, they will. Don't you worry 'bout it."

Nick hung his head. "Oh, well. I guess it was an accident. But next time, you're gone, Otis."

Goal! I could almost hear the crowd roar. Otis takes an issue, bounces it around, fakes to the left, dodges the truth, stomps on Nick and scores again! Otis grinned.

Nick's brows drew together. "Don't put that broken glass in the garbage, Otis. It'll tear the bag and we'll have a bigger mess.

Get a large to-go bag and put it in there.'' Otis went back to sweeping as Nick grabbed my arm and steered me toward the office at the back of the kitchen.

"I can't believe you let him get by with it again,'' I grumbled.

"Me? You're the one who interfered! I would have fired him.''

"All I was going to say is the glasses are two and a quarter, not two dollars.''

"Oh.'' He pulled the office door behind him as I dropped onto the cot. Nick fell into the desk chair and swiveled it around to face me. I stroked his thighs lightly with my fingertips.

"Nuck that off.''

"*Knock*, Nick. 'Ah.' Knock.''

"Whatever. We've got a problem. That party—the retirement luncheon scheduled for next week.''

"What about it?''

"They just canceled.''

"Why?''

"Oh, they gave me some excuse about how some people couldn't come, but when I tried to reschedule it, they got kind of vague. Like they didn't know if it would ever come off. I'm betting they moved it somewhere else. And you and I know why.''

Nick's an up person, always the optimist, believing that tomorrow is a new day. Aside from the miscarriage, I'd never seen him so despondent. I stood up and hugged his neck.

"Better get back to work. We're going to be busy tomorrow, Nick. I can feel it.''

I left him sitting at the desk, head in his hands, and made my way back to the dining room wishing I believed what I'd just said. But it sounded hollow even to me.

Rhonda's car was still in the lot. She was standing, leaning against the open car door, talking to Sam. Much as I liked Sam, I was less than pleased to see him and resolved to keep him away from Nick if possible. Rhonda pulled out of the lot just as I opened the door.

"Your team couldn't possibly have missed anything, Sam, so now what?''

He smiled a little, shook his head. "Not here on business, really. I was looking for Rhonda. Had a favor to ask her, but she can't do it.''

"Something I can do?"

We walked back toward his car. There was movement behind the smoky glass—something darting and jumping. I shielded my eyes and peered inside. A pair of deep brown ones stared back at me, followed by a sharp yip.

"Oh, Sam, he's so cute! Where'd you get him?"

Sam hesitated, stumbled over the words. "He's Bohannon's dog. I was wanting to see if Rhonda could take him. Otherwise, I got to take him to the pound. But she can't have a dog in her apartment and my Crockett would eat him alive.''

He stood on six-inch legs, his black fur an untidy rumple around his square face and prick ears. A carrot-shaped tail spun in a wagging frenzy. As I watched, he leapt across the seat, scurried back and threw his forepaws against the door. A neon green tennis ball stretched his jaws into a wide grin.

"I'll take him." Dogs are no substitute for babies, but he might be just the diversion Nick and I needed.

Again, Sam hesitated, stroking his jaw. "I don't know, Julia. Sheriff Taylor won't like it.''

"Why? Why would he care?"

"Because Nick— He, uh, he just wouldn't, that's all. He's a prickly bastard.''

"Oh, come on, Sam. Are you going to take that sweet little thing to the pound? He's a good dog. Look at him. A Scottie. I'll bet if you go through Glenn's things, you'll find papers on him. Are you going to let them put him down?''

"Well, they don't always do that.''

"You and I both know they've got more animals there than they can handle now, what with the way the students get them and then leave them behind when they move out, or flunk out or whatever. They'll put him down before you're back in your car.''

Sam squinted into the sunlight. "If I let you take him, you got to keep it quiet. Don't say anything that could get back to Sheriff Taylor.'' He opened the door of the car, brought the little dog out on a leather lead. "I'm telling you, Julia, he won't like it.''

I squatted down to read the name on his red leather collar.

"Jack. Black Jack. I guess Glenn must have been a poker player too." I ruffled Jack's head and was rewarded with a big kiss that smelled like tuna fish.

"What have you been feeding him?"

Sam grinned. "Shared my lunch with him. Tuna on whole wheat." He handed me a large basket bed with a plaid cushion that smelled decidedly doggy. "You keep this to yourself, now. Okay?"

"I will, Sam, but for the life of me I don't understand why the sheriff would give a hoot." I held up my hand. "But I'll remember. We won't tell anyone where he came from."

Jack was watering the tire on Sam's car. We both watched him, waiting politely to resume our conversation until he had concluded his affairs. He dropped the ball at my feet, nudged it toward me, darted back, and yipped.

"Julia, since I'm here, there's something else."

I turned back to Sam. His face was serious, with the hard, businesslike expression I had come to know so well in the last two days.

"What? What is it, Sam?"

"I'm going to have to ask you and Nick to come into the station tomorrow. For questioning."

I should have seen it coming, should have realized that the last two days' work were not just idle curiosity on the part of a small, overworked law enforcement team. Still, it hit me hard. For a moment I thought my knees would give way.

"About Glenn. Questioning about Glenn."

"Uh-huh."

"I guess he didn't die of natural causes."

"Autopsy report's not in yet." Then Sam looked me directly in the eye. His own were a clear pale green, rimmed by golden lashes that matched his hair. And their expression was frank.

"No," he said. "I don't think Glenn Bohannon died of natural causes."

FIVE

I NESTLED MY HEAD into Nick's shoulder. The bedroom was dim, but the darkness was pierced by a shaft of light under the bathroom door. Sniff, sniff, snort, snort. Nick had insisted on closing Jack in the bathroom for the night.

"I told him that we'd come into the station tomorrow, after the lunch rush. He just wants to ask us some questions about Glenn."

"About our relationship with Glenn, you mean. And about what we were doing the morning he died."

"Well, yeah. I didn't have a lot of choice but to agree, Nick. He could have come to the cafe to question us, but I didn't really think that was a good idea. We've had enough sheriff's cars parked outside for the last three days."

"I know, Julia. I'm not blaming you. It's just that I can't understand what Sam thinks we had to do with Glenn's death." Scratch, scratch. "Go to sleep, Jock."

"It's Jack, Nick. Aaa. Short *A*. What's he supposed to sleep on? The tile's cold. Go put his bed in there."

Nick reluctantly swung his legs out of bed, stuck his feet in a pair of shoes. "I forgot, I left the bed in the car." In a moment he was back, wedging himself through the bathroom door.

"Stay back, Jock. Here. Lie down. No, lie down here. Here, on the bed! You did tell Sam that we're just keeping him until we can find someone else to take him, right?"

"Yeah. Just for a little while," I lied. I thought Nick might need some time to get used to the idea of a dog. But Jack was such an endearing little thing. A little stubborn, maybe, but... Change the subject.

"Sam thinks Glenn was murdered. He as much as told me so," I called from the bed.

"But how did he die? Right there, Jock. Lie down."

"I don't know. Obviously he must think it's connected with us. He said the autopsy report isn't in yet, though, so maybe he's wrong. It still could come in as natural causes. For some reason, he's getting a lot of pressure from his boss.''

"No, here. On the bed. Cal Taylor. I might have known it. I give up. Sleep on the tile.''

Nick eased himself back out the door and into bed. I curled up against him. "Cal Taylor has no love for me. Or any other immigrant, for that matter.

"You remember a few years ago, the Japanese were going to build an electronics plant here in Delphi? It would have been a boost to the economy and given a lot of people around here steady jobs. But Taylor opposed it on the grounds that foreigners were going to be buying up property here.''

"But that's private enterprise. He couldn't have kept them from buying that land if that's what they wanted to do.''

"No. But there were some ugly incidents if you remember. Someone burned a Japanese flag on the property they were going to buy. And the final blow was that, when the mayor took them on a tour of the city, Cal Taylor refused to shake their hands.''

"Yeah, I remember now. I couldn't believe he was reelected after that.''

Whimper. Whimper. Scratch. "Nuck that off, Jock!''

"He's not going to be happy in there, Nick.''

Nick sat up and switched on the light. He looked steadily at me. His brow was furrowed and his jaws were working.

"What you have to realize, Julia, is that he still represents the majority opinion around here. Foreigners are good enough to do the jobs other people won't do. But let someone like me come in and work his tail off eighteen hours a day, and build a successful business—restaurant, convenience store, it doesn't matter. If he succeeds, he'll be resented.'' He threw back the covers and headed back to the bathroom.

"You're making it sound like someone's out to get you because you're an immigrant, Nick. You don't really believe that, do you?''

Nick was standing in the bathroom door, with Jack dangling and squirming under his arm. "I don't know, Julia. Maybe I do.''

I GLANCED AT THE alarm clock, rolled over and looked into two deep brown eyes. They blinked. I blinked. Thump. Thump.

Six o'clock was long past. I flew out of bed and stumbled toward the bathroom stripping my gown off on the way. Jack was off the bed before Nick knew he'd been there.

"Nick, get up! It's after six. We're late!"

He hit the floor running. I was already in the shower. He pulled back the door and jumped in with me. We passed the shampoo and soap back and forth, scooched around each other, stepped on each other's feet. Through the frosted glass I could see Jack, happily curled up on the bathmat.

"Oh, jeez. You'd better take him out, Nick."

"I'll take him out, all right. I may not bring him back."

"Nick..."

"He can't sleep with us, Julia."

"I know. He'll get used to us, then he'll start sleeping on his bed."

Getting ready, I tried not to think about the day ahead, about the questioning we faced. By the time Nick snapped off the hair-dryer, my hands were shaking and I had little dotted lines of mascara on my cheeks and under my eyebrows. I grabbed a tissue and rubbed at them, finally gave up, turned and curled into Nick's arms.

"I'm scared."

Nick stroked my hair. "Why?"

"There's more to this questioning this afternoon than curiosity, Nick. Sam thinks we're responsible for Glenn's death. But why us? What could we have had to do with it?"

"Julia, let's just try to get through the day. We'll find out soon enough what he wants, and spending our time second-guessing Sam is just going to make us miserable. Like he said, it's probably just routine."

Nick took my face in his hands. "Look, it was almost certainly a natural death. That's the way we're going to think about it, and that's the way we're going to act. Now put it out of your mind and let's get dressed. We're already running late."

We left Jack with a full bowl of food and a tennis ball, but I could hear him howling all the way down the street. "I'll get him some rawhide toys today."

"I thought we were just keeping him for a while."

"Yeah, but he still has to have toys!"

"Now look, Julia. You're getting too attached to him...."

THE DAY WENT relatively smoothly. Cooking and serving a handful of customers was infinitely easier than taking care of a full dining room. Glenn's death was already exacting its toll on business. The "rush" was no rush, but we told ourselves it was just an off day, and left for Sam's office earlier than expected, happy to escape an empty dining room.

"So Morgan was telling the truth. It's definitely Dina's bracelet."

With the arrival of Jack, and my scrambling to justify him to Nick, I had forgotten to tell him about my visit to Roger's shop.

"Definitely. I guess we've learned something here. I just don't know what."

I stared out the car window as we passed through downtown. Delphi is a college town, the home of Parnassus University, a private institution whose name has, in the last fifty years, outgrown the bounds of Southern elitist schools and come to be recognized as a fine institution of higher learning nationwide. The town itself is small and perched atop a series of knolls that form a part of the foothills of the Smokies. Colorful and intense as the set of a Tennessee Williams play, it is relentlessly charming, vibrant, and, at times, suffocating. But despite my occasionally jaded view of its attraction, from the first day I saw it, I—a Yankee born and bred—felt that I had come home.

The permanent residents of Delphi are predominantly white Anglo-Saxon and have been rooted in red clay for a hundred and fifty years. It seems that when the huddled masses arrived here, they were vigorously encouraged to yearn for freedom somewhere else. Until recently, Nick was the only Greek in Delphi.

I met Nick at Parnassus, while studying for a master's in speech pathology. He was there, recruited from a pro team in New Jersey, to coach the fledgling men's soccer team. Soon after we married, funding for the program was cut, the money to be spread between the various sciences and, of course, the first love of the South—football. Delphi was growing, and Nick, being Greek, felt there was only one recourse—open a restaurant. Hence the Oracle Cafe.

I put my own career on hold, ostensibly for a year, to help him get the business started. But the truth of the matter is that I had learned I was not really suited to my profession. I couldn't leave my patients at the office, but brought them home, complete with their disabilities, the devastation that stroke had on a family, or the lingering fear that laryngeal cancer would ultimately erode away the rest of a life. I was incapable of taking the clinical attitude, and my involvement in their lives simply hurt too much. Slowly my interest had shifted to the little cafe that was ripening through our long, hard hours of labor. I liked spending my days with Nick, almost as much as I loved spending my nights with him.

So one year turned to two, three, and four. Outside of the occasional, unusual case, I rarely took a patient. Five years of grueling work—there before sunrise to meet deliveries and start the coffee, late nights cleaning out the fryers and changing table-cloths. Six days a week, sixteen hours a day. And no, as the old joke goes, "Never on Sunday." Before the miscarriage we were operating in the black. Now, again, the debts were piling high.

Nick interrupted my comfortable musings on the past, bringing me quickly back to reality. "I don't think we should mention it to Sam. After all, Morgan didn't come in until after Glenn got sick so he couldn't have had anything to do with it. But if there was something going on between Glenn and Dina we could be opening Pandora's box."

"No, I wouldn't want to do that without knowing more first. It wouldn't be fair to anyone."

Nick pulled into a parking lot next to a long, low building of beige clapboard. Behind the building, a heavy chain-link fence, topped with angry barbed wire, surrounded a second building of the same shape and color. Even from the lot, I could see that the windows were covered with a tight metal grid.

A white bus stood in the parking lot. Across the side, in large block letters, were the words CALLOWAY COUNTY SHERIFF'S DE-

PARTMENT. The windows of it, too, were gridded. It was a road-gang bus.

Sam was waiting for us in his office, and he invited us to sit down in a pair of vinyl-seated metal chairs in front of his desk. I gripped the arms like a dental chair, glanced over at Nick and found him surprisingly relaxed.

Sam arranged a stack of papers on his desk and offered us coffee, which I accepted gratefully. My mug was white, with one of those insolent little happy faces on it.

"Now," Sam said, placing a yellow legal pad on the desk and picking up a pencil. "There are just a few things I want to cover with you.

"To begin with, how did you meet Glenn Bohannon?"

SIX

NICK SAT FORWARD in his chair and rested his elbows on his knees. "He came in one morning with Read Whitehead. Read said Glenn was looking for a piece of property to build on and he was going to introduce him to the Buff—to the businessmen in town."

Sam's lips twitched. Rhonda, it appeared, had shared our private name with him.

"So we started talking, and he told me his plans."

"To open a restaurant."

"Right."

"You must have hated that. A competitor."

"Don't put words on my tongue, Sam. No, I didn't hate it. To begin with, he was opening a Mexican place..."

Glenn Bohannon came from El Paso, Texas. He was a big man, in his mid-thirties perhaps, with strawberry-blond hair that reminded me of the morning sun. His drawl was deep, his smile ready, and Nick and I liked him from the moment we met him.

He had been to Delphi several times, he said, on business with the university. He liked the area, the green kudzu and rolling hills, and would like a reason to settle down here. That's when he'd hit on the idea of a Mexican restaurant—a cantina, really, that served scorching-hot food and ice-cold Dos Equis beer. Just the kind of place college students would love.

Nick and I knew he was right. There was room for a place like that in Delphi. And his would be mainly a night business, so it presented little competition for us.

"So I agreed to help him set up the place—even introduced him to Lee to talk about equipment. But he was a long way from buying, still had to build the place. Read was working on a land deal for him, I think, and Mitch had been hired to do the actual building. You'd have to ask them about that."

"I will. Now tell me about the day he died."

Nick relinquished the floor to me, since I had seen more of it than he had.

"Okay. Well, he'd eaten most of his breakfast. I was on the deck when he left and went to the men's room. When he came out, he didn't look like he felt well. And he was kind of dizzy or something. He ran into Rhonda and she dropped the tray, and..."

I finished telling it, told it more or less again, two more times. But each time, Sam took me back earlier in the day.

"What, exactly, did Bohannon order for breakfast?"

Nick answered. "The same thing he ordered every day—three eggs, over easy, double hash browns, bacon and biscuits. Tammy took the order. You can check with her."

"So when you saw the ticket, you knew right away who it was for."

"Well, yeah. I suppose so."

"Who cooked the food?"

"I did." Nick shifted in his chair. "You know that, Sam. I do most of the cooking—all the short order."

"And who served it? Tammy? Rhonda?"

"No." I was trying to be patient, knew full well that Sam already knew the answer to the question. We'd been over it twice. "I finished what I was doing in the kitchen and took it out to him."

"Anyone else have access to it, besides you two?"

I thought about this, about the way the Buffs crowd the deck, move from seat to seat as they conclude their business and good fellowship. "Of course. Everybody who was sitting there."

"Who was sitting next to Bohannon?"

I closed my eyes. "Read, I think. But then, he got up and moved down to where Warren was, and then I think Sonny sat down with him. Only they all got up and moved around so often...I think Lee was sitting on his right when he started choking, because he was going to try a Heimlich maneuver...."

"He wasn't choking, Julia." Nick stroked his chin. "Or, I don't think he was anyway, because there wasn't any food in his mouth when I got up there."

"Maybe Lee had already dislodged it. I don't know if he tried before I looked up from the mess on the floor."

"So you're telling me that most of those boys had access to his food at one time or another?"

"I suppose so. But I think it would have been hard—hard to get a poison into it without him noticing." I looked over at Nick. He nodded. "That is what we're talking about, isn't it, Sam? Poison?"

Sam sat back in his desk chair, rearing it off the front legs. "Now I don't want to make any statements about a thing like that just yet. But it's one of the things we're looking at."

"But wouldn't he have tasted it, smelled it? Something?"

"Hard to say." Sam glanced up, out the window of his office door. He ground his jaws. I turned around. Cal Taylor was peering through the glass, chewing on the butt of a cigar. Sam sat forward again.

"Gotta ask you some personal questions, Nick."

"Go ahead."

"When did you come to the U.S.?"

"Nine years ago."

"How'd you happen to come here?"

"You know the answer to that. I came here as a soccer player. Went to work as a coach for Parnassus seven, almost eight years ago after I tore the cartilage in my knee."

"You got a green card?"

"Yes."

"Lemme see it, please." Sam walked around the desk, took the green card Nick removed from his wallet. "Just gonna make a copy of this, if you don't mind."

"No. Fine." We watched Sam's back as he lumbered out of the office, pulling the door closed, rattling the window.

"Why would he want your green card?"

Nick's normally olive complexion had turned an odd, khaki shade. "I don't know. But I don't like it."

Sam was back in a minute, and he wasn't alone. He stood at the window, staring out into the parking lot as Cal Taylor perched on the corner of his desk. He thumbed the corner of Nick's green card.

"We got a serious problem here, Mr. Lambros." He adjusted brown horn-rimmed glasses over the bump in his long, narrow nose. His eyes gleamed, and the shadow of a smile twitched behind the grave expression he was trying to maintain. Cal Taylor was enjoying this.

"What kind of a problem?"

His voice had a slightly nasal quality about it, and he tended to laugh through his nose, something he did as he responded. "INS computers seem to be down. We can't access them to verify your documentation."

"What do you mean, verify my documentation? You've got my green card right there in your hand."

Taylor adjusted his glasses again, pretended to be studying the card carefully. He even made a show of comparing Nick's facial features to the photograph on the card. Finally shook his head.

"Can't be too careful. There's fakes of these out there, and not all that hard to get, neither. I'm afraid I'm just going to have to hold on to this until we can get through to INS." He dropped it into his shirt pocket.

"Now wait a minute! I've got to have that. I'm supposed to carry it at all times." Nick was half out of the chair. The muscles in his jaws flexed. This, I knew, was not a good sign. Nick doesn't get angry often, but when he does, he's liable to do something rash. I put my hand on his arm to steady him. Behind Taylor, Sam slowly shook his head. Nick dropped back into the chair.

Taylor turned to me, speaking in a lazy drawl, a wide grin spread across his face. "How long you two been married, Miz Lambros?"

"Six years."

"I s'pose that rules out you marrying him so's he could get a green card."

It moved up from somewhere deep in my gut—a rage that colored my face and put a bite in my words. "I married Nick Lambros because I love him and for no other reason," I said evenly. "And who do you think you are to imply otherwise?"

"I wasn't implying nothing. No reason to get cheeky with me, Miz Lambros. You ain't in no position for that. I'm doing my job here."

"Your job is—"

He turned back to Nick, dismissing me. "How come you ain't

applied for citizenship, you don't mind my askin'? You plannin' to rape this country, then go back to—where is it?'' He pulled the card out of his pocket. "Greece?'' He snarled a smile, pronouncing it "Greasy.''

This, unfortunately, was not an easy question to answer. Nick had no plans to return to Greece permanently. Perhaps he had, before we met, but now we were married and making a life together here. No, he would not be going back.

But I also knew that he was not ready to renounce his own country, and maybe he never would. I had tried to tell him that getting his citizenship would simply give him more rights, and more protection here. But the issue was not that simple for him. For Nick, taking American citizenship was final. It meant he was turning his back on the rocky homeland he loved so much. For Nick, it meant he would no longer be Greek. Others had done it—pragmatists who knew they would never return, believed their Hellenic heritage pumped in their veins. For them a piece of paper was nothing. But for Nick, it was a lot.

"No. I'll get it. Someday. But I'm busy with the cafe right now. Don't have time…'' He stopped, stared, as I did, at the burning hatred unmasked in Cal Taylor's eyes. My stomach flipped, my mouth grew dry. Cal Taylor was unmistakably out to get my husband.

"WHY WOULD HE want to keep your green card, Nick?''

He relaxed, pushed the sailor's cap back on his brow, and guided our little Honda out of the parking lot. "Intimidation, probably. Remember what I told you—about how he feels about foreigners?''

"Yeah, but I guess I didn't quite believe it until I saw it in action.''

"You know, by keeping my green card, he's keeping me from traveling, too. It's kind of a safeguard, I suppose. He knows I wouldn't venture very far without it.''

"Well, I think we should call an attorney. Warren, maybe. He'll know what to do.''

"Taylor can't hang on to it forever, Julia. I don't want to risk making him madder. Let's wait a few days and see what happens. He'll return it. He'll have to.''

Nick's reasoning prevailed. I was glad he was able to keep as cool as he was under the circumstances. It's one of the many things I admire about Nick—his utter confidence in himself. Born poor in Greece, he's relied on himself from an early age. It's made him strong.

"I still don't like it."

"There are a lot of things about this I don't like, Julia. It's pretty obvious that Glenn was murdered—poisoned, as you said. Clearly, they think it was in his breakfast, and they can't connect it with anyone but me. Us. Other people may have had access to the food, but, as you pointed out, it would be hard to slip it in at the table. But it would be very easy for me to do it in the kitchen. Besides, Cal Taylor's got Sam hamstrung. He's convinced that I killed Glenn Bohannon, and all he's got to do is prove it. He's going to keep Sam on me, which means Sam's not going to be looking too hard for other suspects."

"But Nick, Sam's our friend."

"Sure he is, but let's face it, Julia. I'm suspect number one and you're number two. They're going to try to build a case against us, no matter what. Sam's going to do his job and Taylor may have him convinced that he doesn't need to look any further than Nick Lambros. Even if Sam's not completely convinced, don't forget, Cal Taylor's a mean S.O.B. And he's Sam's boss."

"So are you saying there's nothing we can do to protect ourselves?"

"No. We can find out who killed Glenn."

SEVEN

"Now, LET'S GO BACK over what we know. Glenn was probably poisoned, and it was in the food, which means a limited number of people had access to it. Us. The Buffaloes, Rhonda and Tammy, maybe."

We pulled up in front of the cafe, unlocked the door and flipped on the lights, which triggered the sound system. Nick had it rigged that way so that no one, not even I, had to touch it. It's a personal fetish, that system. It plays tapes, CDs, has high-speed dubbing, even an ambient mike that can record what's going on in the room, if you know how to set it. I hadn't even bothered to learn.

Tammy Wynette was back, a clear indication that our Tammy had closed. Nick flipped her out, put in Yanni's *Reflections of Passion,* and started to clear the register.

"And don't forget, Glenn carried a gun. And he had a bracelet in his pocket that belonged to Dina Fox."

"So where do we start?"

"I wish I knew why Glenn was carrying a gun. That would be a good start."

"Well, I'd like to know why he had Dina's bracelet. And I think maybe I know how to find out."

Nick had started counting the register drawer, stacking the money in careful piles. He held his hand up to stop me. *"Octo, enya, theca..."* He stacked the tens to one side, entered 100 on the adding machine, and began again.

I was fidgety as I wandered through the dining room, checking the tablecloths and pulling the stained ones. I snapped open a freshly starched cloth, laid it over a table, and topped it with a blue, plastic service cloth. It smelled clean and new, as always giving me a sense of pride. I looked around the Oracle.

There are three decks, staggered in height, sitting about two feet above the entry level at the door. Each is covered in Mediterranean blue carpeting that matches the service cloths. In the center is an open floor that we use for food bars and, sometimes, overflow seating. It's covered in sienna quarry tile that conjures memories of the outdoor restaurants so prevalent in Greece. Nick and I had worked hard to achieve what we had there—a modest place, but thoroughly our own, and I loved every inch of it. And now, for no explicable reason, it was threatened by outside forces. Anger burned through me, not only anger at the murderer, but anger at Glenn, admittedly a victim himself, but whose death left me feeling troubled and vulnerable.

I looked over at Nick, still counting and figuring at the register, and thought about the long days and nights—how he'd painted every inch of the white walls himself, and carefully laid the carpet while I selected the furnishings. And I thought about the times he'd fixed the plumbing and scrubbed the floors, repaired broken appliances and scrimped and scraped to pay the vendors in the early years. I suddenly felt a rush of love for him that made me blush like a newlywed. I crept up softly behind him and wrapped my arms around his chest.

He's not much taller than I, an inch at the most. And he has an athlete's build, slender and agile like a dancer. Muscular. He's quick on his feet, outstanding on a soccer field. For that matter, with his black hair and classic features, I think he's outstanding anywhere. I nuzzled the back of his neck.

"Nuck it off, Julia. You're making me lose count."

I laughed and tickled his earlobe a little. My hands crept down his chest to his waist. He was wearing jeans, and I slipped my hands into the pockets.

"Julia, let me finish, then we'll go home and—"

The gravel driveway crunched as an enormous gray Pontiac, circa 1968, floated into the lot, hiccuping black smoke behind it. It looked as if it should have been flying a Liberian flag. A little rental trailer followed in its wake. The Pontiac bobbed up and down, ground to a stop at the door, rebounding a couple of times before the wide door swung open and an immense man unfolded himself from behind the wheel. He pulled the black sailor's cap off his head, mopped his brow, then stood back, hands on hips, and stared at the building.

"*Neh, neh. Katse kato.*" As he came in the door, Nick pointed him to a chair at the family table. It looked a little frail. The big man smiled at me and the bushy mustache above his upper lip quivered. He stuck out an enormous hand.

"I am," he said in laboriously careful English, "Spiros Papavasilakis." He folded my hand in his palm and shook it. When I finally extricated it, I flexed it to be sure it still had feeling.

"*Thelis kafe?* Julia…"

I was already in the wait station, and returned with two mugs of coffee and a canister of sugar. The chair groaned under Spiro. I watched as they each emptied half the sugar into their mugs and stirred it into syrup, before I went back to the kitchen to fix him something to eat. When I set the plate in front of him, he smiled and nodded.

"*Evharisto.*"

"*Parakalo,*" I answered mechanically. "How was your trip?"

Spiro faltered and looked at Nick, who rapidly translated it into Greek. My spirits drooped.

"Oh, *neh, kala.* Ve-ry gooood."

The Greek rattled out of them like machine guns. Spiro's brows shot up, lowered, quivered. He ticked his tongue. Nick leaned toward him, sat back, pulled off his cap, then settled it back on his brow. He pointed to the deck.

And on they chattered, yatatatata, yatatata, about Glenn's death.

I quit trying to follow, becoming consumed with watching Spiro. He had a coarse, wide mustache, the tips carefully twisted and curled slightly upward, giving him a peculiarly jovial expression. It hung so low over his mouth that he chewed on it from time to time. He wore thick, silver-rimmed glasses that hung on his steel-wool eyebrows and followed their darting movements, causing him to readjust them on his nose at frequent intervals. Bright eyes, the color of Greek olives, loomed large behind mason-jar lenses. When he talked, all his features moved, shifted, rearranged themselves as though they were made of Silly Putty.

"*Enthoxi.*" They had come to money, had agreed on it. They pushed back their chairs and Nick led him into the kitchen. I followed like a puppy.

"*Po, po, po. Megali!* Is big!" Spiro ran his hand over the steel tables. He picked up a long, carving knife, whipped a crisp dollar bill from his pocket and sheared off the corner. He laughed and the walls shuddered.

"*Kala.* Good. Sharp!"

We wandered back through the kitchen, Spiro testing everything—turning on the ovens, the slicer, the dish machine. We walked into the cooler, then the freezer. His breath fogged the lenses of his glasses and he grinned, flashing teeth like slabs of marble.

We opened the ice machine, poked our heads inside to examine the compressor. Spiro brought out a handful of ice. He smelled it, licked it, crushed it and dropped it over the floor drain. Nick unlocked the office door and the three of us crowded into it. I don't know why I was following along, tagging at their heels, but I couldn't seem to help myself. Like a child trailing a clown at the circus, I watched him, openmouthed and slack-jawed. He was twice Nick's size.

Nick pointed to the cot. Spiro dropped onto it, patted it with his hand, grinned at me. "Is good! Good bed. I try." He stretched across the cot, but his feet hung out over the edge. "Heh, heh." He drew up his knees. The springs screamed, the legs bowed, the little bed sighed and surrendered. I tugged on Nick's elbow, pulling him back out of the office door.

"He's not staying here?"

"He wants to."

"Nick, that bed's not big enough for him. He can stay in the guest room...."

"He doesn't want to, Julia. He's guarding the place for us. We can't be too careful right now. It gives him a place to stay, and it helps us, too. It's only for a few days, until he finds an apartment."

"But Nick—"

"Julia, it's what he wants. He's very independent. Besides, he's from Crete. Don't argue."

We stuck our heads back in the office door. Spiro was already snoring. I hoped the shingles were tight. Nick handed me my purse and picked up his briefcase. He dropped a key onto the desk and switched off the office light.

"C'mon, let's go home."

"But Nick—just leave him?"

He stopped in the kitchen and stared at me. "Julia, he's from Crete."

"Oh, right." I followed him out the door.

AT HOME I opened a can of soup and warmed a loaf of French bread, unwilling to put any effort into doing again what I had been doing all day. I was feeling tense after our afternoon with Sam, and poured us each a glass of wine, curling up next to Nick on the couch. Jack hovered at Nick's feet, looking for all the world as though he belonged to him.

"You know, he kind of looks like you."

Nick stared at me. "Well, thank you so much."

"No, I mean, you know he has black hair, and you have black hair." I twisted a lock of it around my finger. "And you both have square jaws." I ran my finger along his jawline and tickled his earlobe.

He took the glass out of my hand and pushed me back against the couch.

"But Nick, the soup..."

His voice was husky. "Let it burn."

I didn't, of course. I'm far too practical for that. Later, we sat up in bed, drinking soup from mugs and scattering crumbs of French bread all over the quilt. Jack scampered around the bed, nabbing the crumbs that I brushed over the side. I'd put his bed at the foot of ours, but he conspicuously ignored it.

"So I'll be going to the October Garden Club meeting tomorrow after all. It's a luncheon. You'll have to hold down the fort with Spiro."

Jack leapt onto Nick's lap. His ears were up and he was swiveling his head from Nick to me, tennis-match style. He turned back to Nick, waited, then swiped his nose with a long, pink tongue.

"Nuck that off, Jock!" Nick wiped his nose, pushed Jack off his lap and turned to me. "I don't know, Julia. I'm worried. I don't want you to ask too many questions."

"Look, Nick. It's a perfectly natural place to talk to Dina Fox.

I can't exactly call her and invite her to lunch. We've never been friends. But at the meeting, I can casually take her aside..."

"And say what? 'How did Glenn Bohannon get hold of your bracelet? Were you having an affair with him?' I don't think so."

"Well, no. I'll be careful. I'm just going to feel her out."

"You'd better be. Sometimes you're not so... What's the word?"

"Discreet? I know, but I'll be as tight-lipped as Roger Mumford, I promise."

"You'd better be. Once those women get hold of this—"

I bristled. "The women! What about that herd of old men? I've never seen such gossips in my life. Look at Sonny Weaver! You can't shut him up. That's what we have to worry about—"

The phone interrupted what promised to be an interesting exchange of views on gender roles. I snatched it up angrily.

"Hello?"

I thought it was a bad connection. There was a constant shushing in the background, so loud that at first I couldn't hear the caller.

"I'm sorry, could you repeat that?"

It was louder this time, but husky and grating: "I said, 'Tell your husband to go back where he came from. He's not wanted here.'"

My hand was shaking when I dropped the phone back into the cradle. Nick pulled me into his arms.

"What was it?"

"A threatening phone call."

"Who? Did you recognize him?"

I shook my head. I could barely find my voice to repeat what he'd said. And I was angry with myself, angry that he had frightened me and put me on the defensive. "Nick, what have we gotten ourselves into?"

He pulled my head against his shoulder and rubbed my back in gentle circles. "I wish I knew," he said. "But I want you to be careful."

"That's just what he wants, too. To scare us off. Well, I'm not buying into it."

Nick's jaw was grinding. "No, we're not. But we have to be

smart, Julia. I wish you'd leave the questions to me. Don't go tomorrow.''

I hugged him tighter, buried my face in his neck. "I'm in this just as deeply as you. Both our heads are on the block here, Nick. And you said yourself that we're going to have to help ourselves. Heaven knows Cal Taylor's not going to, and he's not going to let Sam, either.''

"Then please, for God's sake, watch what you say.''

He pulled my chin up and looked into my eyes. There was a little twinkle in his. "Dip your tongue into your brain before you use it.''

[faint text at top, partially visible from previous page bleed-through]

EIGHT

A WIDE PUTTING-GREEN lawn leads up to Marjorie Vandemeer's two-story brick colonial. The front porch is flanked by four massive columns. It's a builder's house, a tract home with a faux plantation facade, but somehow it still invokes visions of women in hoop skirts, with parasols, rocking on the front porch and waiting for "the darkies" to serve them lemonade.

Marjorie is fulsomely gracious, the perfect hostess. A size four herself, she's capable of making the most sophisticated and self-confident woman feel like a Viking. I looked down, just checking to be sure I wasn't wearing breastplates.

"We were afraid you wouldn't make it, Julia. We're so delighted you're here!"

I glanced around the room. No one looked that delighted. Some looked positively apprehensive.

I am a Yankee, but there is something about Delphi that has seemed home to me from the beginning. Maybe it's the smoky blue fog that hangs over town in the early morning, or the crisp autumn colors we get here, near the Smokies, that remind me of New England. Or maybe it stirs some memory of a past life, when I was the one rocking on the front porch and waiting. For all that I deeply love this part of the South, I don't think it loves me.

Here was the one frontier I'd not been able to conquer completely—Southern women. Not all Southern women, just that particular breed who cordially keep me at arm's length and are terminally sweet.

"I'm afraid you've missed the business meeting, but we're just about to serve lunch." I congratulated myself on my impeccable timing.

"You will stay for lunch, won't you?" I felt guilty. Marjorie really is a nice person, and her question was put with earnest concern. As if I hadn't planned to stay.

"Come along, ladies, before it gets cold!" Eleanor Mumford

clapped her hands, organizing the women into a line at the buffet table. I spied Dina near the middle of the line, dropped my purse next to a chair and tagged along behind Carol Hunter. I was going to speak to her, but she was deep in conversation with her next-door neighbor.

To my annoyance, they were lingering in front of the utensils. My stomach roared as though I had cued it. I blushed. It's just this kind of thing that always seems to set me apart. How do other women control a growling stomach? Carol turned around, gave me a thin smile and moved on.

Nothing tempts me like food I don't have to cook. The table groaned under hot casseroles and cold salads, warm muffins and dainty little finger rolls. I heaped my plate with abandon, only mildly ashamed in the knowledge that, having missed the business meeting, I didn't deserve to partake of lunch.

Dina was outside on the deck, the second level of four that terraced and spiraled down to a little stream. The way was lined with azaleas.

"Can I join you?"

She started and looked up, then glanced around as if she were wondering whether it was the only available place to sit. An awkward moment for us both, but she nodded and I plumped down on a wrought-iron chair, leaning toward her as though we were old friends.

"It's so nice to see you. Of course, I see Morgan all the time. You're going to have to get him to bring you in for lunch."

Dina giggled a little. She picked at her food as I wolfed mine down. I was doing a really bad job of this. Why had it seemed like a good idea? I dug into a mound of green rice, asking myself what I knew about Dina and what we could possibly talk about.

What I knew about Dina could be summed up in three bites. She's a petite blonde, attractive and beautifully dressed. She has three small children who are equally attractive and quite well behaved in public. And when she appears on Morgan's arm, it looks to all the world like she adores him.

"How are the kids?"

"Oh, fine," she said vaguely. "Corrinne is getting braces this week."

"Uh oh. Soup time."

"What?"

"Soup. You know how they hurt when you first get them."

"Well, uh, no. I never had to wear them." She might have been sniping at me, but I don't think so. She was just distracted, pushing her food around her plate, and looking as though she wished she were anywhere else but sitting with me. I screwed up my courage, resolving to have a go at getting some information from her.

"I'm really sorry about that incident with Tammy."

"Incident with Tammy? Tammy who?"

"Our waitress. You know. Your bracelet. The one Morgan lost."

Her fork slipped from her hand, onto her plate and off, into her lap. She didn't seem to notice. I went on as though I hadn't seen the reaction, or noticed how pale her face had become.

"It really is the most exquisite thing I've ever seen. All that inlay and carving." I looked directly at her. "I'm sorry. Didn't Morgan tell you? Tammy found the bracelet in the cafe, but instead of turning it in, she kept it. If she hadn't worn it to work, Morgan would never have known where he lost it."

"No. I guess he forgot to mention it."

By then I had discovered a Mexican dish on the second layer of my plate and was really beginning to enjoy myself. Dina looked at her watch, carefully folded her napkin and stood up.

"I hope you'll excuse me, Julia. I have to pick Todd up at nursery school."

"No, wait!" My mouth was full, and a little chunk of corn chip flew across the deck. Flustered and embarrassed, I just blurted it out. "Were you having an affair with Glenn Bohannon?"

I looked at my white plastic knife, wondering if I could possibly cut my tongue out with it. Dina flushed angrily and opened her mouth. I knew she was going to deny it. She stared at me, and I tried to arrange my face in a sympathetic and understanding expression. It must have worked, because she calmly sat back down.

"How did you know?"

"Excuse me?"

"I said, how did you know? Did he tell you?"

"No. Glenn would never have done that. It wasn't his style."

She plucked an azalea blossom off a nearby bush and twirled it between her fingers. "No. It wasn't." She tossed the flower down, ground it under her heel, composed her face and said, "Well, then...?"

"The bracelet. Morgan claimed to have lost it, but Tammy said it fell out of Glenn's pocket. Why else would Glenn have had it? You must have—"

"—left it at Glenn's. I know. I'd meant to go back and get it, but they'd sealed his apartment. I was worried about it."

I swallowed hard. "Dina, what will Morgan think?"

She shook her head. "I don't know." She stopped and looked out over Marjorie's terraces. When she became conscious of me again, she shrugged. "Maybe I'll tell him that I lost it after I went to the cafe for lunch."

"Your timing may be a bit off."

"Yes," she said slowly. "Well, Morgan is always very busy. Sometimes he loses track of time. Maybe, next time you see him, you could just plant the idea that I've been in recently..."

I wasn't crazy about being sucked into this little domestic drama. "Well, yeah, I guess I could sort of drop a hint—something about how nice it was to see you."

"I'd be really grateful to you, Julia. You won't mention this to anyone else?"

"Of course not." Gratitude was just what I wanted. It might help to keep the lines of communication open, so to speak. I needed information about Glenn, and Dina Fox, who had been his lover, might just be able to provide some. I wondered how far I dared pursue this conversation. Of course, tact and good taste had not stopped me so far—why let them interfere now?

"How on earth did you ever get involved with Glenn?"

"Oh, Morgan introduced us at the club when he first came to Delphi. But it really started at obedience classes. I met him again taking the dog to obedience classes."

"You're kidding. You mean Jack's been to obedience school?" I was getting off the track and had to bring myself back to reality. "Dina, I'm not just prying, really. I have…had a reason for asking you, and I have to ask you something else. What would Morgan do if he found out?"

An explosion of bitter laughter burst from her throat. "He won't. Because he'll never, ever, be suspicious. He'll buy the lunch story without blinking. You see, Morgan couldn't possibly imagine that I could be attracted to anyone but Morgan! He is, after all, the perfect husband. And I am the perfect wife. As long as he goes on believing that, he'll be perfectly happy. And Morgan will go a long way to make himself believe it. It's all about image. Not substance, Julia. Just image.

"And now, I really do have to go. I'm already late as it is. Todd will be frightened. Besides, it won't look good if Mrs. Morgan Fox is late picking up one of her perfect children. It might reflect badly on Morgan, and we can't have that, can we?"

I had gone as far as I could. Even I have limits, although at that moment they seemed pretty broad. I couldn't ask her any more personal questions. At least not then.

I REPEATED the conversation to Nick later.

"She wasn't embarrassed?"

"Not a bit. At first I thought she was angry, but then it all changed. In fact, she almost seemed happy that I knew. It was like she wanted to dispel her perfect image. Weird, huh?"

Nick scratched Jack behind the ears and lifted him into his lap. "Do you remember when I coached his son? The oldest one, what's his name?"

"Bradley, I think."

"Right, Bradley. Morgan was on the poor kid all the time. On me, too. He wanted him to play forward, but the kid's not right for it. He's a back, and he could be a good one, but Morgan rode him constantly. No matter how well he played, his father thought he could have played better. I tried to tell him that every position is important in soccer, but he just wouldn't listen. And the more he criticized him, the worse Bradley played. But anyway, I think it's a dead end."

"Why?"

"Because Dina didn't deny the affair, and if she doesn't care that you know then she must not have anything to worry about."

"Maybe she's counting on my discretion." Nick's glance said it all. "All right, I know it's not my greatest strength. But according to her, Morgan has a lot to worry about. His image is pretty important to him. I suppose a successful banker has to build that kind of solid appearance, looking trustworthy and family-oriented. Who'd borrow money from someone who can't manage his own house?"

"I would, if the interest rates were good."

"Well, maybe you're right, but I'm not sure everyone in this town would feel that way. There are a lot of image-conscious people in Delphi, and don't forget, Morgan's on his church board. A scandal would turn off a lot of people."

"Mm, maybe." Jack leaped down and closed his jaw around Nick's ankle. "Ow! Are you sure she said obedience classes? Go get your leash, Jock." Nick stretched, then clipped the leash to Jack's collar. "I think the answer's somewhere else," he said, before following Jack out the door.

I was ready for bed and brushing my teeth by the time they got back. Nick tried to coax Jack into his basket, but Jack turned tail.

"By the way," he said, "I'm taking Spiro to look for a place to live tomorrow. Do you want to go?"

"Where?"

"Come on, Jock. Get on your bed. It's a nice bed. I don't know, we'll look at the ads tomorrow. Probably one of those apartment complexes off Broadway."

Nick was sitting on Jack's bed, bouncing up and down on the fluffy cushion. "Look. It's nice."

Jack wagged his tail, sniffed at the bed, then scampered across the room and vaulted onto the overstuffed chair in the corner. Nick thinks of that chair as his personal valet. Jack scratched and nosed until he had two sweaters and a sweat suit comfortably arranged, then gave a final wag and plopped down. Nick ground his jaws.

I pulled back the quilt and slipped between the sheets. Jack had rolled onto his back and was asleep with his head hanging off the chair. Nick stared at him in disgust before climbing in beside me.

My mind drifted over the day, replaying my conversation with Dina, hearing again the bitterness in her voice—Dina, Morgan, and their strange relationship. How far would either of them go to protect it?

At first I didn't even notice Jack's low growl. I heard the thump as his paws hit the floor and wondered briefly if he had been faking sleep, planning to have a nosh on the furniture once we settled in for the night. But neither of us could miss the frenzied barking at the back door. I nudged Nick. He moaned.

"For crying out loud, I just took him out."

"No," I whispered. "I think he hears something."

Nick staggered out of bed. "Probably voices. In his head. This is the craziest dog I've..." He muttered his way into the kitchen, returning quickly with Jack under his arm.

"There's nothing out there but squirrels and rabbits." He plunked Jack on the bed, but the dog was having none of it. Back to the chair with a happy wag.

"Nick, do you think Morgan is the kind of man who'd kill to protect his image?"

He yawned and scooched down in the bed. "I don't know. Maybe. You never know what people will do, what really drives them."

"Well, I'm going to find out. I'm not sure how, just yet, but... Nick?" I shook his arm. He rolled over and rewarded me with a soft, puffing snore.

"WHAT IS THAT?" It was hanging in the center of the doorway between the wait station and the kitchen. Nick blushed and laughed, but I thought the laugh seemed a little forced.

"*Skorda.* Garlic."

"I know it's garlic. Why is it hanging here?" I thumped one of the pods and the string started swinging, kitchen to wait station and back again.

Nick pulled out his worry beads. Click, click. Click, click. "Well, it's because of Glenn."

"I don't get it, Nick. What does a string of garlic have to do with Glenn? And who put it there?"

"Uh, Spiro."

"Why?"

"To keep away evil."

"You're joking."

"Well, not really. See, Spiro thinks there's some evil in the restaurant, since someone died here, and garlic's supposed to... Well, he's a sailor, and sailors are very superstitious."

I suppose I was staring at him. The worry beads spun into a blur.

"In fact, Greeks in general are kind of..." Click, click. "Well, he believes it, anyway."

"But you don't?"

"Of course not."

"Okay, then let's take it down." I reached up to the top of the door frame, but Nick wrenched my arm away.

"No!"

I eyed him with deep suspicion. "Why not?"

"Because Spiro will be upset. He's from Crete, Julia."

"You know, I'm getting a little tired of that oblique answer."

"Well, take it down and you'll see what I mean."

This had the sound of dire consequences. I reached for the string again and gently laid it across the top of the door frame. "There. At least now it will be out of the way. Are you ready? Let's go."

Nick called to Spiro, who was coming through the back door with an empty garbage can. He snapped open a clean bag and carefully arranged it.

"Okay," he said, pulling off his apron. "We go." As we left the kitchen, he grabbed the garlic string and pulled it back into the doorway. "Is good," he said. "No more trouble."

THE SIGN SAID Delphi Rental Properties in faded green letters, and leaned about ten degrees, approximately the same angle as the posts on the front porch. Nick stood on the cracked sidewalk and gaped at the house. Spiro wandered across the tiny patch of front lawn, pulling out weeds by the handful.

"Let's go. This is no place for him. It's horrible."

I looked around the neighborhood, dismayed to see that the bungalows were identical, both in design and condition. Peeling paint, warping porches, shutters hanging precariously by a single hinge.

We had been to just about every apartment complex in Delphi and Spiro had summarily rejected them all—too much noise, too many students, too small, too big, too...

Spiro was on the porch, hammering on one of the posts with the heel of his hand. It actually did seem to straighten up a little. He moved from that to one of the lopsided shutters, lifted it into place and closed one eye, then rattled something at Nick.

"What did he say?"

"He says he thinks it needs a little work."

"With a wrecking ball, maybe. Let's go, Nick."

"Spiro, ella, pame!"

Spiro reluctantly left the porch. At the curb, he stopped and turned around, closed an eye again. Nick was urging him into the car, when the low vibration of a motor came around the corner. A sleek, black Toyota MR2 swung into the driveway and rumbled to a halt. Then the driver's door swung open, and she slid out.

NINE

CONNIE SANTOS had that kind of sultry, steamy appearance that suggested she'd just tumbled out of a centerfold and into her clothes. Her complexion was a burnished olive, her eyes deep brown under heavy lids. Her hair was almost as dark, but with streaks of gold that looked like fingers of sunlight had been stroking it. It had been put up in some type of twist, but the tendrils that had fallen around her face did nothing to diminish my overall impression that Nick could not be left alone with her safely. I instinctively brushed a hand through my own close-cropped curls, and felt deeply that I was the lesser woman.

But when she stuck out her hand and introduced herself, she was all brisk business. I took her hand first, as Nick and Spiro were frozen, their mouths open so wide that I could have jerked out their molars.

"I'm Julia Lambros and this is my husband Nick." I shot him the hardest elbow I could tactfully inflict. "And this is our friend, Spiro Papavasilakis."

"Hi. Fine." Spiro shook her hand and grinned, grinned and shook her hand. She looked quizzically from him to me and finally pulled away.

"Let me show you the house." She turned and was up the sidewalk and on the porch before I could protest.

"Well, we've just about decided…"

"It won't hurt to look," Nick said. Spiro held the door open for her and felt around for the light switch.

Three dim bulbs in a tulip fixture strained to light the room. It was completely furnished, if one could call a gold vinyl couch and matching armchair furniture. One of Sonny Weaver's old wall calendars hung over the couch, proclaiming his slogan, Insure and Feel Secure, in bold red letters. The place smelled musty and cold and I thought I heard something scratching in the walls.

The ad had read "fully equipped kitchen," which apparently

referred to a white single-door refrigerator that shrugged its round shoulders into a corner. It heaved and sighed when I opened the door. I was grateful that the interior bulb was burned out. A random set of stainless utensils rattled in one of the drawers. I opened the rest of the cabinets and inventoried: two saucepans, one frying pan, a large, speckled black spaghetti pot, an egg beater...

"So, there's a four-hundred-dollar nonrefundable deposit on the house. You pay all utilities. Rent is due on the first of the month without exception. If he wants to move in this week, I'll prorate the rent through the thirtieth."

I stared disbelievingly at Nick, but he was following Connie Santos to the bedroom. Forgetting the pots and pans, I was close on his heels.

"And how much did you say the rent is?"

"Three twenty-five a month. Renter pays the utilities."

Nick ticked his tongue and raised his brow at Spiro, a sign to be interpreted by all Greeks as a firm no. The unspoken exchange seemed to throw Connie off, but just for a minute.

She hastily continued. "Let me show you the rest. It has kind of a homey feeling to it, doesn't it?"

Home to what? The scratching in the walls seemed to be getting louder and more frantic. I walked on tiptoe, prepared to vault into Nick's arms at the first sight of anything gray and furry. We followed Connie through the house and back to the living room.

"Does your friend speak English?"

"Not much. A little."

Connie seemed to brighten at this. I suppose with Spiro's limited command of the language, she wouldn't have to worry about him hitting on her. She wouldn't understand him anyway.

"Ohee, agori mou!" Nick and Spiro were in the middle of a brisk exchange. Spiro was nodding yes to Nick's emphatic nos. Connie could read the situation as well as I could. She put a light hand on Nick's elbow.

"If it's the expense you're concerned about, I can probably adjust that a little. Say, to two-fifty a month?"

Spiro demanded a translation, and Nick reluctantly complied. Connie was developing a worried little pout. I was afraid she would lower the rent even more, just to get the lease. I guided her toward the front door.

"How long has the house been vacant?"

"Almost a year. I...I've been searching for just the right renter. We're a little particular about our tenants."

"Why?"

Her eyes grew cold and her lips tightened. She turned back to the men as though she hadn't heard me. I stepped in front of her.

"Just who owns this house, Ms. Santos?"

"Why Delphi Rental Properties, of course."

"Where's their office?"

"Oh, well, we don't have one. I take calls out of my apartment and meet the client at the property. An office would really be an unnecessary expense."

"I see. Well, who owns Delphi Rental Properties?"

Connie's eyes shifted back to Nick and Spiro. The muscles in her face tightened, and her fingers gripped the edge of her shoulder bag until the knuckles turned white. The men crossed the room toward us. Nick was shaking his head, but Spiro was beaming.

"Oh, a local businessman or two. Did I mention that pets are not allowed? Your friend doesn't have a pet, does he?"

"Only a small goat he brought from Crete," said Nick, grinning.

"Oh. Well..." She looked around vaguely, as though trying to figure out how to accommodate the goat. Then she caught the twinkle in Nick's eye.

"YOU KNOW, for a minute I think she really believed Spiro had a goat." I tied on my apron and stuck a sailor's cap on my head. I could smell the coffee, knew it was done. I took two mugs off the shelf, filled one halfway with sugar, poured coffee into both and came back through the wait station door, stopping to rearrange the garlic. Nick was filling the steam table with water. He mopped his brow and took the coffee gratefully.

"It's hard to understand why she'd be concerned about pets with the place in the condition it's in, though. Spiro's already talking about fixing it up. He wants to paint it and put in a garden.

I told him not to start anything. The landlords should take care of that.''

''Well, don't hold your breath.'' I cracked a half dozen eggs into a steel bowl and started whisking them into submission. It was Monday morning. Spiro had spent Sunday moving into his new place. We'd told him to sleep in, so Nick and I had breakfast detail.

''Did you see the condition of those houses? Every single one of them is owned by Delphi Rental Properties except the one next door to Spiro on the right.''

''How do you know that?''

''I asked Connie. She seemed a little reluctant to admit it, but I got it out of her. I never could get her to tell me who Delphi Rental Properties is, though. Whoever they are, they ought to be ashamed of themselves. I don't see how, in good conscience, we can let Spiro stay there. It's a dump, Nick.''

''Julia, he wanted to rent it. I know it's hard to believe, but he was very insistent.''

''I saw, but I'm sure I don't know why.''

Nick laid a dozen sausages on the grill, studying them intently. He looked embarrassed. Of course, I really did know why.

''Connie Santos,'' I said.

''He didn't want to hurt her feelings. Besides, he can take care of himself. He's been all over the world. Just because he doesn't speak English doesn't mean he's stupid.''

''Of course not. I wasn't implying that he is. It's just that I feel sort of responsible for his welfare. He seems kind of vulnerable. I don't want her to get her hooks into him.''

''Hooks? Isn't that a little dramatic? I mean, she was all business yesterday.''

''Yeah, but what business?''

''Julia! You know, I think you're a little jealous.''

A warm blush crept up my neck. I was going to deny it, but Nick and I have always been pretty straight with each other. ''Well, I guess it's just that women like that make me feel so...so ordinary!''

Nick took the whisk out of my hand and set it aside, grasping my hands in his. I gazed into his liquid, brown eyes. ''Trust me on this one. There's nothing ordinary about you." He kissed my forehead lightly and turned back to the sausage, flipping one high into the air and spinning on his toes before catching it with the spatula.

"But, I'm glad you feel that way about Spiro. I wasn't too sure you liked him. And remember, he was a sailor. He's a lot tougher than you seem to think. Besides..."

"I know, I know. He's from Crete."

Tammy sauntered through the kitchen toward her locker and the time clock. She was wearing a filmy, black broomstick skirt and a low-cut top that barely grazed her waist. Anytime she reached up, we'd get plenty of bare midriff. Mental note: Have fashion consultation with Tammy. She got halfway across the kitchen before she turned on her heel and pointed at the wait-station door.

"What's that?"

"Garlic."

"What's it for?"

"To keep away evil."

"Oh. Yeah." She shrugged, pulled a furry hairbrush from her purse, and headed for her locker.

The breakfast orders were dribbling in, slowing down more each day since Glenn's death. As soon as Spiro was settled in, we'd take out an ad, probably with his picture, announcing a new cook. Meanwhile, we were relying on the Buffaloes to bring business back. Rhonda stuck her head in the kitchen door.

"I think they're about ready out here, Julia. Just waiting for the photographer to get here. Do you want to watch?"

"Yeah, I'll be out in a minute."

Two tickets fluttered on the wheel. Nick could handle it himself. "Mind if I go on?"

He glanced at the tickets, sighed, shook his head. "No problem. Go ahead. I'll be out in a minute."

"Aw, shit." Norm threw his napkin down on the table, turned away, uncrossed and recrossed his legs. "They sent Jimmy Olsen. Fresh-faced kid, thinks he knows everything there is to know about journalism. He doesn't know a goddamn thing. Doesn't know how hard it is to break into this business...." I wondered if Norm, who fancies himself a reporter, had ever read Aesop or was familiar with the term "sour grapes."

Billy English, the young photographer from the Sun, climbed the deck and headed for us. Nick, having filled his two orders, had joined us.

"A regular Ansel Adams, that one," muttered Norm. "Don't know what such talent's doing at the Sun." He tossed back the rest of his coffee. "I got to go."

"Wait, Norm. You can't go yet. Don't you want to be in the picture?" Billy said. He leaned his tripod against the railing, closed an eye and squared his hands. "Okay, so the way I get it is you guys eat here every morning, right?"

"Well, more or less," I said. This had been Norm's idea, but the others had quickly embraced it, for which I was trying to be grateful. Their thought was that since they were among the best known and, according to them, most highly respected business-men in Delphi, it would be wonderful publicity for us to feature a picture of them breakfasting at the Oracle in our ad. The fact that they usually brought their own food notwithstanding.

"How about we start with all you guys around the table having breakfast?"

"That would be a novelty," I muttered to Nick.

They shuffled around the table, artfully arranging themselves by height so that no one would be obscured. Sonny, who was the shortest, sat at the end of the table. "Wish I'd worn my *Delphi Sun* hat today," he said ruefully.

They reminded me of a Dutch Masters cigar ad, a cluster of hale fellows, chortling and raising their coffee cups—anonymous, homologous in their little group. And yet, I reminded myself, they were individuals, having wives and families, businesses, mothers. Gathered together, all fifteen of them, they took on a single good-old-boy identity. On closer inspection, however, some stood out from the herd.

Read was unquestionably the most distinguished of the group, with his patrician features and carefully correct language. He car-ried the *Wall Street Journal* with him at all times, always wore suits, crisp white shirts, and glossy leather shoes. For dress and general appearance, he was rivaled only by Morgan Fox.

Buffalo gossip had it that Morgan's reputation had caused ripples far outside the narrow banking circles of Delphi. In his early thirties, he'd taken over the bank presidency and increased loans and depositors at an astonishing rate, putting himself on the fast track to the home office in Atlanta. The ascendant star of the Southern financial galaxy smoothed his vest and picked up the coffeepot—standing as though he were serving the others at the table, as though his mission in life were to serve others.

The beneficiary of this service was Norm Pearson, who writes "This Week In Delphi." Being tall and cadaverously thin, Norm sat at the rear of the group. But in a brown-and-gold plaid sports jacket, there was little chance of his being lost in the photograph. He carefully combed six-inch locks from the side of his head over his bald spot and examined his teeth in the back of a spoon.

Next to, but more or less in front of Norm, Mitch Yoakum held a sugar packet in his hands, poised to tear it open. His face reminded me of chopped meat, red and raw from years in the sun pursuing the gainful business of building. He pulled his chair as close to the table as possible in an effort to hide the paunch that hung over his tooled leather belt. "Put out that damn cigarette, Blaine."

Lee apologized and ground it into an ashtray. With his wholesome, Hubert Humphreyesque manner and casual dress, the cigarette created a startling incongruity. He glanced up, giving me a quick view of his most attractive feature—pale blue eyes bordered by a black rim that created a surreal otherworldliness, as though he had seen a better world to come. The impression was further borne out by his placid features and the dazzling whiteness of the smile he tossed to the camera.

To Norm's right, Warren Hunter dumped cigarette butts and ashes into a napkin, which he held over his head, waiting for me to retrieve it. His feet were flat on the floor, but the muscles of his slender legs jumped and jerked nervously, and his hand twitched as he handed me the napkin. As always, Charley Aldrich was grinning broadly. Maybe it's his utter lack of hair that makes him appear as though he has nothing to hide.

"Settle down, will you, Warren?" Charley nudged his shoulder playfully. "It's just a picture, for crying out loud. Nobody's on trial here."

Billy worked quickly, with a professionalism that astonished Norm. In ten minutes they were finished and relaxing around a final cup of coffee. I calculated it in my mind. A minimum of three cups per person, free refills, for a total of forty-five cups of coffee, netting us a little over ten dollars. And these were the kind of customers we wanted to advertise? Yet despite my antagonism toward them, I was grateful for their help.

Charley patted my back. "Maybe this'll help put a stop to the rumors."

"Rumors?" I might have known it. Rumors are rife in the restaurant business at the best of times, the favorite being that it's a cover for drug dealing. Now, with a customer dead at our feet, I could hardly have expected the mill to crank down.

"What kind of rumors, exactly?"

Charley stirred uneasily in his chair. "Well, nothing anybody could take very seriously, Julia."

"I want to hear them, Charley," I said evenly. "We can't fight them if we don't know what they are."

"Okay, well...there's one about your food quality. That you don't buy from approved sources and that, well, what you served Glenn was bad—"

"Hey, that'd make an interesting story!" Norm fantasizes about investigative reporting. "You know, on pirates who steal the rejects from vendors and sell the goods under the table." I tossed my husband an agonized glance.

"I'll bet they come to you from time to time, don't they, Nick?" Read smoothed his peppered hair back with a square hand. "Must be a temptation to save a little money—well, probably a lot of money. What do you do?"

Nick smiled complacently. "I just say no."

Read stood up, folded his newspaper and clapped Nick on the shoulder. "Glad to hear it. I admire a man with ethics. There aren't all that many of us left in the world." He glanced around the deck. "Present company excluded, of course."

"Well, I think it's up to us to put a stop to these rumors, instead of spreading them." Lee took a sip of his coffee. "We all know that Nick runs his business on the up-and-up. And that business about drugs and tax fraud..."

"What?"

As rumors do, they were growing as fast and wild as kudzu in July. Sonny eyed Nick speculatively. "Tax fraud? Wouldn't be so hard to do, I guess. You just don't ring up some of your tickets, they're not on your register tape. You don't report the sales, you don't pay taxes on them. Simple."

"I report all my sales, Sonny. Right down to the last penny." Nick ground the words out between clenched teeth, a cue to the others that it was time to go. They rose as a body and stampeded toward the door. Sonny and Lee trailed along at the back.

"Drugs, huh? Heroin? Cocaine?"

"Now, Sonny, it's just a rumor. I think Cal said cocaine, but I wouldn't put any stock in it."

My throat knotted as the door swung closed behind their backs.

TEN

I SURREPTITIOUSLY watched Sam and Rhonda from the doorway of the wait station. He was so relaxed with her, reclining back in his chair, quietly observing her animated conversation. A trace of a smile lingered around his mouth as he leaned toward her, speaking quietly. Her face became grave, a worried frown plucking at her brow. She shook her head, as though denying something he said. He took her hands across the table and patted them reassuringly. I felt, in my gut, that he was questioning her—but it was a kinder, gentler treatment than we had received. I reminded myself that he was also very much in love with her.

They kept their relationship quiet, seemingly casual. But I knew Rhonda too well to believe that. She was not a girl for casual affairs. Intensely private, that we knew that she was seeing Sam at all was testimony to the seriousness of their relationship. But nothing spoke more clearly than the light in his face when she entered the room, or the excited twitching of her hands when he appeared. I knew the signs, had experienced them myself. For that matter, I still do.

Rhonda had been with us from the beginning. Five years. It's almost a record in this business. Restaurants attract the transient. No matter how much they like you or their jobs, no matter how much you value and appreciate them, when it's time to up and move, they do it—and without looking back.

But not Rhonda. Her loyalty to us was as intense as her adoration of Sam. She was probably in the toughest spot of her life. Sam knew it. We knew it. We tried not to involve or worry her, but down deep I suppose we all knew it was a matter of time.

Nick checked out the last lunch customer and closed the register drawer. "I'm going to talk to Sam," he said.

I watched him cross the floor, saw Sam's relaxed posture stiffen as Nick approached the table. I followed, joining them just in time to hear him ask the question which had worried him the most.

"What about my green card, Sam? When am I going to get it back? I could bring in a lawyer, but—"

"I don't know that I'd do that, Nick. Sheriff Taylor's a bit of..." He stroked his chin thoughtfully. "Well, some in the department like to say he's a hard-ass. Your lawyer might be able to force him to give up the green card, but it's likely to flash back in your face, you know? You're walking kind of a tightrope here. The sheriff'd like nothing better than to push you off. Besides, he's leaving town, won't be back for a couple of days."

"What about you, Sam?"

He looked away from us all, over the all-too-empty dining room. "I'm trying to keep an open mind. Trying to do my job, too. I got responsibilities to the taxpayers, Nick. All the evidence isn't in yet, but I gotta be frank. It doesn't look good."

"How can you know that if the evidence isn't in?"

Sam hesitated. "You might say there are extenuating circumstances." He shook his head. "Sorry, Nick. I can't say more than that." He pushed up, away from the table, and picked up his ticket. I followed him to the register as Nick turned toward the kitchen to consult with Spiro on tomorrow's specials. Rhonda stayed behind to bus the table. Sam tucked a toothpick into the corner of his mouth and reached for his wallet. I waved it away.

"I know it's not easy for you, Sam. Let us buy today—while we still can."

"I shouldn't—"

I put up my hand to stop him. "No strings. Just a meal with friends."

He adjusted his belt into a more comfortable, postmeal position around his broad girth, chewed on the toothpick and nodded. "Just a meal with friends."

RHONDA WAS a whirlwind the rest of the afternoon, cleaning around Tammy, who sat at the family table picking the polish off her nails and watching the traffic on Broadway go by. There was a nervous, worried energy behind the hard twisted silverware rolls Rhonda produced, and the abrasive scrubbing she gave the wait-station counters. I stayed away from her, letting her work it through her system. She was coming to a decision.

"Julia, got a minute?"

I was inventorying the walk-in cooler. She kicked the bucket I was using as a doorstop aside, pulling the door closed behind her. A chill traveled up my back—whether from the cold air, or Rhonda's face I couldn't say. "I need to talk to you."

I laid my clipboard on top of a case of tomatoes and tucked the pencil behind my ear. "Okay. What's up?"

She stared at the shelves, began rearranging the produce, emptying and consolidating the crates. She wasn't looking at me. "Sam. It's something he said. I guess, well, I guess they think...They're pretty sure of how Mr. Bohannon died."

My heart plunged to my stomach. "How? Oh God, Rhonda, tell me it was a heart attack."

She discarded lettuce leaves, stacked and rearranged perfectly ordered blocks of cheese. "Not exactly."

I already knew, had suspected it from the beginning. "Poison," I muttered.

Rhonda sagged against a shelf. "How did you know? How did you know that, Julia?"

"It's pretty obvious by the way Sam's behaving. And there were no wounds, no knife. No weapon. That's all, Rhonda. Really, that's how I knew."

"I guess they have to identify the poison before they can test the...the body for it. The body, Mr. Bohannon, it went to the state crime lab. Sam says they're not sophisticated enough to do that kind of testing here."

"Did he say what it was?"

She shook her head, turned, and for the first time, faced me. "I don't think they know yet. If they do, he didn't tell me. Besides, he was kind of asking me to...to keep my eyes and ears open. I'm not supposed to be telling you this, Julia, but Nick didn't...couldn't...Could he?"

"Of course not, Rhonda. You've known him for five years. Do you really think he could kill someone? I'd be a more likely suspect than Nick, for heaven's sake! I can't believe Sam could seriously suspect Nick."

She stood silent, slumped over the egg crates for a moment, then straightened her back and pushed her hair off her forehead. "He's only doing his job, you know, Julia."

I put my arm around her shoulder and gave her a quick hug, knowing all too well how it felt to have to defend the man you love. "I know," I said. "And I appreciate your telling me. Did he say anything else? Like what happens next?"

"No. But he asked me if you and Nick did much traveling. Like, maybe, it was important to know. But I asked him, where could they go when they're open six days a week?"

"And he said?"

"In the age of airplanes, almost anywhere."

"I'VE GOT TO GO to that game tonight, Julia."

"Nick, don't you see enough of them every morning at breakfast? Besides, we promised Spiro if he'd work lunch we'd help him get settled into his house tonight."

"I know, but...can't you see? It's closing in on us, Julia. Someone set us up to take the fall for Glenn's murder. We'd better face it. It was one of the Buffaloes."

"Then you could be in danger."

"Are you kidding? Whoever he is, he's not going to kill me. He'd rather see me strung up for Glenn's death."

I knew he was right. Until now, I hadn't wanted to face the fact that one of those men, who professed to be our friends, had ruthlessly served us up to Cal Taylor. Murder suspects à la grecque. *Murder!* The word was as chilling as the walk-in. I stuck my icy hands in the pockets of my skirt and started toward the dining room.

AFTER WE CLOSED, I followed Spiro home, armed with buckets, mops, sponges, and commercial cleaners. I stayed close behind the big, gray Pontiac, watched it float down Broadway, turn left on Delphi Drive, right on Magnolia, and enter the little, down-at-the-heels neighborhood that was now home for him.

On the outskirts of "Markettown," so called because, at one time, it had held a large Farmer's Market and Co-op, a few of the bungalows had been renovated quite attractively. Big Wheels cluttered teaspoon yards, and hopscotch boards crisscrossed the uneven sidewalks. Spiro honked and waved at children playing in their yards who in turn stopped their games to follow the progress of his amazing Pontiac in astonishment.

But as we plunged deeper into Markettown the atmosphere grew depressed. We passed the old Farmer's Market, now converted into a Salvation Army facility. Unkempt houses lined the narrow streets like the elderly in a nursing-home hallway, forlorn and almost abandoned, their porches sunken in like toothless gums. The faces on the streets were more often black than white, old than young. A few bungalows housed students, marked by driveways holding sporty used cars arrayed with Parnassus bumper stickers. In these houses the lights blazed at dusk, and despite their sagging appearance, there was an element of cheerful hope surrounding them. Not so the houses which flanked Spiro's.

The Pontiac sheared the weeds in the driveway, while I pulled to a stop in front of the red shuttered house. The house to the left appeared deserted, wide Venetian blinds drawn closed over the green-shuttered windows. A family of faded plaster ducks plowed through the dandelions and milkweed and into what, at one time, might have been a rock garden next to the steps. A low, cinderblock wall separated the driveways of the two houses.

To the right, an elderly woman pushed a walker up a narrow walkway toward the steps of a blue-shuttered house that was the twin of Spiro's. She carried a string bag that slapped against the metal rails of her walker. Spiro sprang from the Pontiac and vaulted over the low hedge between their houses. By the time I was out of the car, she was screaming and desperately trying to hold on to the string bag. She rocked precariously, one gnarled hand gripping the walker, as the fingers of the other twisted through the bag's handles.

"Go away!" she shrieked, and tried to tug the bag from his big hands. "I'll call the police if you don't! Help! Police!"

Spiro smiled and nodded his head. He tugged gently at the bag, but being easily twice her weight, it must have felt that he would drag her with him. He shrugged and dropped the bag, and as she stumbled backward, bent over and scooped her up as though she were a recalcitrant child. By the time I reached her, he was up the stairs and I could do nothing more than grab her walker and stumble up behind them. Her mouth had frozen open, emitting only plaintive squeaks, and her eyes were round with terror.

"Spiro, put her down!"

His enthusiasm faded at the sound of my voice. He let the old woman down gently, took the walker from my hands and set it in front of her with a flourish. "I help *yia yia*," he said.

She swayed unsteadily, one hand to her breast as though her heart might give out, the other carefully patting a cumulus cloud of silvery blue hair into place. I grabbed her elbow and held it, saying nothing and giving her a moment to recover from the shock.

"He was trying to help you," I said. "He doesn't speak very much English."

She turned snapping brown eyes on him, appraising him carefully from the brim of his black wool cap to the toes of his grease-spattered shoes. "Where...where does he come from?" she said, as though he might have just stepped off some alien craft. It was a close encounter of the Spiro kind.

I pointed to his house, next door to hers. "He's just moved in there. He thought he was being neighborly."

"No. You said he doesn't speak English. Where does he come from?"

"Greece. Crete, to be exact."

Her eyes took on a dreamy quality. "Greece. I always wanted to go there. I used to teach school. Well, it seems like ages ago now, I taught history." She unwrapped the string bag that had become twisted around her arm, and put out her hand to Spiro.

"I am Alma Rayburn," she said. She spoke slowly, for him to understand, and her drawl became deeper. "People here call me Miss Alma."

He took her hand as gently as he might hold a baby bird, smiled and nodded. "Hi. Fine. Spiro Papavasilakis. Signome, Kyria." Miss Alma turned to me.

"'I'm sorry, madam.' That's what he said."

"Please tell him it's all right. I know he meant well."

"I don't speak much Greek myself, but I think he already understands."

I introduced myself and we shook hands. Her hand was trembling, whether palsied or from the shock I couldn't tell. She took a ring of keys out of her bag and selected one, held it, seemingly undecided about using it. "Let me do that for you," I said, reaching for the key.

Miss Alma continued to hold it, carefully assessing us both. I was glad to see that she would not simply accept us and open the door to two strangers. In a neighborhood like this one, it wasn't good policy. At length she tendered the key and stepped aside. I turned the dead bolt and helped Miss Alma get her walker over the threshold. Spiro carried the string bag into her living room and left it on the seat of a Victorian slipper chair. Miss Alma invited us to stay for a cup of tea, but I declined for us both. The thought of her Wedgewood cups in his meaty hands, and the way the slipper chair would bow under his colossal frame required more delicate handling than I could manage.

She followed us back out to the porch and watched as we unloaded our cars of their cargo of cleaning equipment, nodded approvingly and gave us a brief wave. As we were hauling in the last of the load, a white panel truck pulled up in front of the house on the other side of Spiro's. The magnetic sign on the side advertised house painters. The door rolled back, two dark men and a woman jumped out. They had duffle bags slung over their shoulders. I thought I saw the window blinds in the house briefly lifted and dropped again. The door slid back into place and the truck pulled out just as they disappeared inside the house. I turned back to Miss Alma's house. She was still standing on the porch, but she had dropped her hand, and her forehead was creased in a frown.

I PULLED ON heavy rubber gloves and pointed around the kitchen. "I will start here," I said. Prepared to meet the worst, I pulled open the refrigerator door. To my surprise, the light flickered on brightly and the white enamel interior was stunning.

"I clean."

"I see that." It was spotless, and already half filled by a gallon of milk, a chunk of feta cheese, a bundle of grapes, and assorted vegetables.

"All right, then." I examined the rest of the kitchen. The counters had been scrubbed down to reveal gold-flecked white formica. Spiro must have cleaned them with a toothbrush. There was not a speck of grime in the molding between the sink and countertop. The floor had been mopped and the cabinets wiped down. Feeling superfluous, I opened the cabinets and, finally, found something that I could do. I pulled a roll of shelf paper from my bag and waved it at Spiro. "This will make it nicer."

He nodded and pointed into the living room. "I work."

I unloaded the little stock of Melamine dishes, plastic glassware, pots and pans. There were so few utensils that they scarcely took up the first two shelves, but to be thorough, I felt I should cover them all.

The shelves had been covered with contact paper, probably sometime during the Ice Age. I peeled it back, repulsed by what was stuck on the back. Measuring and cutting, I mused that my fellow Garden Club members would probably approve of this activity.

"Zulia, it is Connie!"

I rounded the corner to the living room to find Spiro with a broom in his hand. He had covered the couch and chair with big sheets of plastic and, I gathered from the lace of cobwebs trimming the crown of his cap, that he had been sweeping the ceiling. He stood in front of the window overlooking the porch. I peered out with him.

Connie Santos pulled two bags of groceries out of the passenger side of her car, heaved her purse onto her shoulder, and stalked up the sidewalk to the house next door.

"She live here?" Spiro pointed to the house with the plaster ducks.

"I don't know. I doubt it."

"Look. She is there."

She had come back, followed by the two men I had seen getting out of the van earlier. As she directed, they each hoisted a case of beer from the car and followed her into the house. Spiro and I waited at the window, but when she didn't reappear, we went back to work.

I was down to the last two shelves, had the paper stretched

across the counter to be measured, when a flash of light caught my eye. The kitchen window faced Spiro's weedy driveway. I hadn't noticed it before, perhaps because it was dark out there, but when the lights came on, I found myself staring into an identical kitchen twelve, maybe fifteen feet away.

Connie Santos stood in front of the window, a longneck beer bottle in her hand. She was speaking to someone out of my range of vision, her lips moving rapidly and her face agitated. She was angry, and she was spitting fire at someone. I slipped over to the wall switch and turned it off, the more discreetly to watch the growing drama in the house next door.

In a second, the man appeared. He, too, carried a beer bottle, held it to his lips and emptied it in one final, long gulp before slamming it down on the counter. He ran slender fingers through his wiry, black curls and gestured angrily at Connie. Their voices were raised, vibrating across the drive to my waiting ears. But I couldn't make out the words. They were speaking too fast. He took a step toward Connie and she pulled back, lunged for his beer bottle and smashed it against the side of the sink. I caught my breath as she crept toward him, the broken glass glittering in her hand. He stepped back, his hands up in front of his body. He was quiet now, seemed to have turned compliant and agreeable, nodding his head as she scored verbal points with the help of the broken bottle. At length a hard smile cracked Connie's face. She laughed and moved out of sight. When she returned, her hands were empty. She bent down and removed a platter from the oven before they both turned away from the window.

I pondered what I had witnessed as I finished my cutting and fitting of shelf paper. I did not, I decided, want to go out drinking with Connie Santos. Some people get sloppy when they drink. Some get mean. Clearly, Connie was the latter.

"Zulia? *Skotathi?*"

"Dark," I said, mechanically correcting him as I had during the early years with Nick. "It is dark." Not for nothing have I seen *Rear Window* three times. He flipped the light back on and looked out the window.

"Oh, it is Connie!" She was back in the kitchen. Spiro waved both arms above his head, vainly trying to get her attention. She threw her purse over her shoulder and walked away from the window. In a minute, we heard the low rumble of the MR2. Spiro was crestfallen.

It had grown quite late. Jack was at home, alone, and no doubt wreaking havoc on our innocent furniture. Spiro helped me pack up the cleaning supplies and load the car. A match was struck and a cigarette lit on the porch next door. As I pulled away, Spiro clambered over the cement block wall, bound for his new neighbor.

ELEVEN

"How was the game?" I pried my eyes open, lifted up off the couch on one elbow and squinted at the clock. Two a.m. Nick tossed his hat on the kitchen table and rubbed his hand over his forehead.

"Okay, I guess."

"You don't sound like it was okay."

He lifted a snarling Jack off the couch and dropped down next to me. "It was just hard, you know? Sitting there with them, pretending everything is all right."

"Was it worth it?"

"I don't know. Maybe." Jack returned with an all-is-forgiven wag and gently deposited his tennis ball in Nick's lap. Nick scratched Jack's ears absentmindedly. "We talked about Glenn a lot. In fact, that's all we talked about."

"And?"

"Well, they all agreed on one thing. Glenn didn't seem too serious about his business."

"What do you mean? He seemed pretty serious to me."

"Yeah, me too. But I guess when it came down to putting out the money and making the decisions, he sort of hung back. Take Read, for example. He says he showed Glenn at least fifteen different spots in town—some of them good, some not so good. But Glenn just wouldn't make up his mind."

"Well, there's the issue of the highway to consider. Wherever it goes in is bound to affect business."

"Yeah, that's true. But Mitch and Sonny said pretty much the same thing. That they couldn't get a commitment from him. They took the attitude that he was teasing them along."

"Sort of a financial foreplay."

"Right. But when it came to climbing into bed with them, he just wouldn't do it." He rolled the ball in his hand as Jack yipped and danced at his feet.

"Maybe he didn't really know as much about business as we thought he did. Maybe he was afraid to make a decision."

"You could be right. Remember when we took him to Lee's to look at equipment? He didn't seem to know what he was looking for. I had to show him everything."

"I don't remember it quite that way."

Nick blushed, remembering....

NICK HAD swung the car into a narrow gravel driveway and followed the lane past the side of the large warehouse to a vast parking lot at the rear. A huge tractor-trailer truck was backed up to a platform to the right of the door. A young man in overalls jumped off the loading dock, vaulted into the truck and pulled out, parking it at the rear of the lot. Nick watched the massive creature in silent admiration until it was parked.

"Come on, Glenn, let's go find Lee. He should be able to help you."

We tentatively knocked on a turquoise-enameled door with BLAINE DIVERSIFIED stenciled across it in white letters. A shout echoed from the loading dock and the young man waved us on in. He met us in a narrow corridor between two offices.

"Mr. Blaine ain't here, but I 'spect him back in a coupla minutes. Y'all need something?"

Nick explained that we were looking for restaurant equipment for Glenn and hoped that Leland Blaine could help us out. The young man rubbed his chin.

"I don't knows we got what you're looking for. Why don't y'all just go on out there 'n see what you can find. Mr. Blaine'll be back shortly." He pointed to a door at the end of the corridor, then pulled a clipboard off the wall and led us to the warehouse.

"You'll find restaurant 'quipment on over here," he said. He pointed again, this time to three aisles of floor-to-ceiling shelving to the left of the loading dock. The shelves began about six feet up, leaving room for larger pieces below.

"Look at all this stuff!" Nick wandered up and down the aisles, pointing out equipment ranging from enormous Hobart mixers to freestanding reach-in coolers, grills, and ovens. The equipment was definitely used, some in what appeared to be irreparable condition. Some of it was crated and on pallets, ready, I supposed to be shipped out all over the country. From what I understood from the Buffaloes, Blaine did a moderately successful business in buying and reselling used equipment. But not, I conjectured, without considerable repair. Here and there we found the odd piece that gleamed like new.

"You'll want a medium-weight slicer, probably, and definitely a good, heavy-duty food processor."

"What'll I need that for?"

I gaped at Glenn, stifling my surprise. "You've got to shred cheese, and lettuce for tacos. If you're going to make your own salsa, you'll be chopping peppers and onions."

"Oh. Right. Of course."

"Then you have to consider what kind and size fryer you'll need. For Mexican, I'd say pretty big."

"Electric or gas? Is there such a thing as a gas fryer?"

"I imagine. Ours is electric but we don't do that much deep-frying. Yours will have to be heavy-duty, don't you think, Nick? Nick?" He was gone.

"Find what you're looking for, Julia?"

I flinched and swung around to find Lee Blaine standing behind me, his cool blue eyes appraising us. His hands were shoved into the pockets of neat, blue gabardine slacks and he leaned against the shelves, one Hush Puppied foot crossed over the other.

"I'm sorry," he said, "didn't mean to startle you. Are you finding everything okay?"

"Yes. Well, I'm not really looking for us. Let me introduce you to Glenn Bohannon." I explained Glenn's plans for a cantina, and how Nick and I were helping him organize his equipment.

"But I can't find Nick." I called out his name, to find it echoing back at me in the warehouse. "I don't know where he went."

We walked back up to the end of the aisle near the loading dock. "Buddy?"

"Sir?" The young man in the overalls stopped inventorying the crates and turned to Lee.

"You seen this young lady's husband?"

A slow grin crept across Buddy's face. "Yessir. He's out

there.'' He pointed at the semi in the parking lot. I could barely see the top of Nick's head and the bill of his cap. He was seated in the big truck like a kid, pretending to drive.

"Oh, for heaven's sake!" My husband, a grown man, was turning the wheel of the truck. He reached up and tugged on the horn. I was out the door and in the lot, calling him, with Glenn and Lee following behind me talking business.

Nick waved and leapt down out of the cab, making long strides around the truck. Before I could get there to stop him, he was in the trailer. His voice sounded hollow. "I always wanted to see one of these things."

We stood at the end of the trailer. It was empty, and the end wall of the trailer was lined top to bottom with deep shelves. Nick was examining an insulated panel fitted with latches that leaned against the side wall. Glenn vaulted into the truck with Nick.

"I'm really so sorry about this." I turned to Lee.

Lee pulled out his clippers and carefully trimmed his fingernails. "Listen, I just appreciate your bringing me the business. This fellow, Glenn, building a big place, is he?"

"Sounds like it will be fair-sized. Think he's planning on seating for a hundred, hundred and fifty."

Lee whistled under his breath. "That's going to take a lot of equipment, and a pretty good sized staff." He looked up at the two men in the truck, discussing the merits of shelving in a semi. "Let him know, whatever I don't have I can locate."

"I'll do it."

"Sorry. Guess we got carried away." Glenn was on the ground again, a broad grin stretched across his face. "Trucks like this just bring out the little boy in me."

Lee laughed. "I know what you mean. Sometimes I wish I was the one doing the driving, instead of Buddy. Gives you a feeling of power out on the road—able to see over everybody else, you know? Kind of like God."

Nick examined every facet of the trailer, pulling out the ramp and testing the door while Lee watched with amusement. I stared at him, dagger-eyed, until he got my unspoken message and jumped off the trailer.

He looked back at the semi as we crossed the parking lot. "That cab air-conditioned?"

"Sure. My driver goes all over the South—well, North, too. Gotta have air."

"Jeez, you could practically live in there. There's a cot behind the driver's seat. Julia, there's even a TV and a little refrigerator. If I ever close the Oracle, I'm going to learn to drive a rig."

"Then I'll just buy your place." Glenn clapped Nick on the back.

"Uh uh. Not for sale. Not right now, anyway. I like the business. It's hard, but I enjoy the challenge. And I like the customer contact."

We returned to the warehouse, strolling up and down the aisles, checking out the rest of his stock and listing what Glenn would need.

"I didn't know you handled computers, Lee."

"Oh, I handle everything—auto parts, electrics, heavy equipment. That's what I started with, but then I found I could buy other stuff on auction. Need a computer?"

I glanced at Nick, but he firmly shook his head. "Not yet. When the business gets a little bigger I might think about it."

Behind Buddy, at the loading-dock door, I saw that the sun had firmly set. We were keeping Lee from his dinner. Glenn agreed that the practical thing to do was to assess his needs, then contact Lee to start searching for used equipment.

As we were leaving, Nick stopped at the car door to take a last look at the truck.

"You know, Julia, it wouldn't be such a bad life. I mean, you get to see a lot of new places. Some drivers even take their wives along."

"Get in the car, Nick."

"IT NEVER WENT any further?"

"Well, he didn't buy anything, if that's what you mean. I think he went back to Lee's several times to look, but I guess he just couldn't decide." Nick limply tossed the tennis ball, which hit the fireplace with a lackluster bounce. Jack didn't even bother to chase it. He turned and grabbed Nick's ankle firmly in his square jaws.

"Ow! Nuck that off, Jock! Get the ball." Jack scampered away, returning with that eerie tennis-ball grin of his and nudged it into Nick's lap.

"So, what does it mean?"

"It could mean that he never intended to open a restaurant in the first place." He wrestled the ball out of Jack's lockjaw grip and pitched it across the room.

"But why the subterfuge, then?"

"Subter...what?"

"Why the game? The act?"

"You know, Julia, I have a feeling that if we knew the answer to that, we'd know who killed him. And why."

WE WERE BACKING UP against a wall—a rocky canyon wall, steep and narrow and bordered on three sides by high ledges. Nick pushed me behind him. Over his shoulder I glimpsed the amber eyes of the animal, and its narrow, bony body, the brown-gray of its scruffy coat. A low growl rumbled in its throat. Above us, on the ledges, its companions paced. Waiting. Waiting for the leader to perform the kill.

Nick stepped toward the wolf, challenging it. It raised its snout and bared its teeth in a grin, and the growl grew louder. It moved slowly forward, tension in its hindquarters—prepared to spring.

"Nick! Oh my God, Nick!" I frantically grabbed for his arm as the wolf leapt and the growl swelled into a fierce snarl.

I scuttled backward, pulling at Nick, and the heels of my feet burned against the sheets until I was upright and thumped my head against the headboard. Awake. But the growling went on. My eyes couldn't adjust to the darkness. Nick was up.

"It's okay, Julia. Just a dream." He stroked my face softly.

"The wolf. Growling."

"It's Jock."

The little dog rested his forepaws against the windowsill and pushed his snout between the miniblinds, trying vainly to see outside. "What is it, Jack?"

Tires squealed—close to the house. A muffler throbbed in the night. Nick leapt over me getting to the window in time to see a pickup truck tear past the house, and was out our bedroom door before I could hit the floor. Jack was at his heels.

I peered out the window and caught my breath. Something dangled from a dogwood tree. The figure of a man. And it was on fire. I threw on shoes and followed Nick.

By the time I made the yard, he had pulled the figure down and was stamping out the fire on the lawn. I froze, overwhelmed by a chill that made my body tremble, and stared at the effigy.

It might have been a harmless scarecrow—old jeans and shirt stuffed with hay—but for the hat. Someone had placed a hat on the stuffed feedbag they'd used for a head. It was a black baseball cap. But the crown had been flattened, pulled forward on the brim and stapled there. In the darkness, it could have been Nick's sailor's cap.

The neck of the effigy was encircled by a noose. My stomach flipped, rose up in my throat. The rope was braided. Strips of an old American flag had been used to hang my husband. There was no note, but the message was clear. It said, Go home, you're not wanted here.

Nick dragged the thing into the carport where he could examine it in the light, but found nothing which might identify the terrorists who'd hung it there.

"I'm calling Sam, Nick."

"No, wait. Don't call him."

"Why not? Someone's trying to scare us. Are we just going to sit by and let it happen?"

"Of course not. But right now, I don't want to call any more attention to myself than necessary. Besides, if we call Sam, it might get out. Then they'll know they succeeded." He stuffed the effigy into the storeroom in the carport, locked the door and guided me back into the house. I was still shaking.

"I'm not some bird to be frightened away by a scarecrow. That, I think, is the whole idea. To scare us into leaving town," Nick said.

"So what are we going to do?"

"We have to go on as usual, as though it didn't happen. Make it clear to whoever is watching that we're not going to be frightened away." He took my hand and held it between his own. "I know how hard this is on you, Julia, but I don't see any choice here." I nodded silently.

"Let's go back to bed," he said.

I followed him into the bedroom and collapsed on the bed knowing there'd be no more sleep for me that night. Nick sat down on the floor, scratching Jack softly between the ears. Jack tipped his head back, closed his eyes. His black lips seemed to part in a doggy grin.

"You're a good boy, Jock," Nick said. "I think we'll have to keep you."

TWELVE

"LET ME GET THIS STRAIGHT. He said he's having a few friends over for dinner?"

"Right."

"A few friends.... But Nick, who does he know? Just us."

Nick shrugged. "Well he also knows Rhonda and—"

"Oh, surely not! I don't think I can spend a whole evening with Tammy. Every day's enough. Besides, one of them would have said something about it if they'd been invited."

"Look, let's just wait and see when we get there."

I stared out the window as we turned into Markettown. The way Nick had phrased it—"he's having a few friends over for dinner"—as though we might expect the full complement of drinks and hors d'oeuvres, several excellent courses compatible with lofty conversation. Spiro might preside at the head of the table, graciously seeing to his guests' every need. Perhaps he would be wearing a smoking jacket, and the gentlemen would retire to the study for brandy and cigars. I twisted my denim skirt between my fingers, idly wondering if I would be well enough dressed for the occasion.

But as we turned onto Spiro's street, I was abruptly snapped back into reality. The neighborhood had not improved in the last few days. If anything, it looked more run-down than it had before.

Except Spiro's little house. He had pulled all the weeds, I noted. It had left bald spots in the yard, but was decidedly neater. The windows sparkled, and bright lights glowed behind the venetian blinds in the living room. He had installed a light at the front door which beamed expectantly down the steps. Miss Alma's house had a similar light at the door, as well as spotlights at the corners, which threw an eerie blue light over her patch of yard and seemed to emphasize the stillness around the house. Spiro's Pontiac sprawled in the driveway like a great gray beast, but there were no other cars to be seen.

"Are you sure we have the right night?" I whispered, fully aware that, like my lipstick and handbag, my social insecurities travel with me on every occasion.

Nick pulled a bottle of ouzo out of the backseat and snuggled it under one arm. "Of course I'm sure. Relax, will you?"

I did, as soon as Miss Alma met us at the door. She seemed to glow as she stepped aside and ushered us into the house. She was not using her walker, had parked it in a corner, and seemed to have a light spring in the soles of her oxfords. I introduced Nick, who took her hand and gently brushed his lips against the raised veins and liver spots. A fresh young pink rose to Miss Alma's cheeks.

"Spiro is in the kitchen fixing dinner. Come in, won't you?"

A table stood at the end of the living room. It was not exactly a table, but a door laid across a pair of sawhorses—a practical arrangement. I counted seven placemats, white linen, embroidered with flowers in bright silks that beautifully matched a central arrangement in a low, cut-glass bowl. Each place was set with Spiro's Melamine and flanked by embroidered matching napkins laid with heavy silver. Miss Alma chuckled as I moved closer to the table.

"We combined our resources. He didn't have enough table linens, and I thought my silver might add a nice touch. I haven't used it in years."

Plastic tumblers had been set at each place, and next to them long-stemmed wineglasses of dubious crystal. Spiro's footsteps thundered behind me. I turned just in time to be enveloped in his arms, my nose smashed against his chest. He pecked the top of my head and let me go to do the same to Nick.

"You here! Good. This *Kyria* Alma." I reminded him that I had met her before.

"Who are the others?" I addressed Miss Alma, jerking my head toward the three mystery places.

"I don't know. I thought you'd know. I don't ask many questions because I usually don't understand the answers." I nodded, sympathizing completely.

Spiro guided Nick back into the kitchen, and Miss Alma and I followed, gasping as he threw open the oven door to reveal roasted lamb and, my favorite of all dishes, spanakopita. Nick tugged at a strip of the succulent meat, popped it into his mouth and extolled the virtues of garlic, a string of which was hanging in the kitchen window. He tested the flakiness of the phyllo pastry, and as Spiro stood by and took his compliments humbly, Miss Alma and I fled to the living room.

"In my day, it would have been the women discussing recipes in there and the men in the living room," she said. She carefully lowered herself onto the couch and I dropped beside her.

"Make no mistake," I said. "It's not like this every night. In fact, a lot of nights Nick and I just don't eat at all, because neither of us wants to cook. But you have to understand Greeks. Entertaining is an occasion that demands a certain ritual. This is just the beginning."

Spiro arrived bearing a tray of glasses of retsina, serving each of us in turn. He proposed a rather lengthy toast in Greek, something to do with good wine and good friends. We clinked our glasses and they drank, while I watched in astonishment as Miss Alma downed hers in two swallows and held her glass out to be refilled. Footsteps rapped on the porch and Spiro flung the door open.

"*Bienvenidos,*" he cried.

Voices murmured greetings as I peered around his massive form to get a look at the arriving guests. Nick stood at the kitchen door, a smile teasing his lips and his eyes twinkling. At last, Spiro stepped aside and two men and a woman entered.

The first was a small, stocky young man with ink-black hair falling softly to his shoulders. He wore faded jeans and a plaid, western-style shirt, and he carried a six-pack of longnecks in each hand. A woman huddled close behind him. Her dark hair was pulled back and held by a wide leather band, speared by a pick to hold the hair in place. She had a plain, square face, blunt nose, and slightly almond-shaped eyes—a face evoking ancient cultures. She, too, wore jeans, tightly strained over thick hips and narrow legs. A lightweight black jacket was snugly fitted over a plainly tailored orange shirt. She slipped a tentative arm through her companion's, ignoring the inconvenience of his full hands.

As they stepped away from the doorway, I saw the second man

take a hard pull on the remainder of a cigarette butt and toss it over the porch rail. He wore black pants of a cheap, shiny fabric, very tight across his narrow hips and gradually belling over the tops of his black boots. A gold chain and crucifix glimmered at the open neck of a silky blue and gray shirt. He ran his fingers through black, tightly curled hair, turned on his heel and strode into the room. I recognized him at once as the man who had been on the business end of Connie's broken beer bottle.

"My friends," Spiro was saying as he unburdened the man of his beer. "Ramón and his..." He looked at Nick. *"Yineka?"*

"Wife," Nick said.

"Neh, neh. His wife, Elena." We nodded to one another and Miss Alma shook their hands, introducing herself, Nick, and me.

The other man stood apart, raring slightly back on his heels, arms firmly crossed over his chest. His eyes were watchful, stabbing around the room like stilettos. A hand shot out abruptly when we were introduced.

"Tomás," said Spiro.

His palms were thickened with calluses and his hand wrapped a little too firmly around mine, as though he might rub the knuckles together the way kids do. He flashed me a hard smile and turned to Nick.

Spiro, I saw, had slipped outside and retrieved the cigarette butt, carrying it between two fingers into the kitchen. Ramón dropped into the easy chair and, although Miss Alma and I made a place for her on the sofa, Elena dragged one of the chairs away from the table and positioned herself next to her husband. Tomás turned his chair backward, straddling it as though he were in a western movie. Spiro soon returned, his tray loaded with glasses, beer bottles and a tall, half-filled bottle of retsina. The guests made their choices, Tomás and Elena selecting beer, while Ramón shyly pointed to the retsina.

"I try," he said.

Spiro clapped him heartily on the back, and the round of toasts was repeated. Again, Miss Alma knocked her retsina back like a sailor. Tomás raised an amused eyebrow and sipped his beer thoughtfully. An uncomfortable silence fell over the room. Spiro turned to the three newest arrivals.

"Niko y Julia son mis patrones, y Señorita Alma es mi vecina."

Miss Alma leaned toward me on the couch and whispered, "He said, 'Nick and Julia are my bosses and Miss Alma is my neighbor."

I was too stunned to reply. Nick was watching me from the kitchen door. A grin tickled his ears, but he shrugged as though he, too, were surprised.

"Spiro, you speak Spanish?"

Spiro snatched the sailor's cap from his head, waved it at me, and abruptly set it back on his head. He tapped his chest. "A sailor. We go to South America many times. I learn to speak very good. Good…" His lips curled up around his mustache. "Good Spanish. Not so good English."

Miss Alma patted his hand. "But getting better, my friend." She turned to me. "I'm teaching him English and he's doing things around the house for me. You saw the spotlights?"

I nodded. She went on to describe the little chores Spiro had undertaken on her behalf. Her funds were limited, she explained, but Spiro seemed to have a gift for fixing things without having to buy parts for them. "He should have been an engineer," she said, glancing fondly at him.

"I think it comes from growing up poor. Nick's the same way, good at making do in a pinch."

Miss Alma cited other examples of Spiro's handiwork. I listened with one ear, but strained to hear the Spanish conversation across the room. Two years of Castilian Spanish in high school had not prepared me for the evening, and Spiro spoke almost as rapidly as his neighbors. Nick, still propped against the kitchen door, was watching it all with a pensive expression. I knew he didn't understand the language—he's not doing real well with English—but something was on his mind. He edged closer to the group, finally sputtering a rapid question at Spiro in Greek. Spiro turned back to his friends, clearly translating.

As though in one movement, the three shifted in their chairs. Elena glanced at Ramón, sitting in the easy chair. He was staring at a spot on the carpet. Tomás tossed the beer bottle back. I watched as his larynx bobbed up and down in three hard swallows. He turned to Nick, meeting him eye to eye.

"Estudiantes. Somos estudiantes de la universidad."

"He say..."

"I understood, Spiro. Ask them what they're studying."

Spiro asked the three in turn. Elena fidgeted with her fingers, retrieved her empty bottle from the floor and sipped out some air. *"Educación,"* she said.

"Historia." Ramón mumbled a scarcely audible reply. Tomás watched them both with a half-smile quivering on his lips. When his turn came, his response was loud and clear. *"Economía,"* he said. I thought, for a moment, he was going to laugh. Ramón shot him a wry smile, but Elena's expression spelled anxiety.

Miss Alma nudged my ribs. "I should like to know how they can attend the university when they don't speak English."

"Well, I suppose they start with ESL classes and move on from there."

Spiro had risen and thundered into the kitchen. Tomás, Ramón, and Elena whispered among themselves. Miss Alma casually rose and adjusted the place settings on the table near them.

In a moment, Spiro returned carrying the spanakopita. He set it on the table with a flourish, and basked in admiring remarks in three languages. The phyllo was a perfect golden brown—flaky layers several inches thick, covering the spinach-and-cheese filling. The aroma of dill and cheese permeated the house. The lamb was next to arrive, and at its appearance my stomach rumbled appreciatively. Nick followed Spiro out with hot bread and a Greek salad of tomatoes, olives, and feta cheese.

Dinner was a somewhat confused affair. Spiro carefully explained the making of homemade phyllo, how he stretched it across the table to dry and constructed the spanakopita. He described the making of feta cheese from goat's milk, a dairy product familiar to his guests, if not to me. All of this was, of course, in Spanish, but Miss Alma whispered halting translations to me and Nick. Tomás watched us all closely.

"How is it that you speak Spanish, Miss Alma?" I said.

She patted her blue-gray curls. "I was born and raised in Texas, in the Rio Grande Valley. I couldn't help but learn Spanish there. It's a way of life. I haven't used it in years, but I guess, since it was almost my native language, it's never left me."

We had cleared the table and settled back in the living room with glasses of Nick's ouzo. The Mexicans were tasting it tentatively as Spiro explained how he mixed it with water. He poured a shot of the clear, colorless drink into a glass and topped it with water, swirling it lightly. His guests aahed appreciatively as it clouded in the glass, and were complimentary of its licorice flavor. No one told them that it's the liquid equivalent of brass knuckles, packing a punch that leaves the head reeling for hours.

Elena, however, was already finding out. On her second glass, her coffee-bean eyes grew bright. She stood and began swaying seductively to the Greek music Spiro popped into his cassette player. Ramón flushed and tugged at her hand, trying to draw her back to her chair. Tomás' black eyes quickened and he rose to join her in the dance, turning to face me. My face felt hot. The air grew charged. Miss Alma hastily grabbed Nick's hand.

"Tell Spiro to turn off the music. Quickly, or there's going to be trouble here."

Nick had started to do so when a hard rap rattled the small window in the front door. Spiro switched off the music before answering it.

"I'm looking for some friends of mine. They said they were here."

Spiro opened the door wider and Connie Santos slid in. Her eyes took in the three Mexicans with a quick glance, then turned to the rest of us. She seemed confused, as if she was trying to compose her face into the appropriate expression, but not sure, herself, what that was.

"I just...I needed to talk to Ramón and Elena for a moment." She smoothed her palms over the legs of her scarlet silk pants. She wore a matching shirt, open and casually thrown over a gold camisole of the same, soft silk. The effect was incendiary.

"Ella. Katse, katse." Spiro pointed toward a seat next to me on the couch, and firmly closed the door behind her. Connie hesitated for a moment, then crossed the room and dropped down, hugging the arm and twisted slightly to get a good look at the rest of us. I glanced over at Ramón. His eyes were worrying the spot in the carpet again, the muscles under his cheeks rigid. Elena pouted in her chair, as though a parent had caught her in the act

of jumping on the bed. Tomás leaned forward, his long fingers wrapped around his glass of ouzo. He was watching Connie intently.

Spiro offered Connie a glass of ouzo, which, after a second's hesitation, she accepted. I smoothed the folds of my denim skirt, conscious again of the sharp contrast between her casual seductiveness and my oh-so-Betty Crocker style. I hastily scrambled to make small talk.

"They're friends of yours, then?"

"Yes." Connie swirled the liquid in the glass and took a little sip. "I always try to make contact with the Spanish-speaking students in town. It helps them to know there's someone who can help them if they're having any problems at Parnassus. As it happens, I rented that house to them. It worked out rather nicely, actually. But I really do need to see Ramón and Elena. I'm helping them work out a problem with their schedules."

"How lucky for them to have found you," I said. "And how nice that you speak Spanish fluently."

"I'm of Mexican descent myself. My parents emigrated from Mexico to California before I was born. Spanish is as much my native tongue as English."

I sighed, thought how wonderful it must be to speak two languages fluently. While I understand Greek quite well, putting the words together to phrase my own thoughts is another matter entirely. I said as much to Connie. Spiro was listening carefully, relying on Nick to translate for him. The Mexicans sat in silence.

Miss Alma had gone to the kitchen. When he heard the clatter of dishes being washed, Spiro rose and followed her with voluble protests. Connie moved across the room to her friends and spoke in a low, harsh sputter. Although I could not understand much of what she said, the word *peligroso* appeared repeatedly. "Danger"—I did remember a little high-school Spanish after all. And *migra*, which I did not know. Spiro returned to the room, dragging a reluctant Miss Alma.

"He won't let me help in the kitchen," she said. "I just wanted to start doing a few of the dishes."

"No. A Greek would never let you do that. When he entertains, it means he serves you and cleans up after you. No help is accepted. It would be insulting to him as a host, and to you as a guest.''

Tomás and Ramón were standing with Connie, urging a reluctant Elena to get up. She protested mildly, but finally rose, swaying a bit before Ramón caught her elbow. Connie turned back to Spiro.

"We have to go now," she said very slowly and clearly to him. "Thank you." She led the others toward the door.

"De nada," he said.

Connie stopped, her back to him, rigid. When she turned, her face was the same scarlet as her clothing. *"Habla español?"*

"Un poco," he said, putting his thumb and index finger together to measure "a little." The others protested, clearly saying that he was a master of the language. Tomás was watching Connie, and although his face was grave, his eyes glittered maliciously.

She laughed a little. "Well, then," she said. *"Buenas noches. Gracias."* She slammed the door behind her. I joined Nick at the window as he watched them descend the porch and cross to the house next door. They were arguing. Connie's wrath was turned upon Tomás, who seemed able to give it back in full measure.

"Connie said, 'They said they were here.' Who are 'they'?"

Nick shrugged. "I don't know." He shot the question to Spiro, who answered at length with a full compliment of hand gestures.

"Apparently, those three are the only ones Spiro knows. But he says that there are twenty or more people in that house. They don't go out very often. Connie comes to see them a lot. But when he has gone over to see Ramón and Elena, others have been there, sleeping on bags on the floor."

"Miss Alma, did you hear what she was saying to them?"

"No. I was in the kitchen most of the time."

"Connie kept talking about danger. I caught that word. And *migra*. What does that mean, do you know?"

Miss Alma's eyes clouded and her lips compressed tightly as she nodded her head. "Yes, I know. It means 'immigration.'"

THIRTEEN

SPIRO WHIPPED THE COFFEE in the *briki* until it foamed and poured it into four demitasse cups. We took our cups and followed him back into the living room.

"Delphi's such a small town. You'd think they'd be worried about being conspicuous," Miss Alma said.

"Well, not really. Don't forget, there are a lot of foreign students at Parnassus. In some ways, it's a very neat cover as long as no one is watching too closely." Nick took a sip of his coffee, properly complimented Spiro on it and went on. "What I wonder is where they go from here. We're pretty far north for much Mexican labor."

Miss Alma took one sip of her coffee, swallowed hard and set her cup on the coffee table. "They don't stay long, I can tell you that. In the last two years I've seen hundreds of them come and go."

"You mean it's been going on that long?"

Miss Alma nodded, looked off into space. "Let's see. It's been not quite a year since that terrible fire. The one in Auburn."

"Fire?" I was having trouble following this conversation. Miss Alma certainly held her retsina and ouzo better than I.

"Yes. In Auburn, Alabama. I kept the clipping. It was just a small article, but I thought, with them living in that house, it might be important. I'll get it if you like. Then you can see what I mean."

She left the walker at Spiro's, was gone only a short while before returning with a yellowed newspaper clipping in her hand. "I'm in the habit of cutting articles out of the paper—just random events that interest me. I don't know why, exactly. Maybe it's the teacher in me. You can retire the body, but not the mind, you know." She handed the article to me. I read it aloud.

Auburn, Alabama. In the worst fire Auburn has seen in several decades, twenty-five people died in a three-alarm house fire in one of the city's oldest sections today. The occupants of the house were not known, but were rumored to be foreign students attending Auburn University, police said. Apparently, many of the victims were sleeping on the floor, and the house, a four-bedroom Victorian style, was dangerously overcrowded. Neighbors stated that the windows had been boarded up for several years, due to rampant vandalism in the area. Fifteen of the victims were male, one of whom lived long enough to tell police an incredible tale of being locked into the house and unable to escape when the fire broke out. The victim, who was of Hispanic origin, died before police were able to extract further information. However, arson investigators issued a statement late today indicating that there is no question that the fire was deliberately set. Police are working around the clock to identify the victims and, according to a spokesman, will spare no effort in investigating this tragic crime.

"Those poor people. What a terrible way to die."

"Auburn University. Hispanics. Don't you see, Julia? Another college town and more illegals. I'll bet it's part of the same network."

"You're probably right. But why the fire?"

Nick shrugged. "It may just be coincidence. Or it may be that some, or all of them, didn't pay the coyote when they were supposed to. Hard to know."

"'Coyote'?"

"The smuggler. The guy who brings them across the border."

"Are you saying they'd burn them all out like that? Just because one or two of them didn't pay what they owed the coyote?"

"It's called setting an example."

"My God, Nick! What kind of people would do a thing like that?"

"Murderers."

Miss Alma twisted her gnarled hands in her lap. "I suppose I should have done something about it a long time ago. But I have to be careful, you see. This used to be such a wonderful little neighborhood. When Franklin and I first bought this house... But now, well, it isn't very safe anymore.''

"It's good to be careful and know what's going on in your neighborhood. What about the sheriff?''

She shook her head. ''They hardly patrol the neighborhood at all. I never see them. Well, I haven't really known what to do, you know. They come at all hours of the day and night. Most of them seem to stay about two weeks and then move on. They don't come out of the house very often, except that Tomás. He comes and goes when she's not around. I don't get the idea that she likes it much. I've heard them arguing about it.''

"What did they say? Do you remember?''

"I was coming back from the corner store yesterday afternoon.'' Miss Alma pointed past the Mexican house, down toward Market Street. ''They were out at her car. She was getting ready to leave and he asked when was she going to get his papers and get him a job? Well, she was mad, I can tell you. She slapped her purse on the hood of her car and shook her finger in his face. When she knew she could trust him, she said. If he couldn't follow the rules, she was going to send him back or bring in the coyote. He seemed scared then, but only for a minute. She said she wouldn't have him jeopardizing the rest of them, but he only laughed. That Tomás, he's a cocky one.

"Anyway, I see him coming and going. But not when she's around. She leaves town, I think, because sometimes she'll bring in boxes and bags of groceries, and lots of beer, and then she won't show up for several days. But most of the time she's here every day, checking up on them, I guess.''

"How do they come in?'' Nick was still perched on the edge of his seat, looking intently at her.

"I saw two men and a woman arrive that night when I was here helping Spiro clean,'' I volunteered.

"Ramón and Elena?''

I thought about this, tried to remember how they looked. The woman, I thought, was taller than Elena. And her hair was short. "No, I think it was someone else. They came in some kind of a van. With a housepainter's sign on it.''

Miss Alma nodded. "That's one of them, yes. There are several vans, different colors. And I think they switch the magnetic signs on them, too. Sometimes it's a painting contractor, sometimes it's heating and air-conditioning or a plumber's sign. I made a note of one name but there's no such paint contractor listed in the phone book." She sighed.

"I suppose I could have called the sheriff or something but, well...I guess I was afraid. You know, I've seen how dangerous these people can be—the coyotes, I mean. In the valley...knifings and killings. And the illegals, they're just poor people who need to get jobs. They're just following their dreams. It's the people who exploit them that deserve to be caught. Not the Ramóns and Elenas."

Nick and I assured Miss Alma that she had been right to stay quiet. If what she said, and what I'd heard about the coyotes was true, it would be far more expedient to remove an old lady than to suspend their operation. I realized suddenly that while she had been translating for me, she had not spoken directly to any of the Mexicans. She did not want them to know that she understood their language, and now I knew why. Nick quickly summed up the situation for Spiro.

"Ah," he said. *"Pollos!"*

"Chickens," said Miss Alma. "That's what the coyotes call their victims."

Spiro's hand circled the air. *"Po, po, po! Eine poli epikinthinos!"* He went on, absorbing Nick's attention for several minutes.

"He says it's very dangerous. He's seen them in South America and Mexico. Sometimes they wanted to travel on his ships. One time three of them stowed away, but they were caught and put out at the next port. Spiro says that everyone knows coyotes can be very dangerous men."

"Then why do they go to them?"

Miss Alma supplied the answer. "Have you ever been to Mexico or Central America, Julia? Once you get away from the tourist areas you see some of the worst poverty in the world. These people want a better life, and the risk of a knife in their backs is better than the prospect of living that way forever. Their only hope is El Norte. It must be very painful knowing you have to leave your homeland in order to have a better life.''

I glanced over at Nick and Spiro, and found tears stinging my eyes.

"NICK, THERE'S SOMETHING I don't understand about this. Where does the money come from? If these people are so poor, how do they get the money to pay the coyote?''

Nick pulled away from Spiro's house and nosed our little Honda through the winding streets on our way out of Markettown.

"From what I understand, the whole family saves the money until they have enough for a down payment. Sometimes the new arrivals pay off the balance after they get jobs. Remember, they're very vulnerable. The coyote keeps track of them. He can always report them to the INS, or even easier, if they don't pay up, he just removes them.

"But, to tell you the truth, I don't know all that much about it. I'd certainly like to find out, though. And I'd also like to know who owns Delphi Rental Properties. But not right now.''

"What do you mean?''

"We've got bigger problems.''

"Yeah,'' I said, knowing exactly what he meant. "Like being murder suspects.''

There was nowhere to go but home, and so we did.

WALKING THROUGH the garage, I turned to my husband. "Nick?''

"Hmm?''

"Did you put the garbage out today?''

"Yeah. It's Friday. Why?''

"Well, where's the can?''

"Still down at the curb. I'll go get it.''

I waited at the back door as Nick made it halfway down the driveway, swore loudly and turned back around. "We need practical jokes right now.''

"It's not there, is it?''

"No.''

"It's weird, Nick. I don't like it.''

"Julia, it's just a garbage can. We can get another one. I'm sure it was just a joke. Kids, probably." He took my hand and led me into the house. "You're on edge, that's all."

"I suppose. With everything else that's happened..."

Nick sat down on the edge of the bed and pulled off his shoes. He had put a dog biscuit on the plaid cushion in the basket, hoping to coax Jack off his favorite chair and onto his rightful place. Jack stood a foot from his bed and stretched cautiously toward the dog biscuit. He snatched it up, wagged triumphantly at Nick and vaulted back into the overstuffed chair. Nick ticked his tongue.

"The trouble is, I don't know where to start. Sam's not telling anything."

"Okay, let's go over what we know. We know Glenn was poisoned at the restaurant. It had to have been one of the Buffaloes that did it. They had access to his food on the deck. But Nick, that was the morning they all came into the kitchen. Remember? They were coming out of the kitchen as I came in. What were they doing in there, anyway?"

"They wanted to talk about the poker game. They thought maybe I'd object if we included Glenn in the game."

"Okay, so who, exactly, was it? Who was there? I remember Read and Lee."

Nick closed his eyes. "Sonny, Read, Norm, and Lee. And Mitch. It's one of the five of them, Julia. And I'll bet that's when it happened. Right then, in the kitchen. No wonder Sam suspects me."

"So where do we go from here?"

Nick shook his head. "I wish we could find out more about Glenn. All we know about him right now is that he wasn't too committed to this restaurant thing. If we could only get into his apartment...but Sam's got it sealed off."

We thought about this, silently watching Jack nuzzle in Nick's clothes on the chair. He scooched down in the corner, rustled around and came up with a sweater draped over his ears, looking, for all the world, like the wolf in Red Riding Hood's cape. I grabbed Nick's arm.

"Wait. Maybe there is a way."

FOURTEEN

THE LIVING ROOM held a small Queen Anne desk with a princess phone and a pencil cup, the only concessions to the makeshift office it was. Stacked on the left hand corner of the desk were a few brochures entitled ''Oak Grove Townhouses.'' I picked one up, slipped it into my bag and turned back to the rental agent.

''I will have one coming available. I'm not exactly sure when, though.''

''Could we possibly see it,'' I asked.

She shook her head and smoothed her platinum hair. ''I'm afraid it's... Well, frankly it's off-limits right now. The sheriff has it sealed while a crime is being investigated.''

Nick raised an eyebrow at her and shook his head. She jumped right in. ''Oh, it's nothing that happened here. The man who rented it, Mr. Bohannon, died rather suddenly. I don't think they've ruled it murder or anything but, well, like Detective Lawless told me, they like to be careful. That's all. Maybe you read about it in the papers.''

''No,'' I said. ''We're new in town. My husband will be joining the faculty at Parnassus. He's a...a scholar on the, um, Middle East. Of course, he'll have to recover his voice before he can begin lecturing.'' I laughed nervously. ''He uses it all the time— you know, lectures, that kind of thing. Had this perpetual hoarseness—vocal cord nodules. The doctor has prescribed complete voice rest.

''But back to the townhouse—I'm afraid if we can't see it...''

''Well, mine's just like it, actually. The layout, that is. I'd be happy to show you around so you can get a feel for it.'' Nick inclined his head, gesturing that he would follow her.

We made our way through the living room and trailed after her up the stairs to the master bedroom. I started and drew back, faced by the three strangers reflected in the mirror-tiled walls.

I had forced Nick to discard his trademark sailor's cap in favor of one I'd bought on a whim one Christmas. It was a glen plaid woolen hat that made him look like Rex Harrison. To that I'd added a muffler at his neck and a herringbone sports jacket. The Greek islands could hardly have been farther away.

My own disguise was a bit more extreme. I'd rinsed my hair with a dark rinse that had turned it a peculiar shade of auburn, donned a straight, black wool sheath and added to it almost every piece of jewelry I owned. I topped it all with makeup so heavy I could hardly be sure there was skin underneath. I scarcely recognized myself.

"Are the walls in the other townhouse mirrored like this?"

"Oh no, my husband and I did that ourselves."

I was relieved. I was really getting into the role. "Of course, my husband will need a study."

"Right this way."

We passed a bath in the hall, following her to two smaller bedrooms occupying the end of the house overlooking the carport. I peered down onto her patio and those of her neighbors. She glanced at her watch. "I'm afraid I'm going to have to go. I have a dental appointment at four o'clock." Back down the stairs. She handed me her business card.

"Why don't you give me your number here locally? As soon as the sheriff opens up the apartment, I'll give you a call."

"Of course. We're staying at the Delphi Inn. I'm afraid I don't know the number, but if you just call the desk and ask for our room..."

"I'm sorry, I guess I forgot to ask your name."

How stupid of me! I hadn't prepared for this. "Higgins," I said smoothly. "Eliza Higgins."

"OKAY, THAT'S HER." We watched a Ford LTD pull out of the driveway behind the townhouses. Nick started the car. "Let's go."

He drove slowly, carefully scanning the carports and counting off the numbers. "If that's 201, this must be 203, 205..."

I grabbed his wrist, pointing to a carport that sheltered a low-slung black Toyota MR2. "Well, look who else lives at Oak Grove Townhouses."

Glenn's house was two down from Connie's. Nick parked the car close against the storage area, as though he could somehow shield it from view. Quietly we slipped inside the cedar fence. The French doors were posted with a Sheriff's Department sign declaring it off-limits and the handle resisted our rattling. Above it was a dead-bolt lock.

"I don't see how we can get in there," Nick whispered. "Even if we break the glass, we probably can't open that lock. It's a double dead-bolt."

"How about the window?" I pointed left, to a small window which, I remembered, was over the kitchen sink in the agent's apartment. Nick examined it and shook his head. "Too risky."

We walked back to the French doors, shaded our eyes with our hands and peered in, trying to see through the sheers that covered the doors. If only they'd left a light on. "Can you see anything?"

"Can I help you?"

I jumped, leaned against the door, letting my heart return to a normal beat. "You startled me."

"You looking for someone?"

She was a big woman with a coarse face and tightly curled hair that ran riot over a massive head. She stood in bare feet, wide toes peaking out from under a pair of light blue polyester pull-on pants. Despite the curls and the flowered blouse, I sensed that this was not a woman I wanted to meet in an alley. All muscle.

"No, we're, um, we just spoke to the rental agent about this place." I produced the card from my bag. "We can't get in, but thought we could at least look at the outside."

This was met with a cursory glance at the card, but no verbal response, forcing me to keep talking. Keep lying. "You know, I'm glad we ran into you, though. My name is Eliza Higgins. This is my husband, Henry." We shook hands—Henry, the Hulk, and me.

"Gilda Scoggins."

I explained about Henry's vocal nodules, his voice rest. "It's probably good to get the neighbors' viewpoint on this. Do you like Oak Grove?"

"Yes. Sure. It's okay."

"Well, we're a little concerned..." I pointed to the sheriff's posting.

"Oh, that." She shrugged. "Didn't happen here."

"Yes, well, but is this place safe?"

"Far as I know."

"How about quiet? My husband is a scholar, you see. He needs quiet for his studies."

"No kids at Oak Grove. Quiet as death."

I thought it was an unfortunate metaphor under the circumstances.

"It's a shame about your neighbor. Did you know him well?"

Now this, finally, was a subject she could warm up to. She licked her lips. "I met him a coupla times. Came from Texas, he said. He was planning to open a restaurant."

"Really. How interesting!" Nothing new here. "Married, I take it?"

"Nope. Single. Had a few women in and out, though. Not gay or anything."

Nick latched the cedar fence and we strolled with Gilda toward the car. "Well, I suppose that's just as well. He didn't leave a wife behind to grieve for him." Was I really saying this? Clearly improvisation was not my best thing.

"No, but... Well, there's a couple of women might be missing him...." My stomach knotted. She leaned toward me, lowered her voice to a raspy whisper. "I don't like to gossip now, but one of 'em's somebody most people here in town know. Banker's wife. I've seen her with him, right here, like she owned the place!"

"Maybe she was working for him."

"Right. Probably. Well, I'm not one to tittle-tattle. Her secret's safe with me, you can be sure." Oh, I was.

"Then, there's this other one." Gilda licked her lips again. "I don't know her real well. Met her once or twice." She pointed beyond her townhouse in the direction of Connie's carport. The rear of the MR2 was barely visible beyond the storage closet.

"A neighbor. Well, I suppose it's only natural..."

"More than a neighbor, I'd say. I'd see her coming and going, in and out of his house all hours. And him in hers, too." I glanced at the cedar fencing surrounding the patio. Gilda read my thoughts.

"We're pretty careful here. Watch out for our neighbors. Hear strange noises at night, we investigate."

"Of course. It's good to know. Another point in Oak Grove's favor. I suppose they were pretty noisy, then. He had a lot of visitors?"

"Oh no. Just Connie and the other one."

Nick opened the car door, gestured for me to climb in. I shook Gilda's hand, then rubbed my knuckles. "Well, it was so nice to meet you. Henry and I will look forward to being your neighbors."

"Maybe we can get together for a barbecue sometime."

I smiled brightly. "Can't wait."

"WHAT DO YOU BET her husband's a wimp?" I toweled my hair, shook the damp ringlets back in place and examined it in the mirror. Blonde again.

"Probably. How could he compete with her?"

"So Connie Santos was Glenn's lover. I wonder if Dina knew."

Nick shrugged, picked Jack up and deposited him on his bed. Nothing doing. "Oh, good griff."

"So does Connie figure into this? And if so, how?"

"It could just be coincidence. They were neighbors, became friends…"

"So do we know any more now than we did before?"

"Well, we know he was quiet. That he was telling everyone the same story about the restaurant. We know he was having an affair with the banker's wife, and also with Connie—whose role in all this is not yet clear. We know he carried a gun. We know he was murdered."

"Okay. And someone is trying to scare us. And Sam is asking if we travel, and Cal Taylor is holding your green card."

"Yeah, but like I said, I think that's just intimidation."

I slumped down on the bed, despondent. "I don't think we really know anything yet."

Nick dropped an arm over my shoulder. "Let's think about it

this way. If you were a detective, what would you do? Say you're...Miss Marple."

"Everything's always so easy for her. She just sits in her living room and figures it out."

"Well, real detectives do legwork, Julia. They follow all the leads. That means the Buffaloes first and foremost. And now that we know Glenn was involved with Connie, maybe we should take a look at the illegals a little more closely, too."

I dropped back on the bed, punched and rearranged my pillow, too restless for sleep. Nick switched off the light. "That Connie must be quite a woman."

I felt my face growing hot. It was my turn to grind my teeth. "Well, I suppose if you like cheap women..."

"That red outfit didn't look cheap to me," he said.

"No. It wasn't. But she's cheap, kind of hard and..." I turned to Nick and found that he was grinning broadly. He nuzzled my ear and slipped his hand down my shoulder toward points south.

"Of course," he added, "I like my women soft."

FIFTEEN

"JULIA, YOU EVER HEARD of Those Iggies?"

Tammy slapped a ticket down and stuck her head through the window. Spiro was pressing hamburgers. Something smelled heavily of garlic. I followed my nose, which led me directly to Spiro's big stainless bowl. Twenty pounds of ground chuck lay in the bottom. His big fingers were kneading it, and with it, little slivers of green pepper, onions, garlic and oregano.

"*Bifteki.*" He pointed to the mixture. I'd never heard anyone chortle before.

I smiled and said something inane. We called them our Greekburgers, an idea I had resisted until I saw how popular they'd become. As much as anything, this new burger of his was helping to keep us afloat. Okay, yes. I was ashamed of myself.

I went back to the worktable where I was working backup for Spiro, making hamburger setups for a ten-top on B deck. It was entirely too busy to mess around with Tammy.

"Those what? What are you talking about, Tammy?"

"I think she said 'Those Iggies.' It's a beer."

"Dos Equis. It's a Mexican beer. We don't carry it. Who wants it?"

"Woman on A deck. I'll go tell her."

Nick was in the back checking in a delivery. Like most vendors, New Systems Foods has the annoying habit of arriving during mealtimes, demanding to be checked in and paid during the busiest time of the day. A string of profanity testified to the driver's arrival. I stuck my head out the wait-station door for a quick glance at who wanted the Mexican beer. "Wait, Tammy," I said. "I'll tell her myself. You okay here, Spiro?"

Spiro was elbow-deep in meat. He nodded happily. "*Neh, enthoxi.*"

Connie Santos gazed out the window onto Broadway, giving me time to study her as I approached her table. She wore a pale blue denim skirt and a blazing white blouse with a deep, ruffled neckline. A wide silver concho belt encircled her narrow waist. Her hair was down, tumbling around her shoulders. She might have just crossed the border with the bandidos. Her long legs were crossed, displaying a tan that suggested Cancún. Where did she manage to get a tan like that in Delphi, in the fall? I wondered jealously.

"Ms. Santos?"

She turned, regarding me coolly.

"I think you were asking for Dos Equis beer? I'm afraid we don't carry it. Can I get you something else?"

She toyed with the ruffled neck of her blouse. "Oh, any kind will do. It doesn't really matter."

I dropped into the chair across from her, signaled to Tammy and gave her an order. "I hope you don't mind if I join you for a minute." Connie looked uncomfortable, but I hadn't really given her a choice, nor did I wait for an answer.

"We might think about carrying it," I said. "It's a good beer. I know Glenn developed a taste for it. You knew Glenn Bohannon, of course."

Connie faltered only a moment. Both of us knew she couldn't deny it. "Yes. He lived in my townhouse complex. I knew him. Dated him once in a while."

"Mm. You know, of course, that he was going to open a Mexican restaurant. 'Fried jalapenos and Dos Equis beer,' he used to say. His death must have hit you pretty hard. I'm sorry."

"Well, of course I felt bad. But I didn't know him all that well. As I said, I only dated him a couple of times."

"Really? I had the idea you were more, um, involved than that. He told us about you, you know."

It was a gamble but it produced the desired effect. Connie sat very still, her hands folded in her lap. But the glow had drained from her face, leaving the tan a sickly, ocher color. "I'm sure I don't know what he could have told you. We really didn't know each other all that well."

"Mind if I sit down with you?" Like me, Nick didn't wait for a response, but pulled out the chair next to mine and fell into it. "It's nice to see you again, Ms. Santos."

"Call me Connie." Smoldering eyes, pouty lips curved into a half-smile as she turned to my husband. I grabbed Nick's hand and gave it a light squeeze.

"Nick, honey, I was just telling Connie that Glenn had mentioned her to us."

He's quick on the uptake, that Nick. He pushed his hat back off his brow a little, and leaned toward her, dropping his voice. "Yeah. He said you had some interesting connections."

"Connections?" Her voice was cool, steely, but her fingers plucked the edges of the tablecloth and her body was stiff.

"You see, I have a little problem, Connie. Lucky, your coming in here today. You remember my cook, Spiro? You rented the house to him."

"Yes, of course I remember him. How's he doing?"

"He's fine. And he's fixed the house up quite a bit. You'd hardly recognize it."

She said nothing to this. What could she say, after all? Admit that it was a hovel? She waited for Nick to go on.

"Anyway, back to this problem. Spiro is from Crete, as you know. I'm not entirely sure how he got into the States, but it seems that he's missing some of the necessary documents to stay."

"Documents? I don't understand. I'm just a rental agent. What does this have to do with me?"

"Well, Glenn...suggested that you were an expert in helping people. Like your Mexican students, for example. He said you help them obtain the documents they need to remain in the United States. Like a green card. And a Social Security card. He seemed to think you might have some connection in the INS."

"Here's your Greekburger with cheese. Need anything else?" Tammy set the plate in front of Connie, chewed her gum and tapped her foot.

"Some ketchup, please," she said.

Connie waited until Tammy had brought the ketchup and departed, her feet slapping the deck as though she were wearing flippers. Not for the first time, I could have shot Tammy. Her timing was lousy, diffusing the pressure Nick had succeeded in applying, drawing attention away from Connie and giving her time to think. She carefully prepared her hamburger before responding. "So you're saying that you're harboring an illegal alien." She smiled, thoroughly relaxed and, I thought, enjoying herself.

"I'm saying that he's missing certain documentation that he should have."

"Yes, I understand." Connie dredged a french fry in ketchup, sucked on it lingeringly as she peered at Nick out of innocent eyes. "But I really don't see what I can do to help. The students I work with come here on visas. Sometimes they have problems with their papers, but it's nothing serious. I just help them straighten it out."

"Well, Spiro's prepared to pay whatever it might take to, um, straighten his paperwork out."

Did I imagine the spark that quickened in her eye at the mention of money? I don't think so. She half closed her eyes, as though trying to remember something.

"Hmm. I did have a friend who was in the same predicament a few years ago. I suppose I could call him and find out how he handled it. It might cost some money. There are application fees, legal fees, things of that nature."

"How much, exactly?"

"Well, I'd have to check with my friend, but I think it would run somewhere between five hundred and a thousand dollars to obtain both a green card and Social Security card. Of course, the cost may have gone up since he…applied for a green card."

"I see. Well that could probably be managed somehow." Nick nodded. "Yeah, I think we could take care of that." He pushed his chair back and stood, tugging my hand to follow him. "I'll go and tell him now."

"No, wait. I'll have to check around first. My friend may not be able to help after all. I'll have to call you."

"All right. I'll expect to hear from you." We shook hands, mine brief, but Connie seemed to linger over Nick's. I didn't like it.

"WHY DIDN'T YOU tell me about Spiro, Nick? We can't keep him here…it's illegal. And we're already in a mess—"

"Relax, will you? He's already got a green card. And it's legitimate. I just wanted to see what she'd say. If she goes any further with it, we'll just follow through as though he were illegal. It's okay."

Tammy stalked by us, grumbling under her breath. She was returning a plate to the kitchen. "You'd better go see what that's about."

"I know what it's about." Nick gestured to A deck, where Read Whitehead sat reading a newspaper at the table next to Connie's. As we watched, he wiped imaginary crumbs off the table, unrolled his silverware and carefully buffed each piece with his napkin before laying it out on the cloth. Satisfied that the table was now to his liking, he returned to the newspaper.

"It's Read's. He always sends his order back. There's nothing wrong with it, but Read seems to think that it's a necessary ritual. It's a power thing. Spiro's already wise to him. He'll stick it under the warmer a minute, then send it back. Read'll never know the difference."

In a moment, Tammy returned, setting the plate in front of Read. He examined it, smiled and nodded, folded his newspaper and set it on the floor beside his chair.

"I'm not sure that was smart—letting Connie know what we suspect about her activities. If she had anything to do with Glenn's death, we may just find ourselves with a pair of matched carving knives in our backs."

"Well, you brought it up. Besides, we needed to confirm it. I mean, she could have been an innocent party to the whole operation."

I glanced up at her table. She was fumbling in her purse, laid a thick envelope and keys on the table before extracting her wallet to pay the check. Below the ruffled neckline the full extent of her curvaceous figure was revealed. "She doesn't look innocent to me."

In a minute she appeared at the register. "I'll have to have certain information from your cook. Correct spelling of his name, things like that."

I handed her the change. "No problem. I guess we'll just wait to hear from you."

She was halfway across the parking lot when I noticed she'd dropped the envelope on the floor next to her chair. I sprinted for the deck, reaching the stairs just in time to see Read reach for his newspaper, snag the envelope and casually insert it in between the folds.

"RHONDA, DID YOU SEE that woman Nick and I were sitting with? The one in the denim skirt?"

"Yeah."

"Have you ever seen her before?"

"Sure. She comes in for lunch now and then."

"How often?"

"Maybe once every couple of weeks. Why?"

"Oh, I don't know. I guess I wondered why I never noticed her before."

"Probably because you're usually working backup for Nick at lunchtime."

That was true. Since Spiro's arrival, both Nick and I had spent more time in the dining room than ever before. Big as he was, Spiro was a tornado in the kitchen, moving on lithe feet to push the orders out. He rarely needed much help, and when he did, he usually intimidated Otis into helping him.

Tammy slapped a handful of change down on the family table. "That man holds on to a nickel so tight he's got Lincoln's face permanently printed in his palm."

"Jefferson."

"Huh?"

"Jefferson is on a nickel. Who are you talking about, anyway?"

"Mr. Whitehead, that's who." She fingered the change. "Look at this. On a six-dollar ticket he left me, um, forty-five cents. I'm not serving him anymore, Julia. Outta the whole damn stingy bunch of 'em he's the worst. Greekburger, fries, carrot cake, and ice water. He knows exactly how much it's gonna be and he's always got exact change. Then he leaves me what he's got left in his pocket. Last time it was twenty-two cents—two dimes and two pennies. I'm not serving him anymore." She dropped off her shoe, crossed her leg and started rubbing her foot. "And I got a blister from these shoes, too."

"Don't do that in the dining room, Tammy! How do you think customers feel when they see you rubbing your feet with the same hands that bring their orders? For that matter, how do you think I feel?"

"All right. Fine. I'll go back to dry storage." She snatched up her change and dropped it in her pocket. "Don't get a bit of sympathy around here..."

Rhonda rolled her eyes at me and went to bus Read's table.

"And wash your hands, please," I called to Tammy's back.

"So, he took the envelope, huh?"

I'd told Nick what I had witnessed. "You think he knows her? Maybe he's going to return it to her. Hey, maybe Read's got something going on the side himself. You know, his wife used to be a pretty woman, but she's really let herself go the last few years."

"I think he's got something going, all right. But it's not what you're thinking, Julia. I think Read Whitehead, real estate broker, is also Delphi Rental Properties. What you saw was a payment. And I'll bet my last dollar it was in cash."

"So how do we find out?"

"Well, there must be records. If nothing else, there had to be an announcement, the articles of incorporation, in the legal notices in the *Sun*."

"Guess that means a trip to the library, or maybe to the morgue at the paper. That could take days in the microfilm room."

Nick pushed back his chair. "I've got to go put up that delivery. Think about it. Maybe we should just proceed on the assumption—"

"We've got to have objective proof, Nick. That is, if we're going to convince Sam."

It was an overwhelming task that faced us. I was still pondering it when Billy English arrived with the photographs for the ad, and knew instantly that the answer had just presented itself at my door. I flipped through the photographs quickly, selected one and handed the packet back to Billy.

"No, it's okay. You keep the rest. I just need the one we're going to use in the ad."

"They're really good, Billy. I'm surprised you've stayed at a paper like the *Sun*. Looks to me like you could get a job at a first-rate paper—maybe Atlanta or Charlotte." A rosy tide swept up his neck into his ears. I had to admit, Norm had a point. He was a little like Jimmy Olsen.

"I like it here. And I'm hoping they're gonna let me move out of ads and into real journalism. I'd like to try my hand at a local story or two, or maybe as sportswriter. I'd really like to be a sportswriter. Besides, my girlfriend's still at Parnassus. Maybe after she graduates we might think about moving out of Delphi. Kinda depends . . ."

"On?"

"Well, on whether she wants to get married. I know I do, but she's kind of independent."

"Send her to me. I'll remind her that a woman can be married and stay independent. Tell me, Billy, do you have access to the computers at the *Sun*?"

"Well, sort of. I mean, I don't have a terminal of my own, but I can usually use somebody else's. Especially at night. Why?"

"Well, suppose you ran across a first-class, exclusive story. And say you did all the research on it and wrote it up yourself. Would the editors print it with your byline?"

"Maybe. Yeah, probably. If the story was hot enough."

"Would fraud and tax evasion be hot enough?"

"Sure!" He looked like a kid who'd been promised an extra helping of ice cream. "You have something in mind?"

I led him over to the family table. "As a matter of fact, I do."

SIXTEEN

I WAS CLOSING OUT the register when the phone rang. I could scarcely hear it over the music. Nick and Spiro were playing *tavli*, pushing the checkers over the backgammon board like a shell game. I'd given up trying to follow, and began closing out for the day.

"Julia, it's Dina Fox."

"Oh! Oh, hello Dina." I hit the volume control on the system, or thought I did. The music cut off abruptly, but Nick and Spiro were too deep into their game to notice.

"I was wondering... Uh, you know, Julia, I'd really like to talk to you. Could we meet somewhere this afternoon? Or tomorrow sometime?"

"Well, yes, I guess we could do that." I glanced over at Nick, absorbed in the lightning flash of dice and checkers. "I'll be free shortly."

"Fine. I'll pick you up. We can just go for a drive and talk a little."

I hung up the phone and fiddled with the tape player. I had pressed Record—may have obliterated George Dalaras. Oh well. Nick glanced up from his game.

"What are you doing?" He was out of the chair and crouched in front of the system, delicately adjusting the controls. He flipped a tape over and popped it back into the player. "Please don't mess with the sound system, Julia. It's very sensitive."

"I'm going for a ride with Dina Fox."

His brows drew together in a scowl. "I don't think that's a good idea."

"She wants to talk to me. Maybe I can find out something about Glenn."

"That's just the point, Julia. How do we know that Morgan wasn't covering up for her? That he didn't know she was having the affair with Glenn? He may have her cornered now. She might be desperate. After all, she told you about it. Now she might wish she hadn't. She might do something—"

"That's silly, Nick. Dina Fox is hardly the murdering type. She just wants to talk to me. That's all."

"If we've learned anything, it's that we don't know what 'the murdering type' is. I don't want you to go."

A black Mercedes Benz swung into the parking lot and Dina tapped the horn.

"She didn't waste any time getting here. Julia, I really don't want you to go."

I had already grabbed up my purse and was headed for the door with Nick at my heels. I hopped into the front seat with her as Nick leaned into the door, giving me one of his penetrating stares.

"How long will you be gone?"

I shrugged and looked over at Dina. She was wearing a white, turquoise, and hot pink track suit, and her blonde curls were pulled up in a ponytail. She reminded me of a petit four. She smiled brightly at him.

"Oh, just a little while." I patted Nick's hand. "I'm sure I'll be back by the time you're ready to leave. Go finish your game." We pulled out, leaving a forlorn Nick still standing in the doorway.

"He seems to hate to see you go," she said. "I guess I'm a little envious."

I brushed that off. "Oh, it's just that I didn't finish closing out the register. He hates to do it. But you got here so fast."

Dina smiled a little guiltily. "I was already on my way. I've been at the gym, so I called you from the car phone. After the other day, well, it's been on my mind that I owe you an explanation."

"You don't owe me anything, Dina. Your personal life is your own affa—um, business. I probably shouldn't have asked."

"No, really. I'm glad, in a way, to be able to talk about it. You know, sometimes it's hard to talk about personal things with close friends. They all seem to have some kind of vested interest in what you do—like if a marriage breaks up, it affects the whole group, so maybe they'll advise you to stay together just to prevent that. Things change, between friends, too. I've seen it happen. You know what I mean?''

I nodded. Although not a psychologist, I am in one of the "helping professions" and therefore seemingly fair game for confidences, even when I don't want to hear them. Ruminating about that, her next question almost knocked me off the seat.

"Have you ever had an affair?"

I gulped. "No. I guess I just don't see myself..." I trailed off, unable to think of any answer that wouldn't sound self-righteous.

"But of course Nick's crazy about you."

"Oh, I don't know. Just crazy, maybe." I fell silent, waiting for her to make the next move.

Dina skirted downtown Delphi, nosed the car toward one of the many two-lane country roads that lead into the mountains. The car smelled heavily of cigar smoke. I cracked the window to let in a little fresh air.

"Sorry," she said. "It's Morgan's car. I know it smells of cigars. Yuck."

She said nothing more, set her jaw, and leaned over the steering wheel. Her foot flexed on the accelerator and we took the first major curve at a smooth forty-five miles an hour.

The road was narrow, lined on either side by deep ditches. To my right, the mountains rose up in cliffs so sheer that the naked roots of the trees were exposed and threatening to topple across the road. Left, below Dina, we skimmed above treetops as though she were navigating a small plane. I grabbed the shoulder belt reflexively and braced my feet on the floorboard.

Dina hit the brakes suddenly, spraying gravel for twenty feet and coming within inches of the metal guardrail. A small green sign said Scenic View. I gasped, realizing I had been holding my breath. The muscles in my legs were cramping.

The valley that is Delphi stretched below us. Thick threads of fog spun out across it like strands of gray cotton candy. The wind had picked up, moving the gray bands quickly, alternately enshrouding the valley, then uncovering it again. To the left, the spires of Parnassus peaked over the treetops. We stared silently at the view, I, trying to swallow lunch back down where it belonged.

"I'm angry," she said. She gripped the steering wheel so hard that her arms trembled. I waited.

"I'm furious with Morgan, and with Glenn, too."

"But Glenn's dead, Dina."

"I know. And now I hate him more than ever."

"Why?" My voice seemed to come from somewhere far away.

She turned on me, eyes bright, teeth clenched. "Because he used me. Morgan uses me, and Glenn used me, and I'm goddamn sick to death of it."

She threw the door wide open and sprang out of the car, stalking to the guardrail. In a moment, she pivoted on her heel and glared at me, daring me to follow her. I reluctantly climbed out of the car.

We stood at the guardrail, gazing down into the valley. Delphi was all but hidden, nestled in among massive pines and oaks in the distant foothills, all of it covered by a gauzy blue-gray net. I picked out Parnassus easily, followed the three-mile stretch of Broadway to the Oracle and Nick, but I was too far away to see them.

"Do you see that?"

I nodded dumbly.

"No, I mean do you really see it? The bank...there, west of the university." She swung her finger back toward the east, in the general direction of the Oracle. "And that...those tracts of undeveloped land. Morgan says there's money to be made in Delphi, and power to be had." She swung around to face me.

"And, for Morgan, that's what it's all about. Power and money, money and power. He wants to be the barracuda in a small pond. And he's well on his way."

Dina's crystal blue eyes shimmered, and again I was reminded of shards of broken glass. She took a step toward me.

"It will never do for my affair with Glenn to be made public. It might ruin his perfect career." She spat the words, stepping toward me again.

SEVENTEEN

"YOU DON'T HAVE TO WORRY, Dina. I won't tell anyone. It's no one else's business." I was moving back, now several feet from the guardrail, my hands loose and waiting. She spun away from me suddenly.

"I don't care, Julia. Tell anyone you want to. Take out an ad in the paper. Shout it from the rooftops. No, I'll do it myself." She cupped her hands around her mouth and shouted out over the valley.

"Dina Fox is an unfaithful wife! Dina Fox is not perfect!"

Her laughter echoed behind this proclamation, a bitter laugh with no joy in it. Her voice was dampened by the thickening mist. It was a desperate cry, one that would not be heard by anyone but me. I watched as she wiped her eyes on her sleeve, pulled a twisted tissue from her pocket and blew her nose.

"Do you want to talk about it?"

She shrugged. "What is there to say? I'm a showpiece." She pivoted on the toes of her Reeboks, arms outstretched. "I keep in perfect physical condition, have my hair done regularly, and always in the latest style. I choose the most fashionable clothes, which must be perfect for every occasion. I stay up-to-date on the latest news, fashions, even sports, which I loathe. I take tennis lessons, golf lessons, cooking lessons, have a cleaning woman twice a week. I play bridge, dance quite well, and teach Sunday school."

My sympathy for her was receding. It did not, after all, sound like such a terrible life. A cleaning woman twice a week?

Dina watched me steadily, as though she knew what I was thinking. In fact, she did. "I know," she said. "It must sound wonderful. But Julia, have you ever read *A Doll's House?*"

I nodded.

"Well, maybe it's not quite the same, but... You see, Morgan wants me to be perfect. I told you that before. But it's not because he loves me. It's because I'm part of his image of perfection.

"I was wildly in love with him when we married. I loved his looks, his ambition, his promise, so maybe I'm not so different from him. But it wasn't long before I realized that he had chosen me because, of all the girls he had dated, I showed the most promise. Good breeding stock, I suppose you could say. He could groom me to be what he thought would make him look good. The man has never loved me for myself, not the way Nick loves you."

"And Glenn?"

Dina sighed. "Glenn. You know, at first I thought he loved me. He was so..." She was struggling, I realized, not only with the words, but with the truth. "—tender. He let me be myself. He laughed at my jokes, asked me questions about my childhood and my own children. He made me feel cherished. I thought we might even have a future together. I would have left Morgan in a heartbeat if Glenn had asked me."

I moved closer to her, to the guardrail. "Then why are you angry with him?"

Dina kicked at the gravel, picked up a rock and threw it out over the treetops. "Because he was using me too."

"How?"

She faced me, and her expression was solemn. "I'm not quite sure. I only know that he had some purpose in the affair. He didn't really love me, either."

We looked out over the valley again, now completely blanketed by the fog. It might not have even been there, might have disappeared into another time like a modern Brigadoon.

"He started asking me a lot of questions about Morgan's business affairs and the political and social issues in town. I wouldn't have known, except that Morgan makes a point of keeping me up-to-date on what's happening and where he stands on the issues. That way there's no risk of my committing a social or political gaffe."

"Does he talk about bank business?"

"Not in actual dollars and cents, but how do you separate the bank's business interests from what's going on in town? They're usually one and the same.''

"What about other businessmen?"

Dina shrugged. "Of course I know a good bit about their businesses. They're some of Morgan's closest friends; that is, the closest thing Morgan has to friends. And I know their wives and their kids. Even some of their grandchildren.''

"What, exactly, did Glenn want to know?"

She shoved her hands down into the pockets of her jacket, looked at, but did not see, the valley below her. "I never was really sure. His questions were so casual, so random. I never pieced together any real point to them. In fact, I didn't catch on to his game until just before he died." She smiled. "I was still laboring under the illusion that he loved me, until I found some lingerie in his townhouse that wasn't mine. Black and red—a teddy. Hardly my style.''

"Did you confront him?"

Dina shook her head. "He was in the shower. I just threw on my clothes and left. I was in a hurry. That's why I left the bracelet.''

She continued to pitch little pieces of gravel out over the guardrail as I watched her. "What about the bracelet? Did Morgan ask you about it?"

"Yes. I told him I was at the Oracle for lunch the day before Glenn died and that I lost it then.''

"Did he believe you?"

She shrugged. "I suppose so. If he says anything to you, I'd be grateful if you'd just—"

"Of course. You were there having lunch. But, I guess I still don't understand how you got involved with Glenn.''

"I thought I told you. Morgan introduced us. Then I met him again taking the dog to obedience classes.'' A wry little smile flickered momentarily on her lips. "Even Morgan's dog has to be perfect.

"Anyway, it was a month after Bobby's accident and I was really having a hard time. Still am.''

"Bobby?"

"My brother. Bobby McIntyre. He used to come into the Oracle with Morgan and the others."

"He's your brother?" Bobby McIntyre was the vice president of Morgan's SafeBank branch, and had been hurt in a tragic accident while driving home from working late about four months before. They said he fell asleep at the wheel and went through a guardrail on one of the mountain roads. The last I'd heard he was convalescing somewhere, but the damage to body and mind were serious and permanent.

"Didn't you know that? Well, I don't know why you would have, really. You see, Bobby and Morgan went to Parnassus together—both majored in finance. In fact, he introduced me to Morgan. Bobby idolized him. Morgan was always at the top of his classes. Bobby was no slouch, but Morgan was always—I don't know—quicker, I guess. More clever.

"When Morgan moved up to the presidency at SafeBank, he brought Bobby on board because, he said, he could trust him and he knew the quality of his work. It was such a happy time. Besides being my brother, Bobby was always my best friend. And the three of us together..." She drifted off, scanned the mountains and pointed at a cluster of houses around a curve on the right. They almost seemed to hang on the edge of nothing, suspended out over the valley.

"That's where Bobby lived. You can barely see it, the white one through the trees there. He wasn't married yet—looking for someone like me, he said." She pointed about fifty yards beyond where we stood, to a sharp curve and a steep rockface. "And that's where he went off the road. It almost killed him, and it almost killed me, too."

We stared at the spot together. The trees below the rockface were large and solid. There was little sign—only a few broken limbs, no twisted wreckage—of what had taken place there four months ago. I didn't know what Dina was thinking, but I could guess. My throat constricted. I have a brother too.

"They hadn't been getting along that well. Morgan has changed. He was always a go-getter, always tough and smart. But after he went with SafeBank he got worse. He wants to move up in the system. SafeBank's based in Atlanta and Morgan's got his eye on big things there. He got more aggressive. Bobby didn't like it. He never told me the particulars, but I could tell that something was wrong.'' She shrugged. ''I guess he'll never be able to tell me now.''

We started back toward the car. ''Just how seriously was he injured, Dina?''

''Very. He's in a wheelchair. His left leg is still in a cast. Both arms were broken. But the worst is the head injuries. He can't speak at all, and I don't know how much he understands. It's like he had a stroke or something.''

She climbed up onto the hood of the car facing the valley below. Again, the wry smile flitted across her face. Morgan would not approve of her sitting on his Mercedes.

''What about therapy?''

''I'm not sure. Morgan's taken care of everything from the beginning. I really...I just couldn't deal with it. I think he goes to physical therapy, but that's all. Morgan talks to the doctors and he tells me there's not much hope for anything better. I've tried to get Morgan to have him tested by a speech therapist, but he's adamant about it. He says it's costing us plenty already and he doesn't want to waste money on something the doctors say can't be helped.''

Four months. It was still pretty early to know for sure. The brain can do remarkable things on its own, but sometimes therapy is just the catalyst it needs. Bobby McIntyre was still a relatively young man, maybe in his mid-thirties. Nick says I'm irrationally stubborn, but I never believe there's no hope. I climbed up on the car next to her.

Dina closed her eyes. ''I'd give anything to be able to talk to him and know he really understood me.'' She shivered as the wind gusted, wrapping us in a thicker cloak of fog. Pools glistened in her eyes. Unexpectedly, I found myself reaching out to touch her arm.

''That's one of the reasons I wanted to talk to you, Julia. I was wondering if you would see him.''

''Oh Dina, I...I don't know.'' Her timing could hardly have been worse. With Nick under suspicion of murder, there was no room in my life for further complication. No time to test him, let alone offer him therapy.

"You could go with me to visit him, talk to him, let me know if you think there's any hope. Oh Julia, you're the only one I can ask."

"Dina, I can give you the names of two very competent speech pathologists here in town who'd be happy to see your brother. But I just really don't—"

"No, you see, I can't...I mean, I can't bring anyone else in. Morgan mustn't know about it."

"Why?"

"Because he doesn't like losing control over things. He's already decided there's no hope for Bobby." Tears were streaming down her cheeks. She wiped them away with the back of her sleeve. "It would have to be someone who's willing to see him, um, privately. I mean, I'd have to sort of slip them in, you know? Without Morgan knowing about it. If you won't do it, then he won't get any help."

Great. A guilt trip. My life wasn't complicated enough. But Nick was right about one thing. Dina Fox was a desperate woman. She wanted her brother back and, for some reason, had latched on to the idea that I, and I alone, could accomplish it.

"Well, why don't we do it this way? I'll go with you someday when you visit. After I meet him I may have a general idea of how to proceed. I won't be able to tell you much until I can read his history and test him, but we'll start with a meeting, okay? We won't mention it to Morgan. Then if it looks like he can be helped, I'll refer you to someone else. I really can't take on his case right now, Dina. I've got some other problems to deal with first."

"You'll change your mind, Julia. He's such a wonderful man. I know, after you meet him, you'll see. You're the one who can help him. And then Morgan won't have to know."

"Dina, I really..."

Her eyes were bright with expectation. Hope. I resolved to deal with it a step at a time. First, see Bobby. Then I could refer him to someone else.

Seed pearls of dampness had settled in her hair. I reached up to my own, found it wet and curling out of control. Blue mist obscured everything beyond the guardrail as the fog steadily overtook us. Driving would now be more hazardous. She slid off the car and moved around to the driver's door. "I'd like to go tomorrow. Would you be free?"

"I'll make time, don't worry." I climbed into the passenger's side, fastened my seat belt and watched as she put the car in reverse. When we were safely back on the road and moving at approximately half the speed of our ascent, I returned to our earlier discussion. "You never really explained about Glenn."

"Well, I guess I was pretty vulnerable. Morgan was caught up in bank business—finding a replacement for Bobby, getting familiar with his accounts, and all that. I'd go to the hospital every day—that was before he was well enough to be moved to Northridge. But it was so terrible, Julia. Seeing Bobby all broken apart and not being able to communicate with him. It was the worst time of my life.

"Glenn was friendly and sympathetic. At first we just talked about the dogs, but then I found myself talking to him about Bobby. And then it just led to...to other things. After Bobby was moved to Northridge, Glenn even went with me a few times to see him. It didn't matter if Bobby figured it out—our relationship, I mean—since he can't talk anyway. He wasn't going to tell Morgan."

"No. I suppose not. How was Glenn with him?"

"Oh, very sweet and gentle. He could be that way—make you open up and talk to him."

"Mm," I said. Clearly Glenn had had an agenda of his own. I found it hard to reconcile this with the Glenn I had known—a sincerely kind man.

"I suppose you must wonder why I stay with Morgan. I know I made it sound like I hate him."

"Well," I admitted, "it doesn't sound too good."

"I don't hate him. Not really. I just don't like him anymore. But, in his own way, he's been good to Bobby. Northridge is the best convalescent home around, and it's very expensive. I don't know how long he'll have to stay there. I'm hoping maybe he can go home eventually. He loved that little mountain house so much, I just couldn't sell it. But frankly, Julia, without Morgan's money, I couldn't keep Bobby there. I suppose that sounds ruthless, but it's true. I'll stay with Morgan as long as I have to, just to provide for the kids and Bobby.''

Dina, it seemed, had learned a few things from her husband.

NICK AND I had stopped for a bite to eat on the way home—fast fried chicken in a place that offered us the anonymity of all such restaurants, the get-'em-in, get-'em-out-quick style of food purveyance. I gnawed on a leg and reflected that if we'd chosen that particular mode of business we might not be in the trouble we were in. The road not taken, I suppose.

My trip to the mountains with Dina had left me exhausted, and I returned to find a backgammon marathon between Nick and Spiro, which meant I still had to do the closing. It was long past dark when we pulled into the carport. Deep in conversation about Morgan, Dina, and Bobby, neither of us noticed the pickup truck parked in front of the house next door. Nick went to collect the mail from the box at the street as I fumbled for the light in the carport, poked my key into the door, and pushed it open.

They must have been hiding there, among the garbage cans and accumulation of bicycles, boxes, and refuse of daily living. The hand over my mouth was the first warning I had. It almost smothered me.

He pulled me out of the doorway, letting the screen door slam shut, flipped off the light and spun me around, arms wrenched behind me, to face the driveway. I could see Nick coming, silently screamed a warning about the two hulking men who waited for him in the shadows.

They looked like the effigy—stockings pulled over their heads flattening their features to a dull facelessness. I kicked and twisted, but his grip on my arms tightened until tears of pain pooled in my eyes. The other two were on Nick, one pinning his arms behind him as the other took deep punches to his gut. Jack barked and growled, throwing his sturdy little body helplessly against the screen door.

It was probably only a minute, but it seemed to drag on in an endless nightmare of smothering, battering pain. Nick doubled over with the first blow, took a second one low in the gut. I tried vainly to stomp on the feet of my captor, and was rewarded with more wrenching pain that shivered up into my shoulders. Behind me the screen door rattled, bumped, thumped open, and closed again. From the corner of my eye I saw the little black form leap off the doorsill.

My captor screamed in pain before he cut loose his grip on me. Jack had his ankle locked between square jaws as lethal as a bear trap. I pulled away. Part of me watched him trying to shake the little dog off, part of me searched the garage for a weapon. I darted for a shovel. My attacker was dragging Jack across the garage floor, shrieking and shaking his foot. I spun, raised the shovel over my head, and stopped.

It all went into slow motion then. Nick leaned back against the man who held him, danced lightly, the balls of his feet barely contacting the cement. Then he leapt, delivered a goal kick—one first into his attacker's groin, and as he bent double, a second cutting upward, upward, toes pointing to the stars and landing square in the larynx of the stocking-faced man. He fell back with a rush of breath, grabbing his throat in a silent scream.

My attacker was speeding down the driveway as Jack worried his ankle to shreds. Nick had pulled out of the third man's grip, spun and delivered another kick, catching the man in the shoulder, reeling him backward. He twisted, made a split-second decision, and dashed for the pickup truck. Behind him, his buddy crawled off the cement and reeled across the yard toward the waiting vehicle. By the time he reached it, the motor was throbbing. My attacker had finally extricated himself from Jack's grip, tossing the little dog across the yard. Jack yelped and struggled to his feet as the truck roared away. I dropped the shovel to follow Nick across the yard.

He cradled Jack like a baby, breathed hard and bent double. We stood, silently trying to recover our breath. Jack panted, let a bloodstained shred of cloth drop out of his mouth, and stared up at Nick. His wagging tail thumped against Nick's legs. I picked up the cloth and we stumbled to the house together.

"He's all right."

Nick finished his examination of Jack, feeling for broken bones, then set him down on the kitchen floor. Jack trotted happily away, returning with the tennis ball.

"How about you?"

He shook his head, rubbed his stomach. "Pretty sore. It'll be worse tomorrow, but I'm okay." He took me in his arms. "That was another warning. They're getting more serious. I want you to leave, Julia. Go stay with your brother or your parents."

Hot tears puddled up in my eyes. My arms and shoulders were sore, bruised. I didn't tell Nick. "And leave you alone? No way. I go where you go, and I stay where you stay. We fight together. Let's call Sam."

"We can't." Nick took the shredded cloth from my clenched fist. "It's bloody. Jack did a little damage there. Looks like a sock—an athletic sock."

It was soaked in blood, had once been white. Jack must have left quite a crater in the man's ankle. Somewhere in Delphi a thug was nursing some deep lacerations. And another one was whispering. I hoped Nick's kick had left some lasting damage—a paralyzed vocal cord would be nice.

"Who were they?"

Nick shrugged. "Just some lowlifes. Probably on somebody's payroll."

"Whose?"

"Think about it, Julia. Who hates foreigners? Who wants us to run?"

"Cal Taylor."

"Bingo. Now you see why we can't call Sam. I'm still not sure whose side he's on."

EIGHTEEN

NORTHRIDGE Convalescent Home is an elegant facility built of pink brick in a low, sprawling style. We pulled up the circular drive past the front door and cut off to the right, following it around the building to an unobtrusive parking lot at the rear. Dina eased her Volvo station wagon in between a red Lexus and a long, navy Cadillac.

"I'm glad to be behind my own wheel again," she said. "I never have liked the Mercedes, but the Volvo was in for service."

Dina's small talk was of the nervous variety. I wasn't sure whether she was edgy because she was doing something behind Morgan's back, or whether it stemmed from deeper reasons. Having made the decision to have me see Bobby, she would finally learn the truth about her brother's condition. It could be a frightening prospect. She wanted hope desperately, and I was not at all sure I could give her that. She grabbed a stack of magazines off the seat and locked the car.

I followed her through a beautifully appointed garden, filled with wide walkways, topiaries, and massive trees. It was the kind of landscaping designed to provide color year-round, with pools of sunlit gardens and benches for enjoying them. We entered Northridge through a garden door which led us into a sitting room. A discreet sign next to the door asked visitors to use the main entrance only.

"We're not supposed to come in this way, but they usually let me get away with it. There are a few good things about being Mrs. Morgan Fox. Why don't you wait here? I have to sign the visitor's log, but I don't want your signature on it. And Bobby's room is at this end of the building. I'll come back and get you."

I agreed and dropped into an easy chair where I could see the garden. At the end, past trees pruned to resemble poodles, a small swimming pool shimmered an improbable blue, not in use at that time of the year. There was something vaguely disquieting about the empty garden, so carefully laid out and so utterly deserted. Rather like a cemetery I thought, turning away.

The sitting room, on the contrary, seemed designed for people and pleasure, in its own way another anomalous setting for a medical facility. Six wingback chairs were casually arranged around a white marble fireplace. Each chair was covered in hand-embroidered crewel fabric of a Jacobean design in soft shades of blue, taupe, and green. The fireplace was flanked on either side by wide French doors that stood partially open, allowing the crisp fall air to gently fill the room. No hospital smell here.

I suspected that a television was discreetly hidden inside a cherry armoire—probably complete with VCR and cable. The parquet floor was blanketed by an Oriental carpet that made me want to slip out of my loafers and curl my toes on it. In fact, I was doing that very thing when Dina came to collect me. I jumped to my feet, unfortunately leaving one shoe behind me as I crossed the room. Dina looked away while I went back to collect it. Dina pushed open a door three rooms away from the nurses' station. I followed her in.

Bobby McIntyre sat in a wheelchair angled toward the window. He was looking out into a courtyard filled with topiaries and gardens of marigolds. Across the courtyard, a like row of rooms gazed back. The building was, I surmised, more or less H-shaped, with four short wings of patient rooms. The center included the sitting room, probably the kitchen, and some facilities for OT, PT, X-ray and the like. Bobby pulled his gaze away when he heard the door swish open.

His left leg was encrusted in a cast like beef Wellington, and his slightly edematous, bare right foot sat on the floor. My heart sank at the signs of left brain damage. Bobby's right arm was immobilized, indicating paralysis. His mouth drooped, and a thin strand of saliva spun down to his pajama collar. A collection bag and tube were taped under his clothing. I had little doubt that his speech would be affected, too.

Bobby's face grimaced in a twisted smile when he saw Dina. She set the magazines on his bedside table and drew me toward him, introducing me as her friend and saying my name very slowly for him. I took his left hand in mine and was rewarded with a surprisingly firm grip, but there was no vocal response to my hello.

The room was large, dominated, of course, by a hospital bed, but otherwise nicely furnished with a small sitting area near the window. Besides Bobby's wheelchair, there was an easy chair and a heavy maple Windsor armchair. I drew it close to him and sat back to observe his reactions to Dina.

She talked about the children—Corrinne's new braces and Todd's preschool carnival. He seemed to be listening intently, and following her sometimes kinetic leaps from topic to topic. His gray-green eyes were alert, focused on his sister, and his brows rumpled when she mentioned Brad's reluctant adjustment to a new teacher. When he learned of Corrinne's solo in the fall program, the twisted smile reappeared. Even in the subtle movements of his face there was confirmation—Bobby McIntyre was following some, if not all, of his sister's prattle.

"She's pretty nervous about it, but I know she'll do fine. Unfortunately, Morgan has a board meeting that night, and he says he can't get out of it."

Something quickened in Bobby's eyes—a spark, a flash of anger, I thought. One side of his face grew hard, creating a grotesque imbalance in the musculature. I glanced down at his hand. His left fingers were wrapped around the arm of the chair, the flesh under his nails pressed to white. Dina did not seem to notice the change. She scooped up the pile of magazines and arrayed them on his lap.

"I've brought *Popular Mechanics, Time, Autoweek,* and *Financial World.* That should keep you busy for a while." I wondered at her choices. I was not altogether sure he could read, but he carefully dampened the tip of his left index finger and turned the cover of *Popular Mechanics* open. Then he gave her a thumbs-up sign and another twisted grin. She laughed and grabbed his thumb, shaking it.

"I'd like to speak to his nurse before we leave," she said to me. Bobby was slowly turning the magazine pages. Dina jerked her head toward the door, indicating that I follow her.

"What do you think?" she whispered.

"He definitely understands you, Dina. But what makes you think he can read those magazines?"

She shrugged. "I don't know that he can, but he seems to like to look at them. I'm going to leave you alone with him for a few minutes. Maybe you can find out more if I'm not in the room. He might be embarrassed if he thinks he's failing some kind of...of test in front of me."

I agreed and returned to my chair as soon as she'd left the room. I was no more than seated when a hand flashed out and clutched my wrist, startling me back onto my feet. I met his eyes and knew then that what I had seen there was terror. His lips were moving, pressed hard together, and a low humming vibrated in his throat.

"Mmm," he said. "Mmmor...Mmmorgan."

"Morgan?" My heart quickened. Bobby McIntyre could speak.

He nodded his head slowly and repeated the name. "Mmmorgan. Mmmorgan. D—an—ger..."

"Dangerous?"

"D-an-ger-s. Hhh-elp mmm..."

"Help you."

He shook his head, dashed at the air with his hand. "Hhh—elp mmm-yy sssister."

My own heart was beating so loudly that I was sure it would bring the entire nursing staff down on us. He had my hand again, gripping it with a strength I could scarcely believe he possessed. "Hhhelp mmmyy..."

"Well, that's done. Oh, I almost forgot." Dina popped back into the room. She dug into her handbag and pulled three small frames out, setting them on his table. "I've brought you the kids' back-to-school pictures. Corrinne was glad they took it before she got the braces."

I stared openmouthed at them both. What was going on here? Had fear and desperation opened Bobby McIntyre's mind, or had he been hiding his ability to speak all along? And if so, how much therapeutic advantage had we lost in the interim?

"Dina," I said excitedly, "he—" A flutter of his fingers stopped me. His eyes bore into mine and I thought I noticed a quick shake of his head. I pointed to his collection bag. "—he might need to have that changed," I said.

"ARE YOU READY?"

Nick glanced at his watch for the third or fourth time as I pulled a cotton knit top over my head and pushed my feet into a pair of white loafers. I took a quick glance in the mirror. The skirt and top were solid white, a fact which gave me pause in late October. But then, anyone who might see me in it would probably shrug, attribute it to my notorious lack of fashion sense. For once, I was hoping that reputation would serve me well.

"Did you get them? Where are they?"

I pointed to a pair of crutches leaning into a corner in the bedroom. I had exhumed them from the attic, the remnants of an old skiing injury which had established me as the only person ever to perform a half-gainer off a chairlift. It still made me blush. Nick grabbed them and made for the door. I tossed my briefcase into the backseat and took my place behind the steering wheel of the car.

"Are you sure he understood everything?"

"I explained it all very carefully, Julia. He'll do fine. But if we don't hurry up, we're going to be late. I told him seven o'clock sharp. We don't want him sitting there very long. That car will draw attention."

Spiro was, indeed, waiting when we pulled into the circular drive in front of Northridge. I veered past the pachydermatous Pontiac and stopped to drop Nick at the corner of the building before proceeding to the parking lot. He hobbled from the car, his leg encased in a full-length brace also resurrected from my skiing fiasco. He wore a sweat suit which, I hoped, might be construed as pajamas.

When I got back to the front of the building, he was waiting, carefully concealed behind a high hedge of pittosporum. He pushed the crutches up under his arms and peered around the corner, raising two fingers to his brow in a mock salute. The Pontiac's door swung open and the massive frame of Spiro appeared. He did not look our way, but loped steadily up the drive and through the doors of the convalescent home. We gave him a few seconds' start on us.

"Let's go," Nick whispered.

NINETEEN

THE AUTOMATIC DOORS swished open. Spiro stood directly in front of the little Chippendale check-in desk. As if on cue, he slid his body to the right. He hunched slightly and clutched his arms over his stomach. His big voice boomed through the hallway.

"O yiatros?"

"I'm sorry, sir?"

"O yiatros?" A long spate of Greek followed, complemented by groans and gestures as Spiro swung his body farther to the right, shielding us from view.

"Is hospital?"

"No, sir. This is a convalescent home. If you'll just go back down this street…"

I chanced a glance backward to see the nurse pointing out the door and directing him toward Delphi General Hospital. Spiro's face was a study in confusion, hers in frustration. Nick was swinging on the crutches at a pace too rapid for a serious convalescent. I caught him by the elbow as we turned the corner.

"Slow down. You're going too fast." We were in the main hallway on the right side of the H, passing a variety of therapy rooms. Other visitors passed us, walking with their charges, but no one seemed to take any notice of us. I breathed a sigh of relief, then followed it with a mental groan. Approaching us was my worst fear.

Marta Kaspir was a short woman with thinning gray hair, permed and colored with a red rinse that left it an uncommitted apricot color. She wore a flowered housecoat, snapped unevenly up the front, and leaned heavily on an ebony cane. Just what she was convalescing from was not clear, but the joy of navigating the halls of Northridge and plucking the grapevine seemed to be therapy enough. She was charging toward us with all the speed and determination of an Indy driver, certainly none the worse for her condition.

Dina and I had met her in the hall as we were leaving Bobby McIntyre's room earlier in the day. We'd stopped for a brief chat, covered Bobby's condition and her own, nebulous ailments, before moving on. Marta was, it seemed, Mitch Yoakum's mother-in-law. Dina summarized it neatly: "I think Mitch feels Northridge is a prudent investment in peace at home." It was easy to empathize.

Recognition snapped brightly in Marta's brown eyes. "How nice to see you again so soon," she said. "I'm sorry, I just don't recall your name."

I murmured something I hoped was appropriately vague and spurred Nick in the ribs with a pinch. He shot forward on the crutches, swinging like a pendulum. Marta gasped and scurried out of his way.

"Well, I have patients to see. Take care, Mrs. Kaspir." I hurried ahead of Nick in the hall, trying to look as though we were not together. As I turned the corner into Bobby's corridor I glanced back. Marta was watching me curiously. "I'll remember it yet," she called. "I'm very good at names."

I gestured as though I couldn't hear her, smiled and waved. Nick swung past me, toward the sitting room, doubling back when Marta was out of sight. I studied the photographs on the wall until he came up behind me. We entered Bobby McIntyre's room together.

He might not have moved since we left him, still seated in the wheelchair staring out toward the courtyard. Darkness had fallen and the poodle trees and topiaries were lighted by spotlights. Their leaves looked waxy, as artificial as Northridge itself. A television hummed steadily in the background, and a toothy newscaster looked appropriately grave as he described yet another mountain collision. Bobby was ignoring it, either too much auditory input for his condition, or too many painful memories. When he turned, he did not seem surprised to see us. For a moment, I wondered if he were heavily drugged.

The remnants of a dinner tray sat on the movable table next to him, suggesting that someone would be coming to collect it. I quickly scooped it up and set it outside the door of his room, stopping to hang a Treatment In Progress sign on the door. It was calculated to keep visitors from disturbing us, but a risk that might provoke questions from the nursing staff. I pulled a few testing and therapy materials from my briefcase and tossed them onto the table. I did not really intend to use them, not without reading up on Bobby's history, but thought they might provide a cover story if necessary. Bobby and Nick watched it all with silent interest.

When I had them suitably arranged, I turned to Bobby, but found myself suddenly awkward. His blank expression implied that I had imagined the events of the afternoon. Nick watched me with shadows of doubt flickering across his face. I decided to plunge.

"Do you remember Nick?"

Bobby nodded slowly, willingly shook Nick's left hand with his own. "Y-ess," he said.

"We're here to talk to you about Morgan."

That same spark lit his eyes—fear? anger? Nick saw it too, and nodded briefly at me in confirmation. I pulled a chair directly in front of Bobby and leaned toward him, covering his hands with mine.

"You told me that Morgan is dangerous. We're here to help you—to protect Dina. We won't tell anyone that you can talk, but you must tell us more, Bobby. We must know more if we're going to help her."

He nodded slowly. "Hhh-elp Dina," he said. "Hhhelp..."

"But how? How can we help her? What has Morgan done?"

Bobby looked down at his broken body. Slowly he lifted his hand to tap his head. "This," he said.

"He did this to you?" Nick was leaning forward, watching Bobby's every expression as closely as I was. Bobby nodded again.

"Sss-l-eep," he said. Bobby had fallen asleep at the wheel and gone off the road. He had worked very late and was tired. It was a tragically natural accident. At least that was the sheriff's assumption, and who had known any better? Bobby couldn't talk, or so he let his sister and brother-in-law, the doctors and nurses, believe. But it wasn't true, at least not entirely. Bobby McIntyre chose not to speak. Why?

"Are you saying he drugged you? Did he give you something to make you sleepy?"

"Eeeat." He shook his head and hand in frustration. "No, co-ff," he said.

"Coffee. In your coffee." Nick jumped up and paced the room. "You were working late with Morgan. You were drinking coffee. You think he put something in your coffee."

"Y-ess. Sl-eep."

"But why?"

Bobby closed his eyes. The effort of speech, so long neglected, was taxing him. Perhaps it was too much for him. I was frightened, afraid to push him too far. "Should we stop, Bobby? Are you tired?"

I thought he would leap from the chair. His body grew tense, shaking, and rigid fingers curled around the left armrest. "No!" The answer exploded from his drooping lips. I patted his hand and waited.

"Bank," he said wearily. "B-aad."

"Bad. Something bad." Nick studied Bobby's anxious face. "Was something wrong at the bank?"

"Mmm."

"And you discovered it. Is that it, Bob?"

Bobby lifted his index finger to his nose. "On the nose," I whispered. "It means yes."

Nick withdrew a notebook from my briefcase and began writing Greek characters across the page—notes to himself, questions. "Did you have evidence?"

Bobby's nod was the only answer Nick needed.

"Do you still have it?" Again, the weary nod.

"Where?"

"Bbb-ox. No! D-oor, no..." Bobby squeezed his eyes closed tightly. His voice was humming in a low rumble, and his thick tongue vainly tried to form words. But it was neither his tongue nor his voice that defeated him. The brain, the electrical connections simply could not be made. Not without help. His eyes shot open and he pointed to the stack of magazines Dina had left him in the afternoon. I got them and placed them on his lap. He picked them up, looked them over and discarded them one at a time until he came to *Time*. This he carefully paged through, stopping at a picture of the president in front of the White House. He pointed to the building.

"This."

"The White House?" Nick and I exchanged confused glances. Bobby shook his head angrily.

"Washington?" I ventured. He waved his hand away.

"House," Nick said. "At your house?"

"Y-ess," came the slow reply.

"The evidence against Morgan is at your house." The light in Bobby's eyes made reply unnecessary.

"Does Morgan know?"

He shrugged. "Ca-aan't find."

"It's hidden. Hidden at your house. Do you want us to find it?"

"Go."

"Yes. We'll go there. But you must tell us where to look."

Bobby picked up the magazine and slowly turned the pages. He stopped at page fourteen, pointing to the number in the corner.

"Fourteen," I said. Nick grabbed the pad and wrote the number. Bobby turned to another page.

"Twenty-two." It was followed by two more numbers which Nick carefully noted: six and twenty-one.

"What are these? What do these numbers mean?"

Nick leaned toward Bobby. "It's a safe, isn't it Bobby? The combination to a safe."

For the first time since I'd met him, Bobby McIntyre looked relaxed, almost serene. He gave us that lopsided smile that I had seen earlier in the day when Dina was visiting him.

"A key! Bobby, how will we get in?" My question was interrupted by a voice on a public address system announcing that it was eight o'clock and visiting hours were over. We could not afford to be caught in the building after visiting hours. The staff would be coming around shortly to dispense medication and take vital signs. I stuffed my therapy materials back into my briefcase.

"Is there a key?"

Bobby nodded and closed his eyes again. His face was drawn with deep signs of fatigue. "Fff-ly," he said.

"Fly," I repeated to myself. "Fly?"

Equipment clattered in the corridor. Next door, the raised voice of a nurse inquired whether the patient was ready for bed. Nick tiptoed to the door, listened a minute and hurried back to me.

"We have to get out of here. The nurse is next door."

There was still so much to ask Bobby, so many questions left unanswered. I grabbed his hands and squeezed them tightly. "Did you tell this to anyone else?"

Bobby nodded.

"Who?"

"Mmm-an. Dina. Frrr-iend."

"Dina's friend?" I already knew the answer. "Glenn?"

"Gl-ennn..."

The clattering was coming toward us—an automated sphygmomanometer was being pushed toward Bobby's door. Nick threw open the window and jerked up the screen. He pulled me toward our only means of escape.

"But where is the safe?" I whispered, even as I threw my case out the window and my legs over the window sill.

"Hhh-ello," Bobby said.

Nick ripped off the knee brace and dove over the sill after me, pulled on the window, but finding it caught, dragged the screen down. The door to the room was opening. We sat below the window, our backs pressed against the brick wall.

"And how are we feeling tonight, Mr. McIntyre?" A dubiously sincere voice chirped through the open window. "It's a little cool to have the window open. Oh my, how odd!" she said.

I chanced a peek over the sill. She was standing with her back to the window, staring at the crutches Nick had left tucked in the corner of the room. In one hand, she held my Treatment In Progress sign, in the other, the knee brace. I slid back down next to Nick, my heart doing ninety beats a minute. Her soft-soled shoes squeaked across the room.

"Mr. Fox," she said into the phone. "This is Ms. Webb, at Northridge. Something is odd in Mr. McIntyre's room. Well, no, he seems fine. But, well, the window is open and...I'm not sure that's necessary. All right."

She hung up the phone and crossed the room. "Has someone

been to see you, Mr. McIntyre?'' She was answered with the
silence she must have expected. "You know that Mr. Fox is very
concerned that you not be bothered by unwanted visitors—'' She
snapped the window firmly closed. I held my breath as she turned
the lock.

"Yoohoo!'' A reedy voice twittered across the silent night in
the courtyard. "Hello again...Janet, is it?''

I glanced at Nick. His eyes were riveted on a window in the
other wing. The curtains were open and billowing in the breeze.
Against the light of the room the small form of a woman was
silhouetted. Marta Kaspir was waving at us.

TWENTY

NICK CUT THE CAR LIGHTS and turned to me. "Will you nuck that off?"

My giggling teetered on a semihysterical precipice. I tried to look serious, but Nick's frown deepened, spurring me into uncontrolled gales of laughter.

"Just look at us! It's eleven o'clock at night. We spent forty-five minutes hiding in the garden of a nursing home, running away from a little old lady with orange hair who kept yelling, 'Yoohoo!' Now we're all dressed up in these silly outfits." I fingered Nick's black sweatpants and pulled at the collar of my black turtleneck.

"And we're getting ready to do a little breaking and entering. Why wouldn't I laugh? I'm a speech therapist, Nick, and you're a businessman. We're not Harry Callahan, or Kinsey Milhone, or Hercule Poirot or Miss Marple or even Inspector Clouseau for Pete's sake! What are we doing here? Did you bring your .357 magnum? Go on, make my day." I nudged him in the ribs, slurring my words from the corner of my mouth. "C'mon, shweetharrt. Hey, angel, how 'bout a drink?"

Nick grabbed my shoulders and shook me gently. "I know you're scared, Julia. I'm nervous too. But I don't think Bob McIntyre would find any of this very funny."

It was a sobering thought. The drooping face, the terrified eyes of Dina's brother, swam in front of me. I had wanted to leave as soon as we escaped his room, but Nick insisted that we stay. In less than ten minutes, Morgan Fox was standing in front of his brother-in-law. By then, under Marta Kaspir's watchful eye, we had slipped across the courtyard, positioning ourselves behind the shrubbery one window over from hers and directly across from Bobby's room. Like a persistent itch I couldn't reach, Marta whispered at the window. "Jeannette? Jackie?"

The nurse showed Morgan the sign, knee brace, and the

crutches in the corner. He examined them, slipped the sign into his pocket, and made a place for the crutches and brace in the closet. Perhaps he thought we'd come back for them, like criminals returning to the scene. When Ms. Webb left the room, Morgan grasped the arms of Bobby's wheelchair and leaned close to his face. I could see his lips move, knew that Bobby would give no indication of understanding his brother-in-law. In apparent frustration, Morgan grabbed his shoulders and shook him roughly. Then, it looked like he laughed. Had his laughter been, I wondered, from the same hysterical source as my own? What, exactly, did Morgan Fox have to fear?

We waited until he left, gave him time to return to his black Mercedes and point it toward home to his perfect wife and children. As we were hotfooting it around the corner and out of the courtyard, I tried to ignore Marta Kaspir's raised voice. "Yoohoo, I see you, June!"

The time to strike was now, before Morgan suspected who we were or that we had really learned anything from Bobby McIntyre. We quickly changed clothes at home and followed Dina's route out of Delphi toward the houses in the mountains. And now, the car secreted a quarter of a mile from the McIntyre house, I had lost all self-control.

"I think you'd better stay here with the car. I don't want you in any danger, and I can't afford to have you cutting up out there."

I shook my head. The memories of Morgan Fox and Bob McIntyre had worked their grim magic. "I'm okay," I said. "And I'd rather be with you than stay here alone. Besides, I'm sure I can help, once we get inside."

Nick grabbed my hand and led me as we skirted the driveway leading up to Bobby's house. It ran through a stand of pine, leading to a clearing where the house stood, practically hanging over the side of a cliff.

Even in the dark I could see that it was a lovely place. A wide, brick veranda, bordered by planters of the same red brick, formed the base. Six wide, fieldstone steps led up to a deep porch that wrapped around a white frame house made up, it seemed, almost entirely of windows. Beneath the porch was a crawl space encased on three sides by white lattice. It was a simple house, as Bobby McIntyre had simple tastes.

Morgan's Mercedes was parked at the end of the drive and a dim light glowed through the picture windows. He was in there, moving swiftly and smoothly through the front room. We tip-toed along the edge of the clearing, creeping softly toward the car. Five, maybe six feet from it an ember glowed—a cigar, only partially smoked and tossed as Morgan alighted from the car. Obviously he hadn't been there long. Nick pulled me behind the passenger side of the car, out of sight of the house, and quietly opened the door. We slipped inside, pulling the door closed until the light went off. He skimmed his penlight over the inside of the car.

"What are we looking for?" I whispered.

"I don't know. Just looking." He rummaged through console and side-door pockets, coming up with maps, cigars, but little of interest. The glove compartment wasn't locked. He carefully pulled it open. The interior light glowed brightly until he clamped his hand over it.

"Shine the light in there." I did as I was told. A partial pack of cigarettes, a pair of leather gloves, and an executive planner— the type with appointment calendar, address book, and notebook all in one. Nick tugged open the Velcro on the planner and scanned the calendar carefully. His face was crestfallen.

"There's not much here, just dates of board meetings and appointments at the bank."

"What did you expect to find?"

"I'm not sure." He flipped through the rest—addresses of all the Buffaloes, doctors, local businesses. The notebook was blank. He handed it to me. "Here, hold it." He was back in the glove compartment, removing the rest of the articles—tire gauge, service manual. In all, it looked like a disappointing haul.

I rubbed my hand over the leather of the planner. I had to give Morgan his due—he had nice taste. The leather was smooth and supple under my fingers, nicer than my best leather gloves. A pocket for carrying business cards, made like a coin purse, was sewn to the inside cover. The back cover was similar, but made up of a single deep, accordion pocket that ran the length of the cover. Morgan had put something inside. I opened the snap clo-sure and slid my hand down into the pocket feeling a fold of papers beneath. I pulled it out.

"Nick, look what I found!" I unfolded the papers, letting his penlight catch and hold the words. "It's a loan application. For Glenn. Look, he's highlighted it where it says 'self-employed.' And there's his former address in El Paso." Nick tore a page from the notebook and hastily copied the address. He put a finger to his lips, replaced the application, and tucked everything back into the glove compartment. When we were out of the car, he softly pushed the door closed, making sure the latch was fully caught.

I followed him, up the wide fieldstone steps and ever so quietly around the side of the house. We crouched behind the porch swing and peered through the slats into a window.

Morgan was at a row of bookshelves, systematically removing the volumes one at a time, checking behind them, then shaking the books open. An occasional bookmark fell out, clearly not of interest, and summarily discarded. He did not go through every volume, but moved on to the pictures, jerking them off the wall and quickly replacing them. He tugged at the furniture, tipping back an overstuffed chair, swinging the sofa wide across the room to look beneath. I had the feeling that he had done it all before, maybe more than once. I wondered how he would feel if he knew that he was making our job easier. I tried to memorize where he'd been, knowing that Bobby's safe must be hidden elsewhere. When he disappeared through an open door, I followed Nick back down the steps and across the clearing.

"We've got to create a diversion to get him out of that house before he beats us to the safe," he whispered.

"I don't think he knows where it is; maybe he doesn't even know it exists, Nick. We'll just have to wait him out."

Nick shook his head decisively. "Can't take that chance. He may be more desperate now than ever." He glanced back down the drive, then pulled me deeper into the pines. "Wait here. Watch the house, but don't move. I'll be right back."

"Okay, shweetharrt. If you need me, just whistle."

Of course, I couldn't follow his instructions. Oh, I waited until he was out of sight, but while he was gone Morgan just might find the safe and leave. What then? We'd never know, might even spend the rest of the night searching for something Morgan had already found. Resolved, I slipped out toward the back of the house in the direction I knew he'd gone.

At the rear corner of the cabin, the ground sloped away dramatically and the porch rested on what appeared to be high stilts, angled diagonally and carefully anchored into the side of the cliff. Spotlights arced out into the emptiness beyond. It took me only a moment to realize that I was standing in their glare. Another massive picture window lined the bedroom wall and Morgan, in front of it, was overturning bedclothes inside. One glance up and I would be made.

I should have eased backward into the woods. There I could have watched him, hidden from view, safe until Nick returned. But panic propelled me the other way. I clambered beneath the corner of the porch, pressing my back against the rocky, sloping earth and wishing I'd followed Nick's advice. Morgan's steps echoed hollowly on the floor above and behind me. When he crossed the room, I'd make my break for the woods and safety. In a few heartbeats his steps started moving away.

I gave myself a moment to catch my breath before easing out of my little refuge. Not so easy, that. My foot slipped in haste, sending a rockslide out beneath me and over the cliff's edge. The movement above me stopped, then burst like a jackhammer against the wooden floors above. Sliding glass doors whooshed open, footsteps following out onto the porch. I pressed my back against the earth and gnawed on my fist, sure, for all the world, that I would scream.

He paced silently overhead, from one end of the porch to the other. He was close to the railing, unable, unless he hung upside down over the rail, to see me. But the porch planks were only loosely abutted. I stared up through the gaps at fine leather shoes and soft worsted pant legs. He took the rail a few feet at a time. I closed my eyes, imagined him craning his neck to peer out over the cliff below and into the darkness. But if Morgan Fox was as sharp as I thought, he'd soon realize that any intruder would have to be on the flat land above, on either side of the house. As if in answer to the thought, the footsteps slowly made their way to the corner, directly over my head. I forced my eyes open and stared through the slats above me.

He was there, must have been pressed against the corner of the house, blocking the light that poured through the porch floorboards. He moved, ever so slightly, and the light shifted, briefly catching on something in his hand. Movement and a soft click, and I, who know nothing about guns, knew he had taken the safety off of a pistol. And somewhere out there in the darkness was Nick.

How long he stayed there I couldn't guess, only that it seemed like centuries passed as I stifled my breathing, lay perfectly still against the rocky ground, stones cutting into my back and my teeth into my flesh. He moved. Something had caught his attention, as it had mine. The smell of smoke drifted across the mountain air.

Morgan's feet scrambled above me, and the glass door slammed, followed by retreating footsteps across the house. I scurried out of my hiding place, angling across the side yard and into the pines. There, in the protection of darkness, I slumped against a tree and caught my breath. A hand grabbed my elbow in the darkness, another one smothered my mouth.

"Where the hell were you? You scared me to death! I thought I told you to stay there."

I leaned heavily against Nick. "I know, but I thought—"

"Ssh."

Nick dragged me along the edge of the darkness parallel with the house. At the front, near the Mercedes, a brush fire burned brightly. He grinned at me. "Morgan's cigar had a little help."

Morgan himself was stamping out the fire, wildly glaring into the darkness as though the neighbors might see it and come running. Above all, he would not want to be found at the house. He shoved the pistol into his pocket, pulled off his jacket and beat at the little flames. He kicked at the edges of the fire and the cigar, brightly burning, rolled out. It seemed to give him an idea. A breeze had picked up, and the flames were licking their way steadily toward the patio. Morgan dropped his jacket in his car and strode toward where Nick and I hid in among the pines. We darted further back into darkness, watching as he gathered several armloads of dry leaves and dumped them in a trail across the patio and up under the wooden porch. When he had them arranged fuselike, leading to the house, he pulled something from the glove compartment of his car. Nick and I watched as he dropped a few cigarettes into his pocket. He wrapped the pack in a white handkerchief, crumpled it, and walking halfway down the drive, artfully dropped it in full view. Then he returned to the house, tucked the handkerchief in his pocket, switched off the lights and locked the door. He was whistling when he entered his car.

"Well, I'll be damned." Nick watched the back of the Mercedes as it retreated into the night, then crossed the clearing, scattered the trail of leaves with his feet and grabbed a hose from the patio, turning its full torrent onto the little fire. It sputtered and was gone.

"He actually wanted it to burn. I guess it would have served his purposes just fine if it did."

"What do you mean?"

"Probably about the only thing in that house that wouldn't burn is a safe, Julia. And Morgan, as caretaker of his brother-in-law's property, would have full access to it. He'd have what he wanted then, wouldn't he?"

"Oh. And the cigarette pack would make the fire look like an accident."

Nick agreed. "He'd come out with the fire department and they'd find the pack. Probably assume it was kids, sneaking off to an empty house for a smoke."

"Kids," I said. He walked up the drive and picked up the empty cigarette pack carefully between two fingers. Kool Kings, a brand vaguely familiar, but one which I couldn't connect with anyone.

"I've never seen him smoke anything but cigars."

"Me neither, but maybe they're not his." He stuffed the pack into the pocket of his sweats.

"C'mon. We've still got to find a way in."

"There are sliding doors at the back. Maybe we can take them off their tracks." I led him around to where, only moments before, I had been hanging off a cliff while a would-be murderer paced above me. If I had wanted to laugh, the idea sobered me like an icy shower. Nick examined the doors and shook his head.

"Can't do it. Not without breaking them. Didn't you ask Bobby about a key?"

I nodded. "Yeah, but he didn't tell me where to find it. He said 'fly.'"

"Swell. What does that mean?"

"I don't know."

We went back around the side of the porch and down the steps, searching vainly for a hidden key in planters, under doormats. I even tried a few rocks, thinking they might be the hollow plastic kind contrived for that purpose. At midnight, all rocks look alike. Bobby's clue kept repeating itself in my head. I dropped down on the edge of a planter and watched Nick comb the porch, sliding his hand up and down between each of the railings.

Bobby was brain-injured, like an aphasic, a stroke victim. Although he could speak, sometimes he couldn't find the exact word he wanted. I'd worked with enough aphasics to know how the searching process went, the brain producing related words—like *box,* and *door* when he really wanted *house.* So what did 'fly' mean? I began to search again, this time looking for something related to the word *fly.* It wasn't long before I spotted it, a birdhouse made of a large gourd. It dangled from a metal pole over the driveway. I watched as Nick shimmied up the pole, reached inside and returned grinning with a brass key in the palm of his hand. We were in.

A pulse lubdubbed in my ears as we crossed the threshold. The house was silent, but I could still feel Morgan's presence there, the lingering odor of Gucci and cigars. The floorboard squeaked beneath my feet, sending me romping into Nick's arms.

"Pull yourself together, will you? He's gone."

"I know," I whispered. "But I can still smell him."

Nick pulled two penlights from his pockets and pressed one into my palm as he pushed the door firmly closed behind me.

"Let's not waste time where he's already been. I'll start in the bedroom, you work in here. And keep an eye out the door, Julia. If he doesn't see the fire flare up, he may come back."

This was a possibility I had not considered, and it pricked me into movement. I took a final peek out the sidelight and turned around. Directly in front of me was the living room, a massive fieldstone fireplace dominating the left wall. Chairs and sofa were comfortably arranged in front of it. Beyond the living room was the door to the only bedroom, through which Nick had disappeared. To the right was a bar, and behind that a long, galley-style kitchen. The side walls of the house were lined with wide picture windows of double-paned glass, and the floors that stretched in front of me were satiny pine—dotted, here and there, with small braided rugs.

It was a man's house, with clean-cut lines and simple furniture. There were only these three rooms, but of such massive proportions that the feeling of spaciousness was liberating. Bookshelves lined the end wall on either side of the bedroom door. I did not go to them. Morgan had found them wanting. Neither did I move pictures or furniture, but went directly to the massive fireplace and began pushing against the fieldstones. I suppose I've watched too many movies. I fully expected to hit one and have the entire structure turn to reveal a safe. It didn't, and after a few attempts I blushed at my own naïveté.

From the fireplace, I crossed the room and rounded the bar into the kitchen where I checked cabinet after cabinet. There were no false walls behind the racks of plates and glasses, no secret compartments in the pantry. I could hear Nick in the bedroom, rapping his knuckles against the walls in search of a sound that thumped instead of knocked. No luck there. In frustration, I even tried the refrigerator, not knowing what I expected to find. It held no food, of course, only a box of Arm and Hammer baking soda. I stared at the box and thought about Dina.

"Hello," Bobby had said as I was catapulting over the windowsill. I had thought he meant good-bye at the time, but now I approached it from another angle. Maybe that, too, was a clue.

"Well, I don't find anything in there. Nothing in the bedroom, nothing in the bathroom. What are you doing?"

"I think I've got it, Nick. Bobby said 'Hello,' remember?" I was tugging on the wall phone with all my might but it simply would not come off. Nick pushed me aside, grasped it and slipped

it up off its rack. Beneath it was a wall plate. He grabbed a knife
from the drawer and inched the screws around until he could pull
it loose. There, to my horror, were wires. Wires, but no wall safe.
Nick patted my arm.

"It was a good thought."

I dropped onto one of the bar stools while he screwed the phone
back into the wall. "I was so sure," I said. "Hello. I'm sure it
meant something."

Nick slid the phone back onto the plate. "Maybe it does. It
just doesn't mean the phone."

"How about a desk, letters?"

He shook his head. "I went through it in the bedroom. It's just
not there." Nick looked around the room, his glance taking in
the fireplace, bookshelves, furnishings. There was simply nothing
left.

"Yia sou," he said. *"Kalos orisete."*

"What?"

"'Hello.' 'Welcome,' they're almost the same, right?"

"Well, not exactly. You can use 'hello' anywhere, but you'd
only use 'welcome' if..."

Nick was striding toward the front door. It took me only a
moment to grasp his meaning. He yanked up the welcome mat to
find more smoothly polished pine floors beneath. I sank back onto
the stool in disappointment, but he wasn't finished. He stepped
down carefully and was greeted by the same squeak that had sent
me flying earlier. Nick dropped to his knees and this time I was
right behind him. He tapped on the floor with his knuckles, elic-
iting a hollow sound directly in front of the door and followed it
in a careful pattern until the telltale thump appeared.

"That's it," he said, tapping the floor again. "Julia, get me
that knife." I shined the penlight close to the floor, watching as
he inserted the knife blade between the wide flooring planks.
Something clicked, and the plank dropped. Nick slipped his fingers in and slid the plank back beneath its neighbor. A combination lock stared up at us, like a great eye peering through the
darkness.

"Mana mou," he whispered. "We found it."

TWENTY-ONE

THE SAFE was a long, cylindrical tube about twelve inches in diameter, embedded in a thick block of concrete. From the outside, it was shielded from view by the steps and latticework around the crawl space, cleverly designed to appear as part of the underlying structure of the house. Perhaps Bobby McIntyre was not so simple after all.

Nick spun the combination and hoisted the lid from its place. I tried to take it from him and was surprised at its weight, maybe as much as twenty-five pounds. We sprawled on the floor and pointed our penlights into the dark hole beneath us.

The interior of the safe appeared to be a series of concentric circles, creating a dizzying, spinning effect. It took me a moment to realize that I was not looking at a part of the safe, but its contents, slightly rolled and shoved down into the cylinder where they had expanded against its perimeter. Nick grasped the edge of one of the inside circles and pulled, extracting a sheaf of papers clipped to a document in a black plastic spiral binding. I tried to smooth it flat as he reached back in for more. Within minutes we had a growing stack of documents, variously bound and paper-clipped together in little bundles.

The safe was deeper than I had expected, about thirty-six inches, and layers of documents were stacked all the way to the dark, gunmetal bottom. The safe contained nothing else—no money, jewels, or famous artwork. Ever the romantic, I squelched a pang of disappointment. We were, after all, talking about and looking for bank business. And found it we had.

Nick shined his light over the document at the top of the stack. "It's a profit-and-loss statement," he said. "Company's called Mountain Pine Knitting Mills. Ever heard of them?"

I shook my head and watched as he perused the stack. "They're all P and Ls, and, it looks like loan papers. Wonder what it means?"

"I don't know, but my back's hurting and I'm tired. Close up the safe and let's get out of here. We've got to take the stuff with us anyway. Morgan may come back, and he'll be expecting to find the safe standing in a heap of ashes."

He thumped the lid back in place, spun the lock, and returned the floorboard to its proper place, recovering it all with the welcome mat. I took a quick turn through the house to be sure we hadn't left any evidence of our visit behind, while Nick split the stack into two manageable bundles and slipped them into grocery bags that Bobby had stored in his pantry. The door locked, Nick shimmied back up the pole and returned the key to the birdhouse.

"Let's go," he said, taking one of the heavy bags from me. "We've got a lot of work to do."

I RESTED MY HEAD on my arms, folded on top of the kitchen table. "I don't have the slightest idea what this stuff means, and I don't see how we can take the chance of going back to Northridge to ask Bobby about it." I pulled myself up and tinkered with the stem of my wineglass before raising it to my lips. "Whaddaya think, shweethart?"

Nick raised a full glass to mine. "Here's looking at you, kid." We toasted and he returned his glass to the table, even as I downed the remaining contents of mine. Jack was casually stretched out on the den sofa, on his back, his legs straight up in the air. He reminded me of Snoopy on his doghouse.

"Get off there, Jack." Thump. Thump.

I dragged myself into the bedroom, returned with the basket bed and set it on the floor next to the table. "Come on, Jack. You used to sleep on it. I can tell by the smell." I hoisted him off the couch and deposited him in the basket. It might have been hot coals, the way he sprang off of it, tossed me a darting look and made for the bedroom chair. "I give up. I don't know what's wrong with him. He just refuses to sleep on that bed."

"He's spoiled. You've spoiled him."

"I've spoiled him? I'm not the one who puts him on my lap and—"

"No, but you let him get on the chair and don't do anything about it."

I was on the verge of snarling something at him, but caught myself, knowing that a fruitless argument would follow. I dropped back into my chair.

"I'm tired, Nick. And I don't get any of this. Profit-and-loss statements, loan papers. So what? Banks make loans, it's what they do, who they are. Not that they ever seem to want to make them to us." I refilled my glass and took another sip. It tasted good, good to be alive, good to be out from under Bobby's porch, away from Morgan's gun and in my own, warm kitchen.

"Yeah, but they don't make loans without collateral. Not one of these loans offers anything for collateral, Julia. No land, equipment, stocks—nothing. And look at how Bobby's highlighted all these P and Ls." He pointed to a wide yellow line stretching across the page in front of him. "What we have to ask ourselves is what, besides no collateral, do all these loans have in common?"

I shrugged. "They need money?"

"Obviously, but why?"

He had me there. I was no longer capable of rational thought. It was two a.m. In four hours, Spiro would be unlocking the door at the Oracle and starting breakfast. I could almost taste it. But breakfast reminded me of Glenn, and the reason that we were poring over these papers in the silence of the night. I straightened up, pushed my wine aside, and opened a booklet covered in gray cardstock. Pink highlighting shimmered in front of my eyes.

"Okay, this one's highlighted on the line marked 'Labor.'" I traced my fingers across the line to a column headed "Percent Cost" and whistled. "Wow, this guy's labor is running at forty-two percent! What kind of a business is this, anyway?" I flipped back to the front cover. "Poultry processing. I had no idea it was that labor-intensive. I wonder what it's supposed to be?"

Nick shrugged. "Don't know. Should run about thirty percent in our business. Lower in fast food." He came around behind me, peered over my shoulder and flipped through the pages in the booklet.

"Look at this." He pointed to another pink line in front of us. "Hardly any assets in equipment. Maybe that's why his labor's running so high. Bottom line is he's barely breaking even. One bad year and he's gone.''

Nick flipped through the loan application. "He's applied for money to expand and purchase equipment. He obviously needs that, but he's offering no collateral, the plant's heavily mortgaged and he has virtually no assets listed. Hard to imagine any bank giving him a loan under these conditions. And look at what he's asking for!''

He pointed to a staggering trail of six figures across the application. "No loan officer in his right mind would approve this without collateral.''

"Maybe the equipment's the collateral.''

"Yeah, but if they have to repossess, banks don't want to be stuck with a lot of industrial equipment. Then they've got to auction it off, and they may get stuck taking a loss on it. Besides, that's not all the money's for. He wants to expand the operation, put more money into advertising and marketing his product outside the state. Where's the guarantee of a return in that? And how did it get through a loan committee?''

"I don't know, Nick, but what's your point?''

"Well,'' he said, "if a recommendation is made by someone who has a good track record in making loans, a committee might well trust his judgment. Look who personally approved the application.''

I squinted over the sprawling signature at the bottom of the page. It was very official, underlined and bearing the officer's title beneath. *Morgan Fox, President of the Delphi branch of SafeBank.*

TWO HOURS LATER I had my second wind, and a long list of loan applicants on a yellow legal pad. Beside their names were columns headed "Assets," "Liabilities," "Percent Profit/Loss," and so forth. Bobby had made the work easier for us, highlighting whatever was questionable, and what we had was a picture of weak applicants who had been given loan approval for no explicable reason.

Nick rubbed his eyes and leaned back in the chair. "I'd bet

that if we had a list of depositors at SafeBank, we'd find all these companies at the top.''

''But there's something I don't understand, Nick. If Bobby took all these papers out of the bank, wouldn't somebody notice it?''

''He probably did it slowly, photocopied everything so the files wouldn't be empty. Once the loans are put into effect, they probably don't go back into the files unless something is wrong. The payments are logged on computer. But when Bobby confronted Morgan with the truth, which he must have, Morgan probably started checking. No doubt, these are what he was looking for tonight. And I'm sure it wasn't the first time he's searched that house, either. That's why the fire would have served his purposes so well.''

''So, okay, what do we actually have here?''

''Well, it looks to me like there are several common denominators. First, high labor costs, running anywhere from forty-two to a whopping fifty-six percent. Cuts into profits big-time. Few or no assets, high debt. If you look, Julia, all these companies are doing business. I mean, the product is selling, but their operating costs are really high—chiefly labor.''

''So why would Morgan approve loans for them?''

Nick stroked his chin thoughtfully. At four a.m., his beard bristled black and accentuated the deep circles under his eyes. ''Maybe he's getting kickbacks.''

''Yeah, maybe. But you've heard the talk. Morgan's the local 'wunderkind.' Since he took over, depositors have increased dramatically. For a small bank, SafeBank is doing big business. And nobody's talking about defaulting loans, either. Somehow, he's making them work. Besides, he probably makes a fortune anyway. Why would he jeopardize his position by taking kickbacks?''

''Most people can never get enough money, Julia. But I'm not sure it's all about big bucks, either. Remember what Dina said. Reputation is everything to Fox. If he can increase deposits and good loans, he's on his way up, out of Delphi and probably straight to Atlanta, with his name written in gold.''

Nick emptied his briefcase and carefully piled the documents inside. ''These go into our safe tomorrow morning.''

"You mean this morning."

Nick glanced at his watch and flipped the combination on his case. He grabbed my hand and pulled me up, nuzzling my neck below the ear. "Not much point in trying to sleep now, is there?"

Six years married, and he still makes my toes curl.

BILLY SHIFTED from one foot to the other while I read the contents of the manila envelope he'd brought me. He could scarcely suppress the grin that wanted to break out across his face. "I think," he said, "that's what you were looking for, isn't it?"

I slipped the papers back into the envelope. "It's exactly what I was looking for, Billy. You did a great job. And so quickly! How on earth did you manage it?"

"The wonderful world of computers." He shrugged. "There's a file for articles of incorporation. And, of course, it'll do a search for me. After I gave it Delphi Rental Properties, I just followed the trail. It would have taken a helluva long time in the microfilm room, though."

He was right, there. Probably days. Read had set the company up very carefully, one of four corporations, each a subsidiary of the previous one and spaced months apart, probably so as not to attract attention. Read had a reputation in town for his ethical business practices. It fit his appearance, the classic features that should have been encircled by a laurel wreath. He would go to extraordinary lengths to protect it. The question was, would he kill?

"Now remember, you have to hold the story back until I give you the go-ahead. It may be a few days."

Billy frowned. "That long?"

"That long." My voice was emphatic. "But I may have more for you then. Possibly a lot more. It'll be worth the wait, I promise." His face brightened.

"Give me a hint about it, Julia. I can be doing background work while I wait." His voice was childishly pleading.

"I'm sorry, Billy. I can't do that. There are a lot of people involved and some of them could be hurt. It wouldn't be responsible journalism."

"Oh well, if you put it like that, okay. But I can't wait to turn it in. Won't Norm Pearson be surprised?"

Not just Norm, I thought. We might get rid of the Buffaloes yet. When this was all over, some of them would be spending time in government facilities of an inhospitable nature. Prison gray might be very becoming to Read.

"Yup. I think Norm will be very surprised. I'll get back with you as soon as I can, Billy. And thanks again."

I laid them out on the desk in front of Nick. "Copies of the legal notices from the *Sun,* taken out over about eighteen months. It wasn't just an impulse, Nick. Read planned to go into the slumlord business very carefully. Delphi Rental Properties is a subsidiary of Apollo, Inc. Apollo is, in turn, a subsidiary of Alternative Investments, Inc., which is a subsidiary of Read Whitehead Real Estate."

"Funny. You know, I remember when Read incorporated Alternative Investments. One of the Buffaloes mentioned it. Read claimed it was set up to deal with recreational properties—lakeside lots, Florida beach condos, stuff like that. He even tried to broker a few places in the mountains. Nothing will scare people off like vacation properties. Everybody's got a story about a friend who got fleeced in them. Read must have known that— figured that no one would ever bring up the subject to him. Pretty clever."

I gathered up the newspaper articles and pushed them back into the manila envelope. "Let's get these into the safe." The phone on the desk jangled. "Go ahead. You get it. I'll put them in." I flipped through the combination, listening to Nick's side of the conversation.

"Well, it's nice of you to go to that much trouble, but it could have waited until you were back in town. Okay," he said. "I think we can have it by then. But you haven't mentioned the cost yet." He waited, whistled through his teeth.

"That much, huh? Well, I'll have to ask him. It's a lot of money. No, I don't want to call it off, at least not until I've asked Spiro. It'll really be up to him. Yes. He's very...discreet. Besides, who would he tell? He doesn't speak English. I'll keep your name out of it. All right. We'll see you then.'' Nick dropped the phone back in the cradle and turned to me. His eyes twinkled.

"I guess you know who that was."

"Mmm."

"She'll be back in town in a couple of days. She wants Spiro to have three pictures, slightly different poses and in different clothes, ready for her friend."

"Her friend?"

Nick laughed out loud. "The one she claims works for immigration."

"And how much is this going to cost?"

"Twenty-five hundred dollars. Cash."

TWENTY-TWO

"WE GETTING coffee this morning, Julia? Or just your bright smile?" Charley's voice intruded on my foggy, fatigued thoughts. I grabbed the pot and headed for their table, trying to find my "bright smile" along the way. I tossed the photos on the table. "I thought you might like to see these. You can look at them while you're thinking about what you want to order for breakfast."

Sonny pointed to a package of bagels. "I got mine already. Ask that new cook—what's his name?"

I sighed. "Spiro."

"Yeah, him. Ask him to toss a couple of these on the grill, will you? Make sure he puts plenty of butter on them, too."

I stared from the bag to Sonny.

"Got any cream cheese around, Julia?"

"No...I don't think...I don't know. I'll look when I go into the kitchen." It was bad enough that they brought in doughnuts and fruit. Now they were asking us to cook their food. I was too tired to argue. I moved on to Morgan, carefully filling his cup, studiously avoiding his eyes. He looked as tired as I felt.

"Man, you're surly this morning! What's the matter with you, Mitch?" Sonny said.

Mitch pulled his big hand over his face, brow to chin, as though he were trying to arrange his features more comfortably. "Hard day yesterday. Trouble on the site. Thought I'd go to bed early, right? Well, ten-thirty the phone rings. Wakes me up, of course. Call that late, well, I figure it's an emergency. Like the time those kids went joyriding in my new backhoe."

He shifted in his chair, leaning back so he could see everyone at the table. "It's Marta, my mother-in-law. She's got some tall story about people in the garden at Northridge. Some woman, all dressed in white."

I stiffened, sloshing coffee over the rim of Lee's cup. I hastily sopped it up with a handful of napkins, murmuring apologies to anyone who'd listen. But they were all listening to Mitch.

"And there was some guy with her. He was dark. Woman looked like an angel, she said."

I smiled, pleased in spite of myself.

"So she goes on about how she knows this woman, seen her before. Her memory comes and goes. Personally, I wish it'd stay gone. There are a few things I wish she'd just forget. Last time, she thought she saw Pat's father in the hall. Hell, the man's been dead for thirteen years! Anyway, took Pat an hour to get her off the phone, and then, only with a promise that she'd look into it."

Morgan was staring intently at Mitch. I snagged the bag of bagels off the table. "Anyone else want a bagel for breakfast?"

"Pat's got a theory about the whole thing. Seeing her husband, and now someone she thinks looks like an angel. She says the dark guy represents the devil. Pat thinks she's trying to 'deal with,' as she put it, old age. You know, approaching death. Jeez, I wish she'd quit reading those damn self-help books. Personally, I just think the woman's effin' nuts. Has been as long as I've known her."

I practically leaped off the deck, sure that Morgan's amber eyes were boring into my back. In the kitchen I tossed the bag to Spiro. "Put a couple of these on the grill to toast, will you? Plenty of arsenic and butter."

I found Nick in the office, hanging up the phone. I pulled the door closed behind me.

"We may have a problem."

"Good. We needed another one."

I told him about Marta Kaspir and was floored by his reaction. "It isn't funny, Nick."

"Quit worrying about it. Mitch thinks she's crazy anyway."

"Yeah, but Morgan might not."

"Well, he doesn't have any proof. Besides, we've got other things to do."

He grabbed the car keys and deposit bag off the desk. "Come on. I'll tell you about it on the way."

"So, I THOUGHT it might not be a bad idea to visit some of those companies, and it just happens that this is one that'll be easy to get into." Nick glanced into the rearview mirror, flipped on his blinker and pulled through the bank drive-through window.

"Just exactly what did you tell them?"

"Well, I just..." He retrieved the bag from the pneumatic tube, tipped the brim of his hat to the teller and pulled out around the building, stopping at the exit onto Broadway. "...just said I was interested in—

"Julia, turn around slowly, casually."

I did as he asked, in time to see a dark blue sedan pull up to the exit, leaving a car length between us. "What?"

"You see that car? Did it go through the drive-through behind us?"

"No. It pulled out of the lot when we circled around. Why?"

"Because it followed us in here. No way that guy could have gone into the lobby and be back out already. I'm not taking any chances. Let's drive down toward the university and see what happens."

The car stayed with us, through Delphi's downtown, as we twisted up and down one-way streets, past bars and movie theaters, used bookstores and more bars. There was little doubt about it. The blue sedan was following us.

"Okay, now listen to me. I'm going to make a left onto Magnolia, then a hard right on Webster. Traffic's always heavy in here. Hopefully he'll get stuck on that left and buy us a little time. As soon as I start to turn on Webster, slide down onto the floor of the car and keep your head down. Ready?"

I did as I was told. The blue sedan was lost, but only long enough for me to hit the floorboards in a crumpled heap. "Now that I'm down here, what did this accomplish?"

Nick answered with minimal movement of his jaw, rather like Clint Eastwood. "I'm hoping he thinks I dropped you off somewhere. I'm going to lead him into the parking lot at the Dionysus Center—you know how busy it is over there. When I get out, ease up and see if he follows me. Don't let him see you, but try to get a good look at him."

I felt the car pull to a stop. "He's pulling in too. I'll be back!" With that, Nick sprinted from the car. I slipped up against the

seat to watch his back scurrying across the lot toward the student
center; turned in time to see a man alight from the car.

He was tall and slender, with a dark complexion and hair. He
wore an unobtrusive gray suit and tie. Nothing especially thuggish
about him—just absolutely ordinary. I watched him round the
corner of the Center, then heaved myself onto the seat and out of
the car, racing across the lot to get a look at his car. Nick met
me back at the Honda, short of breath. "Get in, hurry up! And
get back down."

We screeched out of the lot, Nick eyeing his rearview mirror
and me watching him, waiting for permission to rise from my
cramped position. "Okay, we've lost him. You can get up."

I brushed off my skirt and eased into the seat. "He's kind of
dark-skinned, with thinning dark hair. Tall, over six feet, very
thin. Kind of like you'd expect a, I don't know, a salesman or
accountant to look."

"What about the car?"

"Navy Olds Cutlass. License plate started with GV but I didn't
get the rest. I'm sorry."

"It's okay. Write it down anyway. Maybe we can find some
way to use it."

Nick checked the rearview again and eased us into a normal
stream of Delphi traffic. "Okay, now, on to our real mission."

GRANDMA TYLER stared down at us, obviously disapproving, I
thought, from a Victorian frame on the wall of the inner office.
She had a narrowly pointed, rodentlike face, with snapping dark
eyes that reminded me of a squirrel, or perhaps something else
less benign. Dressed entirely in black, an onyx broach circled in
diamonds pinched a high collar around her throat. Judging by the
photograph, the artist who had rendered her likeness for the logo
of Grandma Tyler's Homemade Fruitcake and Cookies had a mer-
ciful eye.

Harve Tyler sat behind his desk, outstretched palm inviting us
into chairs in front of him. His shirtsleeves were rolled up, as
though he might have just been out in the plant, up to his elbows
in candied fruit himself. He raised the palm to his silver hair,
pushing an errant lock back off his sloping forehead.

"She was my great-grandmother, you know. And we haven't changed her recipes in seventy years. My father founded the plant just before she died."

It was going to be one of those long stories, about how Grandma made the fruitcakes in the kitchen, and her grandson, on the bicycle he won selling magazines, peddled them all around the neighborhood. In reality, she probably had underpaid black women slaving over hot tubs of fruit while she shrewdly balanced the books and raked in the profits. Onyx and diamonds didn't come cheap even seventy years ago.

"...and my father, if you can believe this, had won this bicycle selling magazines. He was an enterprising little boy. So, he figured, as much as the neighbors liked Grandma's fruitcake..."

Harve Tyler's office was a study in contrasts. The outer office was what one might expect in a bakery plant. Deep ocher walls that hadn't seen a paintbrush in fifteen years, gray metal desks, and filing cabinets. The single concession to the coming century was the computer with its flashing cursor and the printer that cranked out invoices in the background.

But what his staff lacked, Harve Tyler had in abundance. Thick, squishy carpet of a sweet caramel color stretched across the vast expanse of floor to creamy walls. The furnishings, bookshelves, wide executive desk, and matching credenza, were Danish modern. No wonder Grandma was scowling.

"As I told you on the telephone, I'd like to take a look at the facilities before I decide whether to carry your product. It's probably not necessary—I mean, I'm sure you make a good product, but it's a rule I have. You understand."

"Certainly. Hell, when you put your name on a product, you want to know it's right. Our plant is open to anyone who wants to visit." Harve Tyler glanced at his watch. "Unfortunately, I don't have time to show you around myself, but my secretary will be happy to do it. Let me just call her."

When she didn't answer her phone, he went in search of her, muttering down the hall. Nick was up and behind the desk, quickly studying the papers on top. I glared at Grandma, daring her to say a word about it to Harve. They returned too quickly to get any information.

"This is Marie. She'll show you around and answer your questions."

Nick turned away from the bookshelves and came forward to shake her hand. She was a stocky woman, dressed in navy slacks and a brightly flowered polyester blouse. A pair of half-glasses hung on a black cord around her neck. She raised them up under thinly penciled brows, glanced at her watch, and dropped them again. Marie was not going to give us a lot of time. I gave Grandma a wave as we followed Marie out the door and through the entrance to the main plant.

"Have you been here long?"

"Thirty-eight years come August. Started out back here in the plant." Her voice was noncommittal, no pride of service evident in the crisp words. "What exactly did you want to see?"

"Oh, everything, I suppose."

She sighed heavily and glanced at her watch again. Nick stepped in between us. I could hear the click as he turned on that Mediterranean charm.

"We just want to get a general idea of how your product is made. You know, Marie, I'm glad you're giving us the tour. I'll bet you know as much about this business as he does. Probably more." He flashed her a smile that came straight from his eyes. She was softening like an Aegean sponge.

"Well, I worked my way up, that's for sure. You can't work in a company thirty-eight years and not know what's going on." Pride was floating to the surface now. And Nick knew just what to do with it.

"A lot of the decisions probably stop at your desk."

A twitch of a smile. "I've made a few, time to time."

"A good secretary usually does."

She took us through the storage area, explaining where they obtained the fruit that went into Grandma Tyler's Homemade Fruitcake and Cookies. "Old Mr. Tyler stuck with fruitcake, but Mr. Harve added the cookies. He wanted to stay up with the times. Personally, I thought we were doing fine without... Well, anyway..."

She led us to the sorting area. Here rows of workers sorted

through the fruit, checking for bad product and pits. "They call this quality control nowadays," she said.

There were four rows of conveyor belts, all in use. Closest to us, three women lined up alongside the equipment. At one end, a man dumped huge buckets of fruit on the belt. The women scattered the fruit with plastic-gloved hands, sorting and occasionally tossing chunks into vats below the belt. Their hair was covered with plastic caps, and denim-clad legs peeked out below pink smocks. They turned silent, almost sullen, at our approach. I smiled, and the woman on the end rewarded me with a gaptoothed grin.

"Hello," I said. "What are you doing?"

She turned to the others, her brows scissoring. A second woman stepped toward me. She was young, and darkly complected. So were they all, I realized with a start. Her English was careful and heavily accented. "We check the fruit. For stones."

Marie pushed her way between us and touched my elbow, steering me away from the conveyor belt. Whatever I had done, and I wasn't sure what that was, Marie did not like it.

"I'm impressed by your quality control," I said placatingly.

"We want only the best in our fruitcakes. Grandma Tyler is known for her quality." She spoke of the woman as though she were still alive. Remembering her picture, I wasn't sure she ever had been.

"This is the mixing station," she said.

I gasped. Before us stood five enormous mixers. The bowls were so huge that a man could have stood inside, and swung merrily on the giant hook that churned a mixture of fruit, flour, and Grandma's secret spices. "Look at that, Nick. It's the mother of all mixers. Have you ever seen anything like it?"

Marie watched me with an arch smile, amused that I should be awed by something she considered so mundane. Nick, too, was transfixed. I followed his gaze to the giant motors overhead, swirling in an even rhythm as the hook pummeled the batter below.

Marie whirled on her heel, following a cry back at the sorting area, where the three women were congregated over the conveyor belt. They were chattering rapidly at the man, tossing their hands as he argued with them.

Nick grabbed my hand, pointed upward at a turquoise decal stuck to the whirling rotors. "Do you see that?"

I nodded. "The batter thickens."

TWENTY-THREE

I SLUMPED against a slick avocado-colored wall and watched them mill up and down the hallway—deputies leading handcuffed prisoners, secretaries scurrying with sheaves of paperwork curled in their hands—and tried to make my mind a blank. But the nervous, tingling nausea in my stomach wouldn't let me forget that Nick was in an interrogation room down the hall and I was waiting to know whether he would be charged and booked. And wondering who on earth I would turn to then. Spiro would be no help, nor would Rhonda. Warren was the only attorney I knew, too high-voltage a personality to provide the calm, soothing, take-charge help I was seeking.

Perhaps we should have called him as soon as Sam had informed us that they wanted us in for questioning again. But I don't suppose either of us thought it was really necessary. An innocent person never thinks he needs an attorney. Lawyers are for criminals.

My feet ached, standing on the hard tile, burning and stinging on the soles of my loafers. Cal Taylor's office was across the hall. Three straight-back chairs, oak but stained an improbable mahogany color, faced the secretary's desk. The chairs were empty and my knees were giving way. I stepped across the hall.

"Would it be all right if I sat down here?"

"Why sure, honey." The secretary was a motherly little blue-haired lady as incongruous in her surroundings as Taylor might be at a Garden Club meeting. "Who're you waiting for?"

"Well, my—"

"Sheriff Taylor's office." She answered the phone, rested it against her shoulder and pushed a form into the typewriter. "I'm sorry. Sheriff Taylor's out of town this week. Yes, I'm sure he'd be willing to speak at the meeting. Let me check his calendar." She stacked and restacked folders on her desk, picking among the clutter until she triumphantly pulled out the calendar. "It looks like he's free, but, now, you'll have to check with him about it. I'd say try him the first of next week. Thanks for calling."

She'd scarcely returned the phone to the hook when it rang again and she launched into another search, this time for a duty roster. "You people really ought to make several copies, you know. Your memory's worse than mine, and I'm three times your age. All right, honey, you call anytime."

Her dithering amused me for a while, but I quickly lost track of the schedules, folders, calendars, and forms she was asked to produce, and let my eyes and ears wander back into the hallways. Here was agony, waiting, wondering where Nick was and what they were asking him. Wondering if and when I would see him again in the free world. Wondering about the wives, children, mothers of prisoners who moved down the hall with armed guards beside them. A shriek of maniacal laughter sliced into the general din in the hallway. A slender black man pulled against the deputy who struggled to hold and contain him—obviously way out there on some hopped-up high.

"Sheriff Taylor wanted to see the autopsy report as soon as it came in."

Eyes open. Jimmy stood at the secretary's desk, holding a manila folder toward her. She glanced up from the typewriter, where she labored with a bottle of Liquid Paper.

"Just drop it there on my desk, Jimmy."

"No offense, Miz Lucy, but the sheriff's gonna be real mad if you don't lock that report up."

Miz Lucy blew a lock of hair off her forehead. She had just about hit the ragged edge. "I know, Jimmy. I been working for sheriffs some thirty-odd years. Just leave it on my desk."

He shrugged and dropped the folder on the corner of the desk. I turned away, lest he recognize me at the last minute, turned back in time to see him pass through the door into the hallway. A knot formed in my stomach. Jimmy was limping.

The folder waited there for me. It might not be Glenn's autopsy report, but then again, it might. I had to know. I summoned all my courage, closed my eyes and delved back into my worst nightmare. When I was ready I stood up, weaving unsteadily on my feet and approached her desk.

"Excuse me, I'm not feeling very well..."

It wasn't much of an act. My knees were weak, my stomach tumbling and threatening. I leaned against her desk, let my hand slip and knock the stack of folders to the worn carpet at my feet.

"Oh, I'm so sorry! I just...I'm pregnant you see, and I lost my first one. Now this. It's all such a strain."

She was around the corner of the desk, those old maternal instincts kicking right in. God bless the Miz Lucys of the world. "If I could just have a cold drink—just water. Is there a fountain?"

"You wait right here, honey. I'll be back in a flash." I watched her flowered skirt swirl around the door, then bent down and gathered up the folders. The papers were mixed up, but it took only a second to find it. No time to read the whole thing, my eye scanned the pages quickly and went to the bottom line, the opinion of the medical examiner. I closed my eyes, memorized the spelling, then stacked the folders back on her desk. All except one. That went into the round metal wastebasket next to the typing table. I'd do anything to buy Nick a little time.

"Here you are, honey." I took the paper cup gratefully and sank back into the chair.

"I...I picked them up. The papers. I'm sorry about knocking them off." Her desk looked just as it had, none the worse for my rearranging things.

"You shouldn't have bothered, honey. When are you due?"

"Oh, I just found out. I'm barely two months along."

Miz Lucy nodded her head safely. "But that first three months—they're calling that the first trimester now. I know because my daughter's pregnant. Anyway, that's just about the hardest time..."

Nick appeared at the door of the office. His face was the same sickly gray it had been the morning of the miscarriage. Sam stood behind him.

"Come with me please, Julia."

I agreed reluctantly. I did not want to hear what I knew Sam was going to say. Already my mind was racing ahead. How long, I wondered, would they keep him? Would they let him out on bond? I supposed Warren would be my first call, but should I do it from the sheriff's office, or go home where we could talk privately?

We stopped at a heavy mahogany door. The wood was gouged and marred, the obvious effects of more than one struggle. Sam didn't look at us, but at his shoes, clearly reluctant to face us. "Better get in touch with someone. There's a bail bondsman down the street."

"You can't do this, Sam."

"I got no choice."

"Please, let us have a couple minutes to talk, then."

Sam nodded and opened the interrogation-room door. I followed Nick in, growing sicker by the minute. When the door was firmly closed, I turned to my husband.

"Don't worry. I'll call Warren. I'll get you out as quickly as I can."

Nick pulled me to him, holding me so tightly that I could scarcely breathe. He smelled of aftershave, and garlic, and all the delicious smells that permeate his clothing and seep into his skin. His voice was rough. "Julia..."

"No listen! I found out what killed Glenn. It was a poison. It's called—"

"Julia, you don't understand—"

The door opened again and Sam's wide body filled it. "It's time, Nick. I've got to take her now." He turned to me.

"Julia Lambros you are under arrest for the murder of Glenn Bohannon. You have the right..."

HOLDING CELLS are very cold places. At first I didn't notice it. I was suspended in numbness, desperately trying to forget. Even there, in the sheriff's office, Sam had insisted on handcuffs—cold, hard bracelets that pulled my wrists back until my shoulders ached. Sam probably broke the rules, but he allowed Nick to follow me downstairs to the desk where I was to be booked. They released the handcuffs there, allowing me to turn over my personal effects. I clung to the memory of Nick's warm hand— touched only briefly as I dropped my wedding ring into his palm.

They sent Nick away then. That, I think, is when I started shutting down. A dull roaring in my ears made it hard for me to hear and comply with the deputy's directions. I submitted as best I could, blindly following, standing where they pointed, turning when they gestured. By the time I reached the holding cell, I was moving robotically, controlled by the outside force of a matron who opened the cell and pushed me in. I fell onto an empty bench, only dimly aware of where I was. I stared at my hands and idly wondered why the tips of my fingernails were a little black.

The next hours were a blur. How long was it? Five? Eight? I remember the arraignment. Sort of. I stood before a judge who asked me how I pled to the charge.

"Not guilty." Who said that? Me or Warren?

And there was discussion. The district attorney and Warren, arguing about the posting of bond. "No previous criminal history..." "A capital crime, Your Honor..." "...married, just recently suffered a miscarriage. She has a business here in town, not likely to flee..." "But this is a case of premeditated murder, Your Honor...." "Poses no threat to the community..."

I know that Nick was there, seated just behind me. I couldn't turn around to look at him. I was too ashamed, too worried about the embarrassment I must be causing him.

Eventually the judge pronounced a sum—a staggering six figures which Nick in his wildest dreams could never produce. I didn't even expect him to try, but I did wish I could have asked him to bring me a coat. Struck dumb, my mind would not formulate words, or my tongue articulate them. Instead, images of being searched, photographed, and my fingers taken, one by one, rolled on a pad and pressed to a sheet of paper, played and replayed in my mind. It was as though the procedure had been recorded on a tape loop which would revolve through my mind to torment me from that time forward.

They didn't return me to the holding cell, but took me to another, with four bunked cots and a single toilet squatting in the corner. The seat was cracked and a half roll of damp toilet paper sat on the concrete floor. I stared at it in horror. My God, I thought, an open toilet! They can't make me use that. But they could, and would. I fought the rising hysteria, the overwhelming shame of being forced to perform such a private act so publicly. It was, for me, the worst degradation—the final dehumanization.

But it was also a turning point, dragging me out of my stupor to realize that this cell, or one like it, was to be my home for the next—oh, how many days? months? Even years? I braced myself, slumped onto a lower bunk and looked around. The walls were pale green, the blankets gray. And the fluorescent lighting gave it all a sharp, surreal brightness.

On the top cot across the cell, a young girl sat, eyes closed, legs folded into the lotus position. She wore black jeans and a heavy flannel shirt over a pale blue bodysuit. Her thick auburn hair was pulled up into a ponytail. Anne of Green Gables à la 1990s. I stared at her until she opened her eyes.

"Hi," she said.

I looked away, clearing my throat. "I'm sorry. I didn't mean to stare. Were you praying?"

"Meditating. I'm focusing on staying calm. My folks are going to be pissed off. I'm getting ready for them."

"What are you in here for?"

She shrugged. "Having the wrong friends."

"They can arrest you for that?"

"Well, in a manner of speaking. Name's April, by the way." She unfolded her legs and dangled them over the side of the cot. "It's my boyfriend. My folks don't like him. He's black." April stopped, waiting, I think, for me to react. I didn't.

"My dad. He's a preacher—part-time. Our little church doesn't have enough money to pay for a full-time preacher. Anyways, he grew up here, knows everybody, and he and Sheriff Taylor's like that." She held up two, intertwined fingers. "That's why I'm here."

"I'm sorry, April, I guess I don't understand. Since when is it a criminal offense to date someone of a different race?"

"Well, it isn't. But like I said, my Daddy doesn't like Davon 'cause he's black. Whenever I want to see him, I have to sneak out of the house, and the sheriff's men—they got instructions to pick me up whenever they see me with Davon."

"Okay, but what are you doing here?"

April tugged on the ends of her flannel shirt and looked around the cell. "Little hard to explain. See, they can't just pick me up, so they've got to trump up some charge to take me in. Whenever anything happens in town—oh, like a convenience store gets knocked off or there's vandalism on the school playground, or maybe we're doing a couple of miles over the limit—if I'm out with Davon they pick us up. They call it 'taking us in for questioning.' I call it harassment.''

"And they can do that?"

"Sure. They can hold me for twenty-four hours without charging me with a blessed thing. I've been here four times. My daddy thinks he's teaching me a lesson. Well, he is, all right. But it's not the one he thinks." She shrugged again. "I can take it, but it's pretty hard on Davon. He's come out pretty bad beat up twice."

April stretched out on her stomach and hooked her feet over the end of the cot. "So what about you?"

"Me? Well, I'm not exactly sure...."

April stared.

"I mean, I know *why* they arrested me, but I don't know what the evidence was. I mean, I didn't do anything wrong, so what could they base it on? And, too, they might have told me so I could try to defend myself. But I don't think they did. It's a little hard to remember. It wasn't exactly playing fair. Does it make any sense to you, April?"

"Nope. Not a bit. Maybe you need to rest," she said.

She was probably right. I couldn't remember sleeping in the holding cell. In fact, I could scarcely remember anything, except the tape that played over and over in front of my eyes. I stretched out on the cot and studied the springs above me. They sagged under a restless occupant who seemed to be turning and moving constantly. I closed my eyes and tried to imagine her—a hooker, maybe? or a pusher? Or maybe just another murderer. Like me. Guilt, from every breach of my conscience ever committed, weighed on me. This must be what Hell is like—an eternity of shame. Poor Nick. How could he have known, when we took those vows, that I would lead him to humiliation? Richer or poorer, better or worse. And worse it was, for there was I, accused of the cruelest of all crimes, the taking of another human life. How could I do such a thing? Such a terrible... My eyes shot open.

Wait a minute! I wasn't a murderer! I bolted up on the cot. Why did they think I was? I had never made any bones about serving Glenn his breakfast—admitted it from the start. But it could just as easily have been Rhonda or Tammy who put the deadly meal in front of him. What else could they possibly have connected to me? And how had they managed a grand-jury indictment?

The fear and shame began to ebb, replaced by a pure, cold anger. They had succeeded in dehumanizing me, making me feel guilty and degraded just for being there in that jail cell with other women who, perhaps, were criminals. But from what I'd seen of April, I'd have hardly called her that. I looked around that cold, bleak place and wondered if we were all victims of a justice system gone amok, and for the first time in my life, I felt a kinship with every convicted felon in the world. It almost pleased me to be a member of that eccentric society, feeding as it did, my sense of injustice and rebellion.

Across the cell, below April, an elderly woman dressed like a basket of dirty laundry napped on her bunk. She smelled of body odor and alcohol. She snorted and rolled over, briefly opened her eyes and glared at me.

"Are we there yet?"

"There?"

"Palm Springs. How long before we get there?"

"I'm not sure," I answered carefully. "But I'll wake you up."

"Good girl," she mumbled. "And don't forget my train case, will you. The porter'll see to the rest of it."

April hung over the side of her cot and gaped, raised up and made a circling motion around her ear with a finger. She giggled. "Apparently," she said, "pride doeth *not* goeth before the fall. I still got mine, too."

"Are you in love with Davon, April?"

She sat up and resumed the lotus position. "Nah. I don't think so."

"Then why do you keep seeing him if it means you're going to end up here every time?"

"Well, I'll tell you…What was your name?"

"Julia."

"Well, Julia, the best I can figure is this. When I was a little girl, I used to listen to my daddy preach and I thought he was the most wonderful man in the world. I didn't know he was only preaching for white folks, but I think a lot of what he said sunk in."

"And now?"

"Now I can't get it out of my head. I mean, I see the way he is, and I know he's a hypocrite. But I'm not. So I figure the only crime I've committed is standing up for what I believe. And I'm going to keep on doing it. They're trying to scare me, but it won't work. I won't let it. I'll fight them any way I can." She sighed. "Right now, this is the best I can do."

"And Davon?"

She pulled at her shoelace and stared at the cinderblock walls. "He'd probably be better off without me."

So Davon was to be the sacrificial lamb. I was just beginning to realize how full the world was of them—some, like Davon, on the altar of principle; but most, the Ramóns and Elenas, in the temples of greed. And I was going to be one of them. April's words reverberated in my mind. *"I'll fight them any way I can."*

The matron appeared at the door of the cell. She was followed by a tall, slender man with a dark complexion who looked vaguely familiar. I slipped back into the shadow under my cot to observe him.

"Victoria! Victoria Guzmán!"

The bunk above me rustled, and two small feet clad in heavy socks and huaraches appeared over the side. The attached body slipped from the bunk and into the light. Under worn, baggy jeans and a soiled sweatshirt I could see that she was petite, with shining dark hair falling over her shoulders. I never saw her face, but watched as she moved toward the door.

"The man is here for you."

"*Hola, Señor Navarro,*" said the prisoner. "*Como estas?*"

"*Cansado, Victoria. Muy cansado,*" Navarro said and sighed. "*Otra vez. Vámanos.*"

Victoria passed through the open door, giving me a second, clearer view of the man. I caught my breath. Navarro! So that was his name. I knew him, all right. If only I could tell Nick.

TWENTY-FOUR

My opportunity came sooner than I expected. I wished April well and followed the matron out of the cell. Nick waited for me outside Sam's office. Warren stood with him, but casually moved away as Nick took me in his arms. I wanted to crawl inside of him, to become a part of him and never, ever leave him again. But I couldn't, because whatever was to come I would, finally, have to face judge and jury alone. I pulled away.

"How did you do it? The bail was so high."

He took my hand and led me out the door. "Come on," he said. "We're going home."

We agreed to meet with Warren late that afternoon to plan a strategy for my defense and parted from him in the parking lot. When we were settled in the car I put the question to him again.

"Spiro," Nick said. "It seems he's got some money put away. Merchant seamen do pretty well. Anyway, he was insistent that I take it to post the bond."

Spiro. Who would have known it? Bless his big, superstitious, generous heart.

"Do you want to talk about it? Or maybe we should try to forget about it for tonight."

I looked out the window at the graying dawn and realized that it had, in fact, been almost twenty-four hours. They must have arraigned me in the late afternoon. It was hard for me to get my bearings, made worse by a huge full moon that still hung low in the sky despite the imminent sunrise. A new day was dawning, and I planned to take full advantage of it.

"I don't understand. Why did they arrest me? How could they have gotten an indictment?"

Nick set a steaming mug of coffee on the kitchen table in front of me, and Jack, anxious to welcome me home, deposited his tennis ball in my lap. Nick poured himself a cup and sat down across the table.

"Okay. Sam explained it to me. He was worried about you, since the miscarriage and all, he thought…I guess he thought he owed me an explanation. That's why he took me in for questioning. He wasn't really questioning me. He was warning me."

"And?"

"Julia, remember the night we had dinner at Spiro's? You asked me about the garbage."

"Yeah?"

"Taylor's men took it."

"How could they do that? And why?"

"They didn't have a search warrant yet. They do now," he added parenthetically. "They've been all over the house.

"Anyway, they claim it had spilled all over the street. That puts it in the public do—"

"Domain. Public domain."

"Right. They don't have to have a search warrant to go through it, then, and the can belongs to the garbage collection company, who gave them permission to impound it."

"So what? What could they have found in our garbage that would implicate me?"

Nick hesitated, sipped his coffee slowly. "Julia, apparently there was poison in the garbage can. It was in a salt shaker, like the ones we use at the Oracle."

"Okay, but—"

"Your fingerprints were on it." Jack yipped, as though adding an exclamation point to the statement. Nick let him out into the backyard. "What I don't understand," he said. "Is how they got your fingerprints."

"I don't understand any of it."

He brought the coffeepot over and topped off our cups. "Well, I think I've figured most of it out. First of all, obviously someone put it in the garbage can on purpose. Probably that night when Jock was barking and I thought there was no one out there. And the shaker came from the Oracle. Someone knew you had handled that particular shaker, so they carefully removed it."

He pulled a shaker on the table toward him, holding the chrome top delicately between his thumb and forefinger. "Like this. Then he slipped it into his pocket, wiped his prints off the chrome later and dropped it in our trash. But unless I'm misunderstanding something, your prints would have to be on record with the police, or they wouldn't be able to match them up."

"Well, they are now."

"Yeah, but I'm sure they expected to find mine, not yours. So how did they get them?" We stared into our mugs, the coffee growing cold and the cream developing a nasty skin on top. At length, Nick took them, dumped the coffee and made fresh. He handed mine back to me and I studied the *Far Side* cartoon painted on the side. A bear, with a target on its chest. The caption read, "Bummer of a birthmark..."

"Nick, that's it!"

"What?"

"We had coffee in Sam's office, remember?"

Nick stared at me, nodding his head slowly. His jaws began grinding. "And they lifted our prints off the cups."

WARREN SNUFFED out a cigarette and immediately lit another one. "I'm going to stall as long as I can, but the prosecution's pretty sure they've got the rightum, suspect...so they're going to push for a speedy trial. Sheriff Taylor, for one, is anxious to get this mess over and done with."

"Satisfying Sheriff Taylor's needs is not one of my goals," I said.

Warren ignored me and turned to Nick. "If we can introduce enough doubt to make the prosecution uneasy, they may go for a plea bargain. I'm thinking of playing up the miscarriage—hormones, mental instability... The DA might buy into manslaughter."

"What?" We said it in unison. Warren's left leg bounced up and down, like a rubber band drawn tight and plunked.

"Look, these fingerprints on the shaker, in your garbage. That's pretty heavy stuff."

"And the motive?" I could taste the acid in my mouth.

Warren rotated the tip of his cigarette in the ashtray. He shrugged. "Bohannon was opening a restaurant. He was going to be a competitor. You thought it might hurt Nick so... Not that I believe it, you understand, but the prosecution can make a fair case of it. That's why I'm thinking that mental instability is probably our safest bet.''

"But I didn't kill Glenn! And somebody out there is laughing his head off, thinking he's going to get away with it. I want to know who that is.''

"Well, I suppose we could hire an investigator. But it's going to cost big bucks, Nick. Have you got it to spend?'' Warren looked around the cafe doubtfully. Nick squeezed my hand under the table.

"The plea stands, Warren. Julia's not guilty.'' He stood up, and Warren, taking the cue, closed his briefcase and rose.

"There will be some preliminary hearings. Meanwhile, I'll go over everything you told me. I'll be in touch.''

And that was it. No long, high-powered conferences. No warm reassurances. That, I knew, was not Warren's style. But I also knew that he did not believe me.

"SO, NAVARRO'S WITH the Sheriff's Department?''

"Well, I guess so. Only he wasn't dressed like a deputy. He was wearing a suit.''

"I've never heard of him before, either. Wonder if he's new. Maybe Warren knows.''

"I'd rather not ask Warren anything. Maybe we ought to think about finding another attorney.''

Nick turned into the main gate at Parnassus, passed the statue of Apollo and headed the Honda toward the library. "Maybe. I know one thing—if we don't make any more progress, we're going to have to do as Warren suggested and hire an investigator.''

"First of all, I'd hardly call that a suggestion. He was just appeasing us. He thinks I'm guilty, Nick. And he's so close to that passel of cronies, he'd never believe that one of the Buffaloes could do it.

"Besides, we don't have the money to hire an investigator. We're barely holding it together right now, with the hospital bills and everything. We have to do it ourselves.''

Nick said nothing as he angled the car into a space. When he had cut the ignition, he turned to me. "We can sell the house and the cafe."

"No! We can do this, Nick. I know we can. Come on." I dragged him across the campus, up the wide marble steps of the library and into the main reference room. There we piddled with the computers until we had the information we needed. He followed me into the stacks. I handed him half the list of call numbers. "You go that way." I pointed down one row. "I'll go this way. Meet you at the table."

I dropped a stack of books on the table, handed one to Nick and picked up one myself. It was quite a collection—handbooks on clinical toxicology, forensic pathology, even criminal investigation.

"What do I look under?" he whispered, thumbing through a forensics book.

"I don't know. 'Poisons.' I wish I could remember the name. It started with a *j*, I'm sure. 'Ja-something. Just start looking."

Several hours later I pushed my stack aside despondently.

"No go. I can't find it." I reached for the books Nick had already discarded. "I'll just go back over—"

"Julia," Nick clamped my wrist. "Could this be it?"

He pushed a thick volume toward me, pointing at a boldly printed subheading. It read "Jatrophin."

"I think that's it! Nick, I think you found it!" I read aloud in a carefully subdued whisper:

"'A product of the Barbados nut, especially dangerous because of its pleasant taste.' Listen, it grows in Florida and Hawaii, Mexico, South and Central America, Asia, and Africa." Nick sprinted to the copy machine, quickly photocopied the page and the title page of the book. We shoved the books onto the stands for shelving and hurried back to the car.

"Florida, Nick. Ring any bells? Read's recreational properties? What's the name of that company?"

"Alternative Investments."

"Right."

"A definite possibility. But not the only one."

"MANA THEN..."

Nick was singing in the shower. His mood, like my own, was greatly elevated by the discovery of the poison. I knew with absolute certainty that the type of poison used was inexorably connected to Glenn's death. We were on our way.

"...fitepsoumai..."

I grimaced. The man can dance, but he cannot sing. I reached for the phone on the second ring, relieved to have something else to stimulate my cochlea.

The voice had become odiously familiar—its whispering, rasping tone scarcely audible as it spilled filth into the mouthpiece. It was always the same, calling me by name before detailing what he would do to me. The general tenor of his messages was that I must be a pretty freewheeling kind of gal to be willing to sleep with a foreigner. Those, of course, were not his exact words.

He painted, in lurid detail, the things he imagined we did in our matrimonial bed. And then, to my horror, he described what he wanted to do to me. I would find, he said, that American white meat was the best.

He knew I was innocent and he was sorry I'd ended up in jail. My husband was using me for a foil, a decoy. But he, the man of the rasping voice and the foul tongue, would save me. And then I would show him how grateful I was.

I forced myself to listen to it all, just as I had the three previous calls. I focused on his voice, not his words. The quality was always the same—breathy, flat. I couldn't be sure, but professional instinct told me that Nick had, at least temporarily, damaged his vocal cords. God bless that high kick.

I hadn't told Nick about the calls. We had enough trouble with Sam breathing down our necks. And we needed our wits about us if we were going to stay on target with this investigation. We couldn't afford to have them scattered by a shotgun full of rage. Nick came out of the bathroom just as I was returning the phone to the cradle.

"Who was that?"

I shrugged, tried to steady my voice. "Political survey. Nothing important."

I pulled my robe around me, curled up on the rug beneath the

hearth in front of the fireplace. A cold front to match my mood
had blown in over the mountains, leaving us unusually chilly for
late October. Jack snuggled against my feet, calm for once, his
head nuzzling my lap. Nick was in the kitchen. I could hear him
slamming cabinet doors, opening and closing the refrigerator. In
a minute the coffee grinder began whirring.

"What are you making?"

"Swiss almond chocolate."

Mmm. Perfect for a cold winter's night and an intimate fire.
Would that it might be a lovely, long-stretching romantic evening,
but romance was the last thing on either of our minds.

"I still don't know how it was done, though. A nut's pretty
hard to introduce into food without somebody noticing it. I
mean...it might work if you put it in a jar of mixed nuts, for
example."

The coffeepot glubbed as Nick rattled mugs from the cabinet,
unplugged the grinder, and shoved it away. He pulled it back out
and stared at it. He opened it, dropped coffee beans into it and
let it run an extra couple of seconds. In a minute, he stood in the
den. He held a small shaker in his hand, fingers curled around so
it was scarcely visible.

"Hold out your hand."

I put it out, palm up, and was rewarded with a softly sifted pile
of coffee.

"That's how he did it."

IT ADDED UP. The shaker the police had found contained the res-
idue of a deadly poison, held by a Buffalo in the kitchen and
casually shaken onto Glenn's hash browns when no one was looking. Nick mixed and turned the potatoes several times, making
sure they were crisp, the way Glenn liked them. He didn't know
he was mixing in a deadly seasoning, nor did I know, when I
cleared the mess off the table and righted the pepper shaker, that
it was not pepper at all. I had stamped that shaker with my fingerprints, possibly convicting myself of murder. But the killer
would not want the shaker found on the table. It might, after all,
implicate him, or the others in his merry band of men. So he

palmed it, as Nick described, and later left it for the police to find in our garbage. It could scarcely have been simpler.

"And you know, Glenn kept talking about how good his potatoes tasted. Now it makes sense. Do you remember what the book said? 'Particularly dangerous because of their pleasant taste.'"

"Pleasant and deadly."

TWENTY-FIVE

"OHEE, OHEE, OHEE! Min pirazes to skorda!"

Otis's screams brought me running from the dining room. Nick tore out of the office, screeching to a halt next to the dishwasher. Spiro's big hands were wrapped under Otis's arms and he was bouncing him on the kitchen floor like a basketball.

"Miz Julia, help me! Please, ma'am. He's gonna kill me!"

"Spiro, stop! Nick...It's not funny, Nick."

But it was, actually. We watched, slack-jawed, as Spiro tossed him into the air like a toddler, bellowing all the while. "No touch! No touch...*Ti lei?*"

"Garlic," Nick said.

"No touch garlic!"

Otis's head bobbed sideways in little jerks. "No, I won't. Never again! Never, never, never..."

Spiro's anger was spent as quickly as it had exploded. He shook his head. "*Neh. Enthoxi.* Nev-ver." He stalked away, still grumbling, leaving Otis suspended from a pair of pothooks on the overhead rack. Nick and I helped him down.

"What on earth did you do?"

Otis was trembling from the soles of his mismatched sneakers to the roots of his impossible hair. "I...I just threw that old string of garlic away. It was getting in everybody's way, hanging there like that, in the door. And he weren't using it to cook."

"No. It's his good-luck charm."

"Ma'am?"

"He thinks it keeps evil away."

"Well, I don't know about that. But if it works, I'm gonna tie me a coupla strings 'round my neck. Maybe it'll keep him away from me. He's always blaming me for something. Know that big carving knife?"

I nodded.

"Well, he's gone and lost it. Can't find it nowhere. Now he's blaming it on me! Says I throwed it away, but I didn't. And he thinks I been stealing tomatoes, too. What the hell do I want with tomatoes, anyways? He's—whatcha call it?—paranoiac.''

"Paranoid."

"Right! I'm afraid of him, Miz Julia. Do we have to keep him?" he whined.

Spiro stepped out of the grill, into the kitchen doorway. "Otis," he called. Otis's trembling resumed. Spiro's grin split his face in half. "You come, *agori mou*. Help Spiro."

Otis eyes were pleading as he looked from Nick to me. Nick, who had said nothing, turned on his heel and whistled his way back to the office.

"Miz Julia?"

"You'd better go on, Otis. He needs your help to strain the grease. You don't want to make him mad, do you?"

When I passed them, headed for the phone at the register, Otis was crouched, a filter cone extended at arm's length over the bucket. Spiro was loping toward him with the fryer vat. Otis squeezed his eyes closed, and a shrill squeal fluted in his throat.

"JULIA, this is Alma Rayburn. I wonder if I might speak to Spiro?"

"Speak to Spiro?" I hesitated, wondering how this might be accomplished over the telephone without the benefit of gestures and facial expression. Although his English was improving under her tutelage, it was far from phoneworthy.

"Just for a minute. I won't keep him long."

"Well, certainly. But...Miss Alma, do you think he'll really understand you?"

It was her turn to hesitate. When she spoke again, her voice was ragged. "It's just that I don't know what to do. You see, it's Elena and Ramón. They're here, at my house. They were next door at Spiro's looking for him, fairly pounding his door down. I went over to explain that he was at work, but they were so upset... Well, I don't really want them to know I speak Spanish. I'm a little frightened, you see. But I brought them here and I thought maybe, if Spiro was free to leave... Well really, Julia, I just didn't know what else to do."

"Miss Alma, do you have any idea what's wrong?"

"They were speaking very fast. I had trouble following, but I think it concerns Tomás. If I understood them correctly, Tomás is missing and they're very worried about him."

I glanced at my watch. It was past closing, but a couple of students lingered on the smoking deck. Spiro and Otis were still straining the fryer grease, a task I was loath to interrupt, and Nick was writing checks in the office. Most of it could wait until later.

"As soon as we get the last customers out, Nick and I will bring Spiro and come over. Try to keep them there, Miss Alma. Tell them in English that Spiro is on his way. Don't use Spanish unless it's absolutely necessary."

"Yes," she said. "Yes, I'll do that. I'm sure I can keep them here somehow."

SHE WAS WAITING at the door when we pulled into her driveway. Spiro bounded over the hedges from his house, his face hard as the marble images of his forebears. It had taken several translations, me to Nick, Nick to Spiro, to explain the situation. At the mention of Miss Alma, he twisted his hands in agitation.

"Ella, bame. Grigora! Kyria Alma..."

I put my hand on Spiro's arm. "We're hurrying, Spiro. Miss Alma will be all right." But it was little comfort to him. The Pontiac stampeded through the winding little streets of Markettown, our Honda scarcely able to keep up. And then we were standing at her door.

"Are they still here?"

Miss Alma nodded and ushered us into her house. Elena was sitting in the Victorian slipper chair. She twisted a dainty lace handkerchief in her hands and started nervously as we entered. Beside her, on a mahogany piecrust table, sat an empty brandy snifter. Ramón was replenishing his brandy from a cut-crystal decanter on the dining room table. Relieved though he was to see Spiro, his expression became guarded when he spied Nick and me. Miss Alma drew us into her kitchen, leaving Spiro to take charge of the couple.

"They've been arguing," she whispered. "Elena is afraid, but

Ramón thinks it's a mistake to bring anyone else into it. He's been trying to convince her to leave."

"Why is Elena afraid?"

Miss Alma was frank. "My dear, you don't know much about coyotes, do you? They're dangerous men. Ramón and Elena are afraid that something has happened to Tomás. As I told you, I don't think he was the most cooperative of *pollos*. I don't know the whole story, only that Tomás is gone and Elena is afraid for him."

"What does Ramón say to that?" Nick asked.

"If Tomás has been hurt, none of them are safe. He thinks they should keep their mouths shut and pretend they suspect nothing. But he's worried about Elena, I think. She's so jittery she may give them away."

When we returned to the living room, Elena had moved to the sofa where she sat, like a frightened bird, hovering under Ramón's arm. Spiro was seated on the slipper chair facing them, his wiry brows tied up in a knot. He put a finger to his lips and nodded to Ramón to continue.

At Miss Alma's direction, Nick brought chairs from the dining room, placing two in a row and one behind them. Miss Alma took her seat behind us and quietly translated as best she could, still careful not to be overheard.

"Tomás has been gone for over twenty-four hours. They've been given their documents, but Tomás did not receive any. He was to have gone to the same job, with Elena and Ramón, at a garment factory. They were to leave in a few days. But when Elena asked Ms. Santos about him, she replied that he has gone back to Mexico. Ramón says that Tomás would never have gone back. They think he was in some trouble there. And he says that even if Tomás had decided to leave, he would have told them."

Spiro, whose Spanish was confident, but a little slower than the Mexicans', was speaking. Even with my limited knowledge, I understood his question. "How," he asked, "did Tomás leave? Did he just walk out of the house?"

"He was picked up in a panel truck, like the one they arrived in," Miss Alma said. "They had been playing cards. In fact, they were in the middle of a game when the truck arrived and the driver came to the door to call for Tomás.

"Tomás was very angry at being interrupted during his game. Ramón couldn't hear what the driver was saying, but Tomás came back to the table, threw down his cards and said he would be back. That was the last time they saw him."

"But why would anyone want to hurt Tomás?" I whispered.

"Spiro asked the same question. Tomás was not easy to handle. Apparently they were told to stay in the house and out of sight, but Tomás insisted on going out when Ms. Santos was not around."

Ramón made placating gestures with his hands, smiling almost shyly at Spiro. "It seems that it was Tomás who insisted they go to Spiro's for dinner. It got them in trouble with Ms. Santos, but Tomás took the blame. And there were other things. He insisted on asking too many questions...who made their documents—I suppose that means false birth certificates and Social Security cards—and who the coyote really works for. He was in El Norte and he wanted to see it, to live like an American, he said. That's what they were promised."

Spiro leaned back in the slipper chair and stretched his legs out in front of him. He tweaked his mustache and chewed on the ends, deep in thought. Elena watched him from behind swollen eyes. Ramón resumed pounding his fist in his open palm and staring at the mottled carpet beneath his feet. Nick and I watched, smothered by the silence. In a minute, Spiro leaned forward and spoke again.

"He wants to know how they came to be here, in Delphi."

"Don't we all?" I mumbled to Nick.

Elena explained it to us through Miss Alma's translation. "The coyote does not pick his pollos up in bus stations and on the streets. They're carefully recruited and interviewed. They must have some skill, more than strength and the ability to pick crops. And they must intend to stay in the U.S. for at least five years. That's why they often come as couples or with other family members. Then the temptation to go back is not as great. They met Tomás at the beginning and have traveled together the whole way. I gather they've become close friends.

"She says that it is very costly—five hundred dollars to cross the border, be brought to a safe house, and given false papers. Two hundred dollars each per week to live in the safe house, and another five hundred dollars after they begin to work."

"Then how can these people afford it?"

Miss Alma shrugged. "The family. They all save, so that one or two may go. After they get jobs, they'll send money home for another to come here, maybe a younger brother or sister. They think they'll make a lot of money here, but the risks are great and the reward is little. If they don't pay the last five hundred, the coyote will find them, and the cost may go up. It may even be their lives. I don't really think they understand that until they're too deeply involved to turn back."

"We've got to find out how they got here. Who brought them?" Nick spoke in a low voice, but the urgency of it filtered across the room.

Although Spiro continued to question them, their answers became vague, their manner, unresponsive. Ramón's guarded mask had dropped back over his features. Elena studied us intently, and I felt her fear. She did not know us. Could she trust us? America must have seemed to her a land fraught with danger and exploitation, and Americans, users, manipulators or, at best, apathetic to her troubles. Tomás, her friend, was missing and she was trapped.

Spiro stretched and stood up. *"Tengo sed,"* he said. He sauntered into the kitchen, gesturing to Nick to follow as he passed us. Miss Alma jumped up, grabbed the brandy and busily refilled their glasses, smiling and gesturing to them both. Nick slipped into the kitchen where Spiro was noisily drawing water. Their conversation was brief, but emphatic, before returning to the living room.

Nick dropped back into his chair as Spiro took his place across the room. "They won't say any more about how they got here. They're afraid of us, and afraid of what will happen to them now."

"Well, what did they hope we could do about Tomás?"

Nick shook his head. "I don't know, really. I suppose they had some idea that we'd go out looking for him. Spiro told them that we'd check all the bars in town, but frankly, I don't think there's much hope of finding him. Meanwhile, they have to make a choice. Either we can find them a safe place to stay, call immigration and get them back to Mexico, or they'll have to go back to the house and pretend they don't notice that Tomás is missing.''

I studied Elena's face. She seemed more in control, or perhaps it was only the brandy's calming effect. Both Spiro and Ramón spoke earnestly to her, in softly consoling tones that seemed to be reassuring. She nodded her head slowly, all the while smoothing the lace handkerchief across her knees. Finally, she took Ramón's hand and let him pull her off the couch.

Ramón shook Spiro's hand gravely as Elena crossed the room to Miss Alma. She held the handkerchief up and smiled. "I wash," she said. "Bring to you. *Es muy bonita.*"

Miss Alma wrapped her thin arm around the girl's shoulder. To herself, more than to Elena, she said, "You keep it, dear child. It will be something to remember me by." Tremulous sadness undermined her voice.

TWENTY-SIX

I HADN'T KNOWN there were so many bars in Delphi. The yuppiest of them merited no more than a cursory check. Regardless how cocky he seemed to be, it was improbable that Tomás would appear in a place that catered to students and white up-and-comers. And the places that boasted of local artists twanging country tunes through the jukebox were, if anything, even more unlikely havens for a man with Tomás' skin tone and heavy accent. Despite the probabilities, Nick checked them all while I wrung my hands, swallowed up in the backseat of Spiro's Pontiac. When we reached the seedier places, the bars on dark streets that supplied the disenfranchised of Delphi, I insisted that I was safer inside with the two men than alone in the parking lot in the Pontiac. Nick and Spiro reluctantly agreed. By the third dive, I was beginning to wonder.

The fourth was the Silver Chariot bar, an obvious allusion to the Parnassus theme, but I doubted that any students, other than those who were known troublemakers or had run out of credit, ever passed through its cloudy glass doors.

We sat at a wobbly table nursing warm beer served in greasy steins. Fragmented faces peered at us through the mirrors behind the bar. Two burly black men in dazzling white shirts sat at the end of the bar talking quietly. Next to them, a long, thin man wearing a fishing hat elbowed the bar. Even in the darkness, his face was crimson, eyes red and blue, swollen nose protuberant. He was the thinnest man I have ever seen, gaunt and stretched looking, as though he slept on a rack. An empty stool stood between him and a woman on the corner. She wore a flowery, filmy dress that strained across the bodice and accented the lines of her bra underneath. Now and then, she threw back her head, blew smoke in the bartender's face, and brayed.

The booths were variously occupied by couples and foursomes—young, heavily made-up girls, who couldn't have been old enough to be served. They sat unnecessarily close to older men of dubious intentions. The booth at the very back of the room was occupied by a single man. Only the top of his head was visible over the back of the booth—blond hair with a buzz cut that left me with the impression that he was young—perhaps too young to be served, ergo the darkness of the rear booth.

"Well, he's obviously not here, either, so why are we staying?"

Nick took a sip of his beer, grimaced and pushed the stein aside. "Maybe they know him here, anyway. If they could just give us a lead."

"Okay. Well, you didn't finish telling me about Ramón and Elena."

"They're sticking it out. I think Elena's hoping Tomás will still show up."

"But you don't think he will?"

Nick stared into his glass, not answering. Spiro toyed with a matchbook and stared at a girl in the corner booth. She was not more than fifteen, with tawny skin and a wide, flat nose that suggested mixed parentage. Her companion was white, heavyset, with graying hair that receded sharply from his high forehead. He took the girl's hand off the table and placed it indelicately inside his upper thigh. Spiro ticked his tongue and shook his head sadly.

"Why didn't Ramón and Elena just go back to Mexico? We could've arranged it for them."

"Ramón says they wouldn't be safe there. The coyote would be looking for them. They know too much and besides, they owe him money. Spiro advised them to go back and act as though they believe Connie—that Tomás has returned to Mexico. He promised them we'd help. Somehow."

"How're y'all doing? Need anything else?" The bartender-cum-waiter picked up Spiro's empty glass and pulled a bar mop out of his apron, making a few careless swipes at the wet ring on the table. Spiro pointed to his glass, indicating that he'd have another beer.

"We're supposed to meet a friend here, but he's late. Maybe you know him. His name's Tomás."

"Wiry guy? Spanish? Yeah, I know him. Haven't seen him for

a coupla three days, though. He was comin' in pretty steady for a while.''

Nick pushed his stein toward the bartender. ''Think I'd rather have something else—how about you Julia?'' I ordered a gin and tonic. Nick pulled a roll of bills from his pocket and pealed off a ten and a twenty. ''Here, that'll cover our drinks and buy you one, too. Why don't you join us?''

The bartender studied the bills, glanced around at his customers and shrugged. ''Be right back with those drinks.''

He took the empty chair next to Spiro and set a bowl of popcorn in the middle of the table. ''I would'na remembered your friend except that he talked a lot. Pretty much to anyone who'd listen.''

''Talked about what?''

''I don't know. Didn't speak English. Coupla times he met this other guy and they'd sit and talk in Spanish, ya know?''

''Other guy?''

''Yeah. Wadn't a regular or nothing, but he came in a few times. Always sat with the other one—what was his name?''

''Tomás.''

''Yeah, Thomas. Funny though, the other guy didn't look Spanish. I was real…like surprised, ya know?''

Nick's knuckles were white around his glass. He looked down and seemed to consciously try to pry them loose. ''This other guy, what did he look like?''

The bartender shrugged. ''Ordinary. Kind of a big guy, reddish, sandy hair. White, not Mexican. Always wore cowboy boots.''

''Where did they sit?''

He pointed to a booth in the rear of the bar. ''Back there.''

''Did they ever leave together?''

The bartender scratched his head, shrugged. ''I dunno. I mean, I wasn't watching them that close. No. I doubt it. That Thomas, he'd usually hang out for a while. Tried to pick up a coupla girls. Think he mighta went home with one of them. One night some hot number came in here looking for him. Hell, that mighta been the last time he was here, come to think about it.''

''What did she look like?''

He whistled. ''Hot. I mean scorching! Dark hair, big— Oh,

'scuse me, ma'am. Anyway, they had this loud fight. In Spanish.
She was like a cat, all hissing and spitting. She got him outta here
finally, but man was she pissed! If she was his lady, he musta
been nuts to leave home.''

"How did he act?"

"Bad as her. I thought he was gonna belt her, but he didn't.
She pulled something outta her bag. For a minute I was scared
she had a gun, but it weren't no gun. Mighta been a knife, though.
Anyways, he went 'long with her after that. Didn't even finish
his beer. Left his cigarettes right there on the bar. You want
'em?"

"You've still got them?"

The bartender shrugged. "Don't smoke. Think I put 'em under
the bar, thinkin' he'd come back. Lemme go look."

He was back in a minute, dropping a pack of Marlboros on the
table in front of Nick. It was almost a full pack, and a book of
matches was neatly tucked into the side, behind the cellophane.
Nick fingered the pack pensively, pulled out the matchbook and
flipped it open. He stared at it for a moment before passing it to
me. Inside, Tomás had penciled an equation: $AN = BD$.

WE CROSSED the railroad tracks and turned left, following the
tracks as they ran down the center of the main street past a Piggly
Wiggly grocery store, a lumberyard, and a hair salon advertising
a seven-dollar cut in letters painted on the plate glass in lime
green. The tracks served as a kind of esplanade, bisecting the
main street in town and confirming that Industry was, and is,
essentially a mill town. The papermill, although on the outskirts,
breathed a putrid fog over downtown. I held a tissue over my
nose and mouth.

"I don't know how long I'll be able to stay here, Nick. This
makes the grease trap in the kitchen smell good."

"Well, hopefully we won't be here that long anyway. Keep
your eyes open for the knitting mill. What time did you say the
shift changes?"

"Midnight is what she said."

The fog was thick and yellow, swirling around modern street-
lamps that the residents must have considered newfangled. Nick

started to roll his window down, got one whiff, and changed his mind.

"Wish I could have thought of an excuse to tour this one."

"Yeah, but I can't think of a single, credible reason that a restaurant owner would want to visit a knitting mill."

"Me neither. That's the problem. Look—isn't that it?"

Nick pointed to a dark, cinder-block building spewing steam from three large smokestacks. It looked to be three stories high, with a single row of lighted windows marching across the top. On the roof, a fading billboard read Mountain Pine Knitting Mills. We'd reached a forlornly blinking stoplight. Nick swung the car across the tracks and doubled back. Before we reached the mill, he angled into a conveniently deserted gas station. From there we could see the security booth and gate into the parking lot, and beyond it a large metal door. I thought I could make out an Employees Only sign above it.

"How'd you find out about the shift change, anyway?"

I shrugged. "Easy. I called the office and told the receptionist that my sister works there and I was coming to town to surprise her for her birthday. I said I thought she worked the late shift and I wanted to meet her at the gate."

"Didn't she ask for a name?"

"Sure, but I said if I told her that, she might spoil the surprise. I was sure she wouldn't mean to, but you know how that kind of thing goes. You start smiling and giggling and pretty soon you've blown it. I told her I'd come in with my sister tomorrow and we'd take her to lunch. Her name's Ms. Gibbons."

"She bought that?"

"For a free lunch? Sure."

Nick eyed me pensively. "You know, you're getting pretty good at lying."

"I think so too. It's an acquired skill, more easily acquired under pressure, and right now we've got plenty of that. I do feel a little guilty about Ms. Gibbons, though. I hope she's not counting on lunch." I yawned.

After leaving Spiro at his house and collecting our Honda, we'd run home and changed our clothes. I'd have given anything for a nap, but we had to strike at night when there would only be workers and security guards to deal with, not secretaries and administrators. An hour's drive into the mountains had brought us to this squalid little town and its deserted gas station.

"Tomás must have been meeting Glenn there for some reason, Nick."

"Or expected to, anyway. He probably didn't know Glenn was dead. The way Connie keeps them locked up, it would be hard for him to find out." Nick fingered the matches from Tomás' cigarettes. "What is 'AN'?"

He repeated it several more times under his breath, then held the penlight over his watch. "We've still got twenty minutes. Come on."

I followed him out of the car and across the driveway toward the plant. The security booth was empty. A radio blared hits of the fifties and sixties, and a half-empty pint of bourbon was tucked under the counter. The gate, though latched, was not locked. Nick swung it open just enough for us to pass through.

"You're not planning to go in," I whispered. "Nick, I don't think we can pull that off, and this isn't the kind of town I want to get arrested in. The police chief is probably the Grand Wizard or Dragon, or whatever they call him."

"Just act like you know what you're doing."

"I do. I'm following you to disaster."

TWENTY-SEVEN

NICK PULLED on the Employees Only door, a vast metal affair that weighed a ton. Surprisingly, and to my disappointment, it opened. We stood at the end of a long hallway flanked by darkened offices. On the wall to the right was an immense time clock and a three-column rack of cream-colored time cards. At the end of the hallway was another door. Through a small, wire-gridded window I could see the main plant. The whirring, cranking, crashing of machinery was loud even there in the hall. The noise must have been overwhelming inside. I wondered what OSHA thought about it all.

Nick tentatively tried the office doors, predictably finding each locked. I was starting to feel trapped. "Let's get out of here."

It was no more than out of my mouth when the official-looking blue cap of the security guard appeared in the window. He was turned, talking to someone, as the door swung open.

"My shift's almost over. Gatlin comes on at one. Tell him about it. No way I'm staying here all night."

A hand over my mouth, arm around my waist, I felt myself falling backward through an open door. Nick put a finger to his lips and pointed. Behind me stood a row of urinals and beyond it a booth. A pair of hightop sneakers were flexed on either side of a porcelain base.

"*Quién está?*"

Nick's eyes grew wide. He walked over to the sink and turned on the water to its limit.

"Carlos."

He hit the hand dryer. It roared to life, making further conversation impossible. I poked my head around the bathroom door. The guard was gone, but the plant door was open and the first of its employees were milling out. At the other door, small groups were straggling in, listlessly punching the time clock and rubbing their eyes. The graveyard shift was coming on.

I motioned to Nick and found him scrutinizing the hand dryer. He pointed to a turquoise decal on the front: For Service Call... In the booth, the toilet flushed, the sneakers moved. The lock was being thrown. We hit the hallway, trying to blend into the group.

Some were laughing, jostling one another, others arguing. But relief that the end of the workday had finally come was palpable in air being rapidly filled with cigarette smoke and spray perfume. Combs were run through hair, lipstick applied. Suddenly conscious of my blonde curls, I wished I had thought to throw a bandanna scarf over them.

Nick threw his arm over my shoulder and pulled me close to him, as though we were lovers reunited after a grueling workday. He whispered to me in Greek, mistakenly thinking, I suppose, that they would think it was Spanish. The theory was fine, but failed to account for the fact that ninety percent of the people in that hallway spoke Spanish as their native language. We drew a few curious stares, but I wasn't worried. These people would do nothing to call attention to, or compromise, themselves.

The hall seemed to go on for miles, the seconds drag to hours. Then we were at the door. Eau de papermill became a welcome scent, the smell of safety. The orange vapor lights shimmered in the parking lot just beyond the door.

"Hey, you two!" The security guard stood just next to the time clock, until then hidden by the press of the crowd. His hand was on my upper arm. I turned back, and felt Nick's arm go rigid and slip off my shoulder.

"*Sí?*" I said.

"Just who the hell are you? Never seen you before." He glanced over my shoulder at Nick and his eyes narrowed in suspicion. "Wait a minute," he said. "Wait just a damn minute, you."

I turned to Nick, shocked to find him grinning to his ears. He pivoted around to face the crowd and reared up on his toes.

"*Migra!*" he shouted. "*Andale! Migra, migra!*"

They started shoving, screaming, and scattering through every available door. Nick grabbed my hand just as the crowd jolted me out of the guard's grasp and launched us both out the door. We scrambled across the parking lot, laughing, as the panicky guard bellowed in broken Spanish. It did him no good. The building emptied as both shifts took flight.

WE WAITED in our darkened car, watching cars screech from the parking lot. When a big, old Chevy pulled out, Nick threw the Honda into drive.

"Too close, Nick. Way too close."

"Yeah...But it was kind of fun, wasn't it?"

I peered back over my shoulder at the Mountain Pines Knitting Mill. The guard stood outside his booth, blindly shaking his raised fists at the fleeing workers. "Salsa's in the fan now. Where are we going?"

"Following them."

"Why? Didn't we find out what we wanted to know?"

"Maybe. I just want to see where some of these people live."

Ahead of us, the Chevy Impala sagged under six tired, probably overworked bodies. It reminded me of Spiro's car, badly in need of shocks and alignment, floating down the main street of Industry.

Nick said nothing, but concentrated on following the escaping Impala through dark, twisted streets. If Markettown looked depressed, this neighborhood was positively suicidal. He braked as a rat darted across the street and scurried into a sewer. This was a neighborhood with no illusions—no pink flamingos or plastic sunflowers, no rock gardens. No pretense at cheerfulness. Just down-and-out poverty. We didn't stop when the Impala turned into a short driveway in front of a tiny, asbestos-shingled house.

Nick drove to the end of the street and made a three-point turn in front of a darkly vacant house. The sign in the yard was odiously familiar: For Rent—Call Delphi Rental Properties. Neither of us commented. We followed the same route back out to Industry's main drag where Nick pulled into the parking lot of a garishly lit convenience store.

"I'm hungry. Want a Coke or a candy bar?"

"No, but I don't want to sit here alone, either. I'll come with you."

The store had a coldly sterile look to it, artifically bright under fluorescent lights. A rotund man in a blue cotton vest stood behind the register. His mama must have called him Bubba.

Nick headed for the candy rack, while I, deciding I might be hungry after all, checked out the other consumables. There were tortilla chips, cans of bean dip, and jars of salsa with more authentic-looking labels than the usual grocery-store offerings. The little cooler on the side wall held a vast selection of fruit, some of which I did not immediately recognize.

"Nick, come look at this fruit. What's that?"

Bubba answered. "That's one of them papayas."

"Kind of an odd selection for a convenience store," I said, selecting an apple and walking toward the register.

"Spics. All we gots round here's spics." He shrugged philosophically. "Gotta give 'em what they want. That's the business."

"Where do they come from?"

"Over there." Bubba pointed to the mill. "Oh, you mean where do they come from—original?"

I nodded.

"Hell, I don't know. Mexico, Cuba. Who knows? I don't ask. Mosta the whites around here don't like 'em. But they's cheap labor and they buy our stuff." Bubba took my money and handed me a receipt for the apple. "Employ a few of 'em myself from time to time, for the heavy labor—cleaning up the parking lot, stuff like that. They do a passable job. I don't hold with bearing a grudge."

Especially, I thought, if you can get them cheap.

I STARED at the telephone, loath to pick it up, to once again endure a swim in verbal sewage. I was tired—too tired to deal with threats. It had been a long night spent at the mill, then following the workers home. One of many long nights in the recent past when, even if we did manage to grab a few hours of sleep, they were fitful, full of nightmares and anguish over what was to come. Nick had taken Jack out for a quick walk. I was turning down the bed when the shrill ringing of the phone began. I knew who it was and I was in no mood for a chat.

But maybe this time I would identify it. I set my mind to listen carefully, to imagine how it had sounded before Nick had stunned it into breathiness. Concentrate, Julia. Listen to the accent. How does he phrase his words?

"It's almost time," he whispered. "You're all alone, aren't you?"

I didn't answer. He chuckled. "I know you are. I have something for you." The phone clicked. I dropped onto the bed, shaking, then flew up at the sound of breaking glass. It was in the den. I moved slowly, picking up the only weapon I could find— a heavy Greek vase, a reproduction piece from the Attic period. I crept toward the door, wondering if, somewhere out there, they were holding Nick and Jack.

I listened. No discernible movement in the den—only the night sounds of crickets and owls seeping through the broken window, and behind them the familiar rumble of a pickup truck moving away. Blood rushed from heart to head and pounded in my ears. I cautiously peered around the corner.

The room was well lighted, waiting cheerfully for Nick to return. My caller had broken only a single pane out of the window, one too small for anyone to get through. Something lay in the middle of the carpet. Afraid to be seen through the open window, I dropped to the floor and shimmied on my stomach across the carpeting to the object.

It was a rock, nothing especially noteworthy, except that it was wrapped in glossy paper, held on by a rubber band. I could see the familiar slogan for a men's cologne fade around the ragged edges of the rock. Satisfied that there was no one in the room, I sat up and unwrapped the rock with trembling hands.

There were three pages, torn from a magazine. The breaking glass had sliced through the one wrapped around the outside. Unfortunately, the two inside were perfectly intact. I didn't know anyone published such smut, photographs so disgusting that I wanted to vomit on them. Where, in God's name, would anyone find such pictures? And what kind of deviant would ever do such things to a woman? Any woman.

I was still sitting in the middle of the floor staring at them when Nick's key turned in the lock. He took it all in a single glance and was beside me before I could hide them.

"Oh my God, what is this?"

I handed them to Nick, went to the bathroom and bathed my face in cold water. When I returned, Nick was cleaning up the broken glass. His skin was pale, and his face as hard as a marble statue. We said nothing as he carefully nailed a square of plywood across the window. Jack sat in front of my feet, as though he sensed that danger waited to assault me.

"That's it, Julia. You're leaving tomorrow."

I shook my head, rooting my feet in imaginary cement. "I can't. Spiro would lose the bond money."

"To hell with the bond. I'll make it up to him."

"Nick, you'd never be able to pay him back. Besides, they'd arrest you for aiding and abetting. And I won't leave you alone. You can't make me. I won't go."

"You have to!" Nick's voice was hard. Angry. I knew he felt helpless, and the helplessness was turning to an anger that he directed at me. "You are so damn stubborn." His words were even. I almost didn't know him.

"Maybe. But I love you and nothing, absolutely nothing," I shouted, "is going to make me leave. Let him come for me. Just let him try!"

Jack growled, pricked up his ears. I patted him. "We're so close, Nick. Don't you see? The closer we get, the more they threaten us. The beating, the phone calls—"

"Phone calls?"

I bit my tongue, silent, as he waited for me to explain. He outwaited me.

"There've been a couple. Obscene calls. He called again tonight, just before he threw the rock through the window. He's trying to scare us away, Nick. And the closer we get, the harder he tries."

Nick dropped onto the couch, pulled out his worry beads. "Maybe. But this guy is sick, Julia. Don't you see? You could be in real danger. He might just do those..." He stopped, not wanting to finish what I knew he meant. Those terrible pictures.

I snatched them off the floor, shredded them, and marched into the bathroom, flushing them into the sewer where they belonged.

When I returned, Nick was turning off the lights. He took my hand and led me to the bedroom.

"I'm calling a travel agent first thing in the morning. Your brother or your parents?"

"Neither." I looked into the stony set of his face and counted on the morning sun to wash the threat away. "Give me just a little more time. If it happens again, I'll consider leaving. But we're too close now to let him win."

TWENTY-EIGHT

NICK WHISTLED and turned off his calculator. "Unbelievable!" He pushed a page of figures across the desk to me. "Just take a look."

"What am I looking at?"

Nick hesitated. "Profit. The profit to be made from modern slavery." He dragged his chair around next to mine and pointed to the figures in front of me.

"Take, as a conservative estimate, Grandma Tyler. She has forty employees who each work a forty-hour week. Say they make six bucks an hour. Now, you have a chance to hire someone who'll do the same work for half as much, and work sixty hours instead. Are you following me?"

"So far, go on."

"Okay, you have to pay your regular workers overtime, right? At time and a half. But the other guys, the illegals, don't demand overtime. You pay them straight time at three bucks. Here's the difference in your weekly payroll for a sixty-hour week—ninety-six hundred dollars." He pointed to a row of tallies. "And your monthly, and your yearly."

I was stunned—over $499,200 for a year's savings on labor. Money. The great motivator. The scheme was starting to make sense.

"Now, on top of that, you have to consider Social Security. That's worth almost thirteen thousand on that same forty people. Remember, the employer has to match Social Security payments. He's paying them less than minimum wage, but he reports it as though it were a forty-hour week, instead of sixty, so it looks like he's right in the ballpark."

Nick turned the sheet over and started scratching a few additional figures. "These people aren't going to demand any fringe benefits, so you can eliminate medical and dental, retirement policies, sick pay. How much is that going to save old Grandma?"

I thought about Grandma Tyler's picture and wondered if she'd cooked this little scheme up herself. The old bitch.

"Grandma Tyler probably employs at least twice that many employees, and it's a relatively small company. Look at the knitting mill. Mountain Pines runs three shifts a day, at least six days a week. By the look of it, they had at least that many employees per shift, so you can triple the savings there. Oh, and you don't have to worry about unions, which, in itself, is worth it to the employer. The illegals live in constant fear that they'll be discovered and sent back. They'll do whatever the boss wants."

"Okay, I get the idea. So Mountain Pines Knitting Mills could be saving as much—with wages, Social Security, and benefits all figured in—as several million dollars a year on using illegal aliens. But I'm not sure I know where that fits in."

"Julia, the biggest common denominator on all those bank loans Bobby had was high labor and low profits. A savings of a million dollars can shift things on a profit-and-loss statement pretty radically, don't you think?"

"Yeah, but the fact is, they were showing high labor and low profits."

"When they applied for the loans. Have you heard of any of those companies going out of business or defaulting on the loans? Any repossessions in the paper?"

"Well, no."

"Exactly. Don't you see? The loans are approved, with the stipulation that they reduce their costs. Well, if they'd known how to do that, they wouldn't be in the mess they're in. That means they get some advice. And probably someone helps them make the right connections."

We had popped the top and they were slithering out—worms, worms of all types. And somewhere in that can had been a snake.

"But who? Morgan?"

"Maybe. Or maybe he's just a wheel in the machinery."

"So what about Glenn? Where does he fit in?"

"Everywhere. He was having an affair with Morgan's wife, living in Read's townhouse complex near Connie, who he was also involved with, and he was meeting with Tomás, an illegal. I have an idea how it all fits together, I'm just not sure how to find out."

I DROPPED THE PHONE back into the cradle and handed Nick the notepaper he'd taken from Morgan's planner. "Well, information still shows him listed in El Paso, so I guess he didn't sell his house."

"Let's try the number." Nick punched in the number I'd given him, waited, and raised an eyebrow when the phone was answered on the other end. He asked for Glenn, listening closely to the response.

"I'm so sorry to hear that. I only knew him briefly, through our work. Please give all the family my regrets. My name? Uh, Carlos. Carlos Martinez."

"His wife?"

"Sister."

"Listen, Nick, I have an idea. Hand me the phone." I called El Paso information again, then dialed the number they gave me and told them what I wanted.

"I'd really like to have a copy of it. For the family records. Could you fax me one? At the *Delphi Sun*. Great, thanks."

I dialed again and asked for Billy English. "More on the story, Billy, but you've got to intercept this fax when it comes in, okay? Don't let anyone else get their hands on it. Bring it to the cafe when you get it."

I turned back to Nick, but was interrupted by a knock on the office door. Rhonda twisted her apron between her hands. "Sam's here, Nick. He wants to talk to you."

He was waiting at the family table, stirring thick cream into his coffee. His face was sober and his expression didn't change when we joined him.

"Hey, Sam, what do you need?" I tried to sound light, ignoring the tingling nausea that his appearance evoked, and the somber set of his mouth.

"Gotta ask you a few more questions."

The coffeemaker glubbed and the ventilating fan whirred in the grill, but silence seemed to descend on the dining room. When Nick finally spoke, his voice was so hard I barely recognized it.

"Not without Warren. Look, she's been charged, arrested, and is out on bail. Julia's not answering any questions, and neither am I."

"Whoa! Hold on. It's something else, Nick." He dropped his spoon on his saucer. "Bohannon's house was broken into last night. They tore the place up pretty bad."

"Did they get anything?"

Sam shook his head. "Not so far's I can tell. My deputy inventoried it the day after Bohannon died. Nothing's missing."

"So what does this have to do with me?"

"I gotta ask you where you were last night."

I could see Nick's thoughts spinning through his head. Tell Sam, and put Ramón and Elena in jeopardy? How about Miss Alma? She might be compromised, maybe in danger. Whoever the coyote was, he didn't hesitate to kill. I longed to tell Sam the truth—all of it—about Dina's affair, and Bobby's attempted murder. About Tomás, Ramón, and Elena. My throat grew tight and sore holding my tongue. Too many people, innocent people, would be at risk.

"We were at home. In bed." I nodded my head in rapid agreement.

He studied us carefully, but he could hardly have missed the dark rings under our eyes. "Anybody else who can verify that?"

"Hardly. We don't usually have observers."

Sam stroked his jaw, took a sip of his coffee, and looked out the window onto the parking lot. "I'm trying to hold back, Nick. Sheriff Taylor's been out of town."

"Yeah, with my green card."

"He's coming in this afternoon. I can't hold off much longer, Nick. I told you before, I never wanted Julia. I don't think she did it. But if I can put you at Bohannon's last night, I'm going to have to take you both in. And Julia's bail's going to be revoked. Count on it. Why don't you just cooperate?"

"I am cooperating, Sam."

"Yeah. Right." He hauled up, pushed in the chair and glanced at his watch. "About four hours. I gotta meet his plane." The implication was clear. He stopped at the door, and turned back around.

"Either of you know a Henry or Eliza Higgins?"

"Higgins? No, I don't think so, do we, Nick?"

"Higgins. Mm, nope. Never heard of them."

Sam shook his head, his expression a mixture of resignation and disgust. He passed Billy on his way out.

"Here it is."

Billy handed me a manila folder, flipping it open to reveal a cover sheet from the *El Paso Times*. I scanned the obituary quickly.

> ...Mr. Bohannon was employed by the Border Patrol sector of the Department of Immigration and Naturalization. He is survived by two sisters, Mrs. Sandra Thayer of Houston and Miss Ellen Bohannon of El Paso. A memorial service...

"That's it, then. INS. An undercover agent. And I'm an immigrant, in the right place, at the right time. No wonder they're holding my green card."

"But shouldn't INS be in on the investigation?"

"I have the feeling they are." Nick stepped to the phone at the register, made a call, and noted the number. I thought I knew where he was going. His next move verified it.

"Agent Navarro, please. Oh, he is? When will he be back? I see. No, I'll try him some other time."

He dropped back into the chair. "Well, now we know."

Billy looked from Nick to me. "What do we know?"

"Almost everything. Almost, but not quite."

"I don't get it."

I paged through the fax again, looking for anything I might have missed. All it held were the bare bones of a man's life—it told nothing of what he'd died from or, more importantly, for. I'd liked Glenn Bohannon. A surge of anger coursed through me.

"There's a story here for you, Billy. But you're going to have to wait a little longer for it, okay? It'll be a big one when it blows, I promise. And you'll have an exclusive. Promise me you'll wait."

He was crestfallen. He was young and wanting to be in the action all the way. I needed to give him a job—something he could do while he was waiting. And hopefully, something that would help.

"Have you got your camera with you? Okay, then here's what I need you to do." I wrote down a series of addresses and passed them to him. "Get good pictures of these places. If you can, get photographs of people coming and going. But make sure you're not seen, okay? It's undercover work, get it?"

He was already out the door, and turned back only for my admonishment.

"And be careful."

I FOLLOWED NICK back into the office, stretched out on the little cot and closed my eyes. "My head's killing me. I don't know how much longer we can take it, Nick. I guess I'm scared, too."

He grabbed my hand and brought it up to his lips. I rested my palm against his cheek. He looked so tired. Tired and worried, probably more worried than he'd admit.

"It's like trying to untangle a bowl of spaghetti—all those separate strands, tied up together, slippery."

"A Gordian knot," he said. "We've got all the threads but we just can't get it untied."

"Maybe we don't have all the threads yet. For example, who broke into Glenn's and what were they looking for?"

"I don't know. Something important enough to risk breaking in when the sheriff had it sealed."

"Do you think they found it?"

He was slow to answer, distracted. I repeated the question. "Doesn't sound like it. I doubt that Sam would let anything slip past him in that apartment. Obviously he knows that Glenn worked for the INS. He's got Navarro hanging around."

"Well, whatever it was, he probably passed it on to Navarro before he died, Nick.... Nick?"

He was staring at the office wall, sitting with his palms up and gesturing, as though he were weighing the points of his argument. "Nick?"

"Unless he had it hidden in a place that no one would think

of, Julia.'' A slow grin spread across his face. He grabbed my hand, pulling me off the cot. ''Come on.''

''Where are we going?''

''You'll see. You won't believe it.''

TWENTY-NINE

JACK HUDDLED behind my feet, peering around my ankles at Nick. Every now and then he yipped. "I think this is upsetting him," I said.

"Why? He never would sleep on the damn thing anyway."

"He used to. You can tell by the smell."

Nick extracted a penknife from his pocket and turned the little plaid cushion over. He looked at Jack. "If I'm wrong about this, I'll eat this cushion." Jack's response was a stiff wag and a growf.

"Look, it's been sewn by hand." Nick held the cushion under the kitchen light for me to see. He was right. The seam had been opened and neatly slip-stitched again. He inserted the point of the knife and picked at the stitches. Once a few were cut, the seam opened easily. He slipped his hand into the top of the cushion, felt around but came out empty-handed. The hand went in again, this time at the back, but emerged empty again.

"I don't believe it. I was so sure." He dropped into a chair and stared at Jack. "You steered me wrong, Jock. I thought that's why you wouldn't sleep on it anymore." Jack yipped, as though reminding him of his earlier promise.

I picked up the cushion and peered inside the casing. It was not a single foam-rubber pillow, as I had imagined, but a thick circle of polyester batting composed of layers. I grabbed the cushion with both hands, pushed them together and twisted. Something crinkled. I smiled.

"I think it's going to be all right, Nick. You won't have to eat it after all." I pushed my hand between the layers of batting, extracted an envelope and dropped it on the table. "Sorry, Jack," I said. "It might have been fun to watch."

It was a business envelope, bearing the initials AN in the upper left corner, followed by an address in Ciudad Juarez, and addressed to Consanza Santos. The top had been neatly slit with a letter opener. Nick pulled the letter out, scanned it and groaned.

"What's the matter?"

"Take a look." He passed it across to me.

"Oh jeez. I could probably translate it, if I had a dictionary. But it might take awhile. It's some kind of schedule, I can tell you that. And some of these names are in English. Look, Nick— here's Auburn, Alabama! And there's Athens, Georgia, and Chapel Hill, North Carolina. They're all college towns, Nick. Just like Delphi. Come on. Let's go see Miss Alma."

Alma Rayburn adjusted her glasses on her nose and sat down at her dining-room table. She shoved a pad across the table to me. "You may want to write this down, Julia.

"It begins by saying, 'Here is the schedule for delivery of merchandise for the next six weeks.'" She looked at the top of the paper. "Dated five weeks ago. Now, this is the actual schedule:

September 28, a.m.	Twenty-two articles shipped from Juarez.
September 29, p.m.	Baton Rouge, Louisiana. Five delivered.
September 30, a.m.	Jackson, Mississippi. Three delivered.
September 30, p.m.	Mobile, Alabama. Three delivered.
September 30, p.m.	Auburn, Alabama. One delivered.
October 1, p.m.	Athens, Georgia. Five delivered.
October 2, p.m.	Chapel Hill, North Carolina. Three delivered.

"The remaining two are delivered to Delphi the next day. And the schedule is repeated about every five days. Five days of deliveries, five days off. Do you want me to translate all the dates?"

"Not right now," Nick said. "But I may ask you to do it later."

I made some quick calculations on my pad. If the schedule was repeated as Miss Alma said, six weeks meant approximately five deliveries. And if the deliveries were all twenty or more people, and I was sure that the articles were people, that meant over a hundred illegal aliens had been brought into the United States in the last five and a half weeks. At five hundred dollars per person...I whistled.

Nick nodded. "I thought the same thing. Over fifty thousand

dollars. That's a lot of money—almost ten thousand a week. And remember, Julia, it doesn't end there."

Miss Alma looked down at the letter. "Hmm. The last delivery date on the schedule is the day after tomorrow. Here, in Delphi. And there's a note on the bottom. Look it's written by hand."

The handwriting was scrawling and angular, written in bold black felt-tipped pen. *"Al lobo no le gustan tus amigos."*

"What does it mean?"

"It says, 'The wolf does not like your friends.'"

TAMMY HELD her wrist to her forehead, a dramatic gesture that evoked little sympathy in me. "I just can't go on, Julia. It's a migraine, I just know it."

I might have believed her, had I not seen the ad for a One-Day Sale at a local department store poking out of her purse. But I'd had a headache earlier in the day, and had complained of it in front of Tammy. It was a mistake that gave her an edge. She looked at me from under lowered eyelids.

"Or it may be some kind of a bug. Like you have."

"My head's fine now, Tammy."

"Oh, well.... My mother gets migraines. This feels just like what she describes." She was warming to her subject. "And I can't see! I mean it's closing in, like a tunnel. If I don't go now, I won't be able to drive!" Her voice was rising to an hysterical pitch. A few customers lingered over afternoon coffee and stared. Trust Tammy to play her little drama to an audience. Rhonda intervened.

"Let her go. I'll bus her tables."

There wasn't really all that much to do—a couple of tables on A, one on B. We gathered up the dishes and wiped down the tables quickly. One of the customers had left a copy of the *Sun* on his table. Preoccupied with the schedule Miss Alma had translated, I pitched the paper into the trash, turned around and retrieved it. The front-page headline plunged straight to my heart. UNIDENTIFIED MAN FOUND STABBED NEAR THE CALLOWAY.

I didn't have to read the article. I already knew, but I forced myself to wade through the text.

The body of an unidentified male was found late last night
in the woods near the Calloway River. A young couple, who
wish to remain anonymous, were parked at one of Delphi's
more popular scenic points along the river when, the young
man said, they decided to take a walk. They stumbled on the
body in the woods near the river's edge. Police describe the
victim as slender, having dark curly hair and an olive complexion. He was carrying no identification. He was stabbed
in the chest with a large carving knife which was found
nearby in the woods. The Sheriff's Department has announced that the body will be sent to the state crime lab for
a full autopsy and they will pursue every avenue to identify
the remains.

Poor Tomás. I took the paper back to the kitchen to show Nick
the story. The set of his jaw and curving frown of his brows told
me he was worried.

"Things are getting hot now. That's two murders. It won't be
long before Sam connects Tomás to Glenn. Maybe he already
has. Navarro may be watching the safe house. If he is, he's seen
Spiro—who works for us. So now we're connected to two murders instead of just one."

The phone shrilled. I darted across the kitchen, but found
Rhonda had reached it before me. In a minute she was in the
kitchen, Spiro in tow. Her face was the pasty white of cottage
cheese, and nervous fingers plucked at her hair.

"Julia, that was Sam. Sheriff Taylor's back in town."

"Yeah?"

She glanced around the kitchen, lowered her voice. "He called
to tell me to leave. It seems…I mean, I guess…Taylor's gone for
an arrest warrant. They're coming for Nick."

"For Nick? Why?"

"You read about the guy they found in the woods? The carving
knife—it was the commercial kind. With Nick's prints on it."

My heart plummeted to my shoes, bounced back up into my
throat. "Oh God, Nick. What are we going to do?"

He was already speaking rapidly to Spiro. I listened for a moment before turning back to Rhonda. "Listen carefully to me. It's

almost Halloween. Nick and I are going to drive out to a farm for pumpkins.''

"Pumpkins?" Her glance said I'd lost my mind.

"We're going to be gone a couple of hours, then we're coming back here to the restaurant with them. A couple of hours, Rhonda. Do you understand?"

She hesitated, nodding her head slowly. "I think so."

"Tell them Spiro clocked out and went home. You're just here finishing up, okay? Try to buy us as much time as you can."

"Right."

I wrapped my arms around her, hugging her tightly. "I know you're putting a lot on the line here for us. I'll never forget it."

She returned my hug, turned on her heel and hurried toward the dining room. Spiro and Nick exchanged keys.

"Enya!"

"Neh, neh. Enya!"

Nick grabbed my hand, guided me out the back door of the restaurant and around to Spiro's Pontiac. It growled to life, lurched, and bobbed out of the parking lot, headed toward Muse-wood. We parked several blocks from the house, darting through neighbor's yards, over fences and through hedges. The driveway and street were empty when we reached the house.

"They'll send at least one car here. If Taylor's gone for the warrant already, we don't have much time." Nick glanced at his watch, then the clear October sky overhead. "Several hours until dark. Hurry up, let's get moving."

I HAD COME TO THINK of them as our breaking-and-entering clothes. I jerked the turtleneck over my head and thought only a minute before pulling on the black knitted cap that Nick insisted I wear.

He had changed his mind, deciding to go alone on this one. For the first time, I thought he would leave me at home. But I was determined, more than ever, that whatever we got ourselves into, we would do it together. And we'd fight them any way we could.

Six years of marriage, even in today's world, is no great record. But I take the vows pretty seriously. I mean, we were married twice after all, once in a traditional ceremony here and a second time, an Orthodox "blessing" in Greece. The vows were different. In America we made the commitments to each other: richer or poorer, better or worse. In Greece we were crowned with the *stefana,* the flowered wreaths joined by a ribbon that signify the inevitable union of two lives, two spirits joined by God, intertwined and never ending. They hang behind glass in a shadowbox on our bedroom wall.

"Okay, the tools are in the car. Are you ready to..."

I was holding the crowns, fingering the seed pearls and silk *stefanotis.* I could still catch the faint smell of incense that clung to the flowers. Nick's voice was gentle.

"Are you sure you want to go, Julia?"

"More than ever," I said, snapping the shadowbox firmly closed. "Have you got everything?"

"Everything but you." He pulled me into his arms.

"You'll always have me," I said.

THIRTY

"WHERE CAN WE HIDE a thing like this?" I gestured at the immaculate interior of the Pontiac. We pulled out of Musewood, skirting Broadway and downtown. "It's so conspicuous—like trying to hide an elephant in a chicken house."

"Well, hopefully they won't expect us to be in Spiro's car, but you're right. We're going to have to get off the road until after dark. When we don't show up in an hour or two, they're going to start looking for us."

"What about Spiro?"

"I told him to get in the car and just drive. Get as far out of Delphi as he could. If they pick him up, they'll take him in for questioning."

"They'll probably arrest him, Nick. As an accessory."

"I warned him. He's prepared for the possibility. But I hope it won't come to that. He's a pretty clever guy. Besides, he doesn't speak English. That should buy us a little time."

I grinned as I thought of a frustrated and perplexed Cal Taylor trying to wrestle information from Spiro. I had to agree with Nick. Spiro was nothing if not resourceful. And totally unpredictable, a fact that would work in his favor.

"All right. Where are we going to hide?"

"I don't know. It needs to be somewhere where an old car doesn't look out of place."

Hide in plain sight. That was the best way. A used-car lot? The bus station? Maybe a junkyard. "Wait, Nick—I've got an idea."

We pulled into the commuter parking lot for students about four blocks from the campus and circled through, looking for a space. "There, next to that old Volkswagen bus." We huddled between the bus and a Dumpster at the end of the lot, scooching down in our seats to await sunset.

"If we don't get the answer tonight, I'm going to have to turn myself in. I can't risk jeopardizing you any further. And we have

to think about Spiro and Rhonda." Nick took my hand and
squeezed it gently. "I wish you'd stayed home," he continued.

"And face Cal Taylor by myself? No way. Nick, I wouldn't
know what was happening to you and I couldn't stand it. I'd go
nuts. Besides, it's part of the vows. Better or worse."

"I know." He squeezed my hand again. "Have you ever re-
gretted them?"

I thought about that. Like most marriages, it hadn't always been
easy, not always happy. But Nick knows me, all my quirks and
foibles, my good and bad moods, the things I love and the ones
that drive me mad. Amazingly, he loves me anyway.

I looked over at him, studying the face and body I know as
well as my own—the slight strawberry stain on the back of his
neck, and the one in a more intimate place. The ears that stick
out a little too prominently, and the juttingly square jaw that re-
minds me of Jack. The coarseness of his black hair—I could
almost feel it under my fingertips. I love him, too.

"No. Never."

He grinned. "Did you have to take so long to decide?"

The sunlight seemed to go on forever, daylight that would
never end. We stayed low in the seat, quietly talking, making
plans for the evening and carefully reviewing them. Students
came and went, shouldering backpacks, revving up other clunkers
in the lot. Fortunately, the owner of the bus had a late class or a
commitment that kept him on campus past sunset. When the vapor
lights came on, flooding the lot with orange light, it was time to
move.

"Are you ready?"

I took a deep breath and nodded, watching Nick heave the
Pontiac into gear. We cruised out of the lot, turned left and started
up Broadway. Hiding in plain sight.

"Now SHINE the light right here." He pointed to a spot on the
window frame, slightly below and to the right of the lock. "We're
lucky they're aluminum windows. We'd never get through a
wooden frame."

I did as I was told, watching as Nick cranked the hand drill at
an angle through the light metal frame. We both wore plastic salad

gloves, a smart precaution but clumsy for the kind of work he was doing.

"You're sure there's no alarm?" I whispered.

Nick looked over the window again. "No wires, no sensors. We're going to have to take our chances, but we have to move fast. Remember what we decided—you take the office and I'll take the warehouse." He'd finished the drilling. "Hand me that skewer."

It was stainless steel, about nine inches long and a little wider than a large needle. We occasionally used them for souvlaki at the cafe. I watched as he inserted it through the hole he had drilled. It was not an easy task. It was the type of lock that swings under a metal lip—the type we have on the windows on our home, a disquieting thought as I watched Nick apply gentle pressure to it.

"We're in," he said, raising the window. "Now, we've got to move it."

Nick helped me through the window, then crossed quickly to the office door, gave the warehouse a quick visual check and was gone before I'd even oriented myself. I was in the outer office. I swiveled my flashlight across the room—copy machine and fax on the right, filing cabinets dead ahead. A metal desk took up the left corner of the room. The door to the inner office was directly behind it.

The secretary must have beat a hot retreat at five o'clock. Her desk was scattered with stacks of paper, catalogues, and dirty Styrofoam cups. I hoped she did a better job of keeping her files than she did her desk. I knew what I was looking for, knew how I would organize it, but there's no accounting for filing systems. They're as individual as the people who set them up.

To my relief, the cabinets were not locked. I'd not solved the knotty problem of how to spring them, had hoped to find a key in a desk drawer, but one look at her desk had dissolved all hope of that. I pulled open the top drawer, delighted to find that Ms. What's-'er-name was substantially more organized in the records department. Her standing files included a green suspended folder called "Accounts Receivable." I pulled it out, quickly thumbed it and set it on top of the cabinet. Behind it, a second file was labeled "Active Sales Leads." It was a thin folder containing nothing more than a handwritten list of names and addresses. But I knew the handwriting, had seen it before on the bottom of stacks of loan papers. I set that file with the others. The remainder of the top drawer contained operating licenses, permits, accounts payable. Nothing of interest to me. It was in the second drawer that I hit pay dirt.

The folder was marked "Wire Transfers." At first, I didn't know what it was, skimmed it, and stuck it back in the drawer, making for the copy machine with the other files. I put the documents into the automatic feeder, watching them shoot through the machine with precision. But my mind was still occupied with the file that remained in the cabinet.

The letterhead read "Aparatos Norteamericanos," followed by a Juarez address. RE: EQUIPMENT PURCHASES, it said. The letter that followed was a form letter, directing a wire transfer of money to an account number in SafeBank, Delphi branch. The dates, amounts of money, numbers and descriptions of equipment varied, but the form remained the same, clearly computer-generated. At the bottom of each letter, a series of numbers gave date and station number, indicating that the letter had been faxed. An idea was forming in my mind.

"Have you got what we need?"

"Almost." I led Nick to the filing cabinet. "Look. What do you make of this?"

Nick sifted through the letters and handed them back to me. "Copy them. We'll talk about it later."

"Okay. What did you find?"

"Specifically, not much. There's a lot of equipment out there. Looks like they're ready to ship it. A lot of it's crated to go to Mexico. A couple of them were still open—a small cooler and an ice machine. They've got no compressors in them."

I gathered up the copies I'd made and replaced the file folders, then started copying the wire transfers. "So what does that mean?"

"I don't know. Who'd want an ice machine without a compressor? It doesn't make sense." He paced up and down in front of the fax machine, snagged a piece of paper off the feeder and rolled it up, tapping his chin. "There's something here," he said. "Something I'm missing."

"What's that?" I pointed to the rolled sheet in his hand. He looked as though he had forgotten about it.

"I don't know," he said, unrolling it. "It's a letter... Oh shit! Hurry and finish that up. I'll be right back."

By the time he returned, I had all the folders put away, the copies in a large, flat totebag I'd brought, and the skewer and drill nestled in the bottom. I checked the windowsill for metal filings and swept it clean with my glove. Nick shot the letter through the copy machine, kept the original, and dropped the copy back on the fax.

"Let's go." He grabbed the bag and helped me into the window frame.

"Nick, the door!" We'd left the office door standing open. It wouldn't do. Everything had to be left as it was. He strode across the office, and had nearly closed it when he stopped and dropped to his knees.

"Come on," I hissed. "Let's get out of here!" I slid to the ground below, with Nick bolting after me.

"Hurry up. Give me the hook!"

I produced a thin metal crochet hook. He made the hole the first time, snapped the lock back into place, grabbed my hand and dragged me toward the Pontiac. We shot out the driveway and onto Broadway at breathtaking speed. Traffic was heavy. It was a relief to slip into anonymity.

"We've got trouble," he said.

"What do you mean?"

"No alarm on the windows; but the office—it had a carpet trap at the door. Somewhere out there a silent alarm is ringing. Loud and clear."

I was feeling pretty good. "But we didn't get caught. It's probably not working. You know, sometimes people string wires around, just to make it look like they've got an alarm. It's like the decals they put on their windows."

"Julia, if he were going to do that, he would have put them on the windows. But maybe you're right. Maybe it wasn't working. Or maybe they forgot to arm it tonight. Anyway, at least no cops showed up.''

I snuggled back into the seat of the Pontiac, starting to enjoy our criminal activities, feeling the rush, the power of taking the law into my own hands. After all, I'd already been to jail—wait, make that "the joint." In fact, I was getting downright streetwise. We'd pulled off this caper and made a pretty thorough job of it.

"What was that letter on the fax machine, anyway?"

Nick laughed. "It's to a customs broker in Mexico, directing him to fill out the claim forms for the equipment he's shipping. The ice machine and cooler were on the list. That's why I went back to the warehouse. To check the serial numbers. He's got them valued as if they were new equipment, but they've got no compressors in them."

"Why would he do that? It doesn't make sense. Won't he have to pay more duty on them?"

"Sure. But nobody will question it, either."

"But what do you think he's going to do with the equipment? Drugs! Nick, I'll bet he's shipping drugs where the compressor's supposed to be."

WE TURNED into the driveway of the restaurant and parked in the rear. "Shipping drugs into Mexico? Julia, really. What's that expression about coals?"

"Coals to Newcastle. Yeah, I guess you're right."

"No, it's not drugs. It's people he's shipping. I'm going to put these in the safe. Then I think it's time to call Sam." I left him in the office, went through the kitchen and into the dining room, flipping on the light along the way. It wouldn't matter now. We had what we needed. Sam and Taylor would be a welcome sight.

"...po, po, po Maria, s'agapo."

I fumbled under the cabinet looking for a Yanni tape. His music never fails to lift my spirits. With its haunting Greek undertones, it seems written especially for us.

The pounding startled me. They'd wasted no time. Sam must have left someone to watch the cafe. I glanced back in the kitchen. The office door was open.

"Nick, there's somebody at the door," I called, swallowed hard and prepared to meet Cal Taylor, probably at gunpoint.

"Wait, Julia. I'll be right there."

It wasn't the first time I'd failed to heed his advice. It probably won't be the last.

"Find out who it is before you open the door." Nick halted mid-stride next to the register.

"Hello, Lee," he said. "What can we do for you?"

THIRTY-ONE

"THINKING of becoming mimes?"

"What?"

"Your clothes. The two of you are dressed up like a pair of mimes."

Nick glanced at our clothes. "Oh, these? Halloween party. We're going as cat burglars."

Lee seemed to find this inordinately funny. "How very appropriate," he said.

"What do you mean?"

He casually ambled away from the register and sat down at the family table, his hands folded in his lap. In the background, a bouzouki and a clarinet poured out a haunting song.

"I went to bed early tonight. There I was, enjoying a peaceful sleep when something startled me right out of the bed. What do you think it was?"

"Hmm. I don't know," I said. "Telephone?"

"Nope. Worse. It was my alarm system. The one I've got hooked up at the warehouse. It's a silent alarm, you see."

"Really?" Nick looked very concerned. "Did you check the warehouse?"

Lee laughed. "Didn't have to. You see, I was just coming down Broadway when I saw a car, a big old thing, tear out of my driveway. It looked familiar, so I just followed it. And where do you think it led me?"

Silence. I caught my breath, stared at the pistol he had trained on me. Nick casually took my arm and pulled me away from the register, stepping in to take my place.

"Never mind," Lee continued. "I think we all know the answer to that."

A pulse was pounding in my brain. My chest was tight. I nearly soared through the roof when the music changed.

"Maria me ta kitrina, pion agapas kalitera..." A bright, happy song, so loud it rattled the windows. Lee pointed the gun at Nick.

"Turn that damn thing off."

Nick frowned. This, I thought, was no time to worry about the controls.

"I said, turn it off." He did so, fumbling with the switches, extracting the tape. He laid it on the counter.

"There. Satisfied?"

Lee smiled. "Almost."

"Lee," I said, as artfully as I could, "why are you pointing a gun at us?"

His eyes were clear and their startling color seemed to shimmer under the house lights. The eyes that I had thought of as other-worldly had turned cold and cruel. The features were still placid, the smile almost pretty. "Because you're in my way."

"In your way? I don't understand."

He flushed, angry. "I don't like stupidity in a woman, Julia. Especially not in a white woman."

Nick hastily jumped in. "All right. So we do understand. But there are a few points I'd like to clear up."

"Fire away." I didn't particularly enjoy the play on words, but Nick's lips twitched in a half-smile.

"Well, let me lay it out for you the way I see it," Nick said. "Feel free to correct me—jump in anywhere."

"Go on."

"Let's say I own a bakery—Grandma Lambros' Baklava and Fine Pastries. Well, I'm barely breaking even. My equipment's in bad shape and my labor's real high. I've got to modernize, expand, but I don't have much working capital, and I'm pretty heavily mortgaged. How am I going to do it?"

"I don't know. Thorny problem, isn't it?"

"Maybe. But then I hear about this bank—right here in Delphi. The president, Morgan Fox that is, he likes the small business-man. Wants to see him make good. So, I go to him with my profit-and-loss statement and hat in my hands, looking for a loan. How am I doing?"

"Sounds about right to me. What else could you do but shut down?"

"Good point. So I talk to banker Fox about it, and he goes over my P and L. Well, Mr. Lambros, to begin with, your business is too labor-intensive. All those people you need to brush butter on those phyllo leaves. You'll never make it like that."

Nick shrugged his shoulders, held his hands out in supplication. "Well, I say, what can I do about it? They don't make a machine to butter phyllo.

"'You're sure about that?' asks the banker. Well, I say, 'Pretty sure.'"

Nick stroked his chin. He was really getting into this monologue. "Hmm. Let me put you in touch with a friend of mine. He owns a used-equipment company and he's an expert in controlling labor costs. Man by the name of Leland Blaine. You've heard of his company—Blaine Diversified. In fact, I'll call him for you myself. We'll get this thing worked out.

"That's where you come in. We meet, and I explain my problems to you. Perhaps you'll tell me how you handle it."

Lee grinned. "Sure. Why not?" He was enjoying the game as much as Nick. I alone seemed to find it bizarre. "I might suggest to you that we check out what equipment's available out there. You'll want a new, bigger oven—probably two; convection, of course. And you've got to have coolers, smallwares. Raise your productivity level—more baklava per hour."

"Right. But how am I going to handle the labor problem?"

"Well, that's a little more difficult. You pay a lot out in Social Security?"

Nick nodded. "And benefits. Insurance is skyrocketing."

"Don't I know it!" Blaine said. "Maybe you need to hire people who don't expect benefits—and none of this union shit, either. Maybe squeeze more hours of work out of them, too."

Nick shook his head. "Can't pay overtime. No way."

"No. But there are people out there dying for work." The irony of that statement was not lost on any of us. Lee grinned and went on. "There are people willing to come to work for you without overtime, no benefits, and they'll work for half what you're paying your present employees."

"No way!"

Blaine nodded. "Oh yes, I have a way. But you'll have to come up with an initial investment. These people have travel and relocating expenses."

"How much?"

"Fifteen hundred dollars per person."

Nick blanched. "I can't pay that! What do I get in return?"

"You've got to think of it as an investment, Mr. Lambros. And with it, you'll get my personal guarantee that each and every worker will stay on the job a minimum of five years. What do you think about that?"

Nick strolled over to the family table, apparently deep in thought. Lee kept the gun trained at his chest. "Sounds good, but I don't know where I'll find the money for the initial investment."

"Not really a problem. With our understanding, SafeBank is sure to let you have that loan."

"And, of course, banker Fox will get a cut of the investment."

Lee shook his head. "Let's not impugn the banker's integrity! I prefer to think of it as a finder's fee. It's a one-time payment, for putting me in touch with a new customer. Of course, more loans and depositors—you do understand that you would have to move your account to SafeBank? Good. As I was saying, more depositors can only add to Mr. Fox's already sterling reputation as a go-getter."

"Sterling reputation," I repeated.

Nick leaned toward Lee. "All right. Now the question is, where will these workers come from, and how will they get here? There's plenty of cheap labor to be had in Mexico."

"Unquestionably."

"But crossing isn't easy. And let's face it—I don't want farm workers. You've guaranteed me that they'll stay five years."

"Right. They have to be carefully screened. But there's an...employment agent in Mexico who specializes in this kind of thing."

"Still, you've got to get them across the border. And the cheapest way is to move a lot of them at one time. But you can't take any risks—it's all got to look legit. How are you going to do that?"

Blaine waved the gun at him. "You tell me."

"Well, suppose you set up this dummy company—say an equipment company—in Mexico. We'll call it Aparatos Norteamericanos. That means 'North American Equipment.'"

Lee patted his pockets and pulled out a cigarette pack. Kool Kings. It was Lee who had been in Morgan's car, of course. Not that it mattered anymore. He stuck a cigarette in his mouth and flicked his Bic. "Good name."

"Say they buy equipment from a similar company in the U.S. The equipment's not in great shape, maybe the cooler has no compressor, but it doesn't really matter anyway. The equipment comes in regularly on a big semi. People at the border are used to seeing it come and go about every ten days or so. It comes in loaded with equipment, and it always goes back empty. But is it really an empty truck? I don't think so."

"Why not?"

"Because it's specially built with a false back panel and a set of deep shelves—wide enough for two people each, lying down just long enough to get across the border, and stacked up to carry maybe twenty people at a time."

"Possibly even more. Some people don't mind a little crowding to get them closer to their dream. Hell no, it's not empty. But it doesn't look empty, either. You're forgetting about weight, my friend. Gotta account for that extra weight. So we load it up with junker car parts and electrics, with the heaviest parts removed, of course, and haul it back into the U.S." Lee shrugged. "But it's all in pursuit of the American dream."

Nick sighed sadly. "Yeah. Some dream. But to get back to business, the employment agent charges a fee—around five hundred dollars per person to cross, and another five hundred when he starts his job. Is that about right?"

"Usually."

"The money goes into the account of Aparatos Norteamericanos, and is wired back out to the American company. It looks like payment for the equipment."

"You missed a step."

"What?"

"How do you account for the money going into the AN account in the Mexican bank in the first place?"

"Hmm. That's a good question."

Lee crossed his legs and leaned back in the chair. But the gun never wavered. "It's simple, really. You sell the equipment to businessmen in Mexico. They won't pay much for broken equipment, but you don't really care anyway, as long as you break even on the cost. And the businessman loves it. You give him an inflated bill of sale that he can show on his profit-and-loss statement and it comes out of his expenses—nontaxable."

Nick laughed. "I suppose it works the same way here, doesn't it?"

"You got it. My clients love it. Absolutely nobody loses."

"'To make the worse appear the better cause.'"

"What?"

Nick shook his head sadly. "They accused Socrates of it—promoting evil by making it seem good. In his case, it wasn't true. But in yours... Well, nobody loses except the laborers. And they lose big."

Lee's face darkened. "Hell, they're barely human beings anyway. You ever been around some of these Mexicans? They drink, beat their women. Animals."

Ramón and Elena 'animals'? Didn't Nick see how dangerous he was? But the game went on.

"Well," Nick said. "Now they're across the border. But they've got to stay somewhere—at least until they get papers and start their jobs.... Hey! I've got it! Why not try to pass them off as foreign students? People move in and out of college towns all the time. Who'll even notice?"

"If you do it right, and they cooperate, no one."

"Except maybe the cops. In our case, the sheriff. So you've got to brush a few more palms with pesos."

Lee shrugged. "Just one. But I've known Cal a long time. We're old friends. He doesn't charge much."

"And you can always find somebody who wants to make a little money helping out foreign students. Somebody like Connie Santos—a rental agent for a slumlord."

"Not just one. Connie's got connections all over the South. Smart girl, Connie. Until she got mixed up with our buddy Bohannon."

"I'm coming to that," Nick said. "So Connie moves these people in, gets them forged papers and moves them on to their jobs. It's all done very quietly—you send a couple to this factory, a couple to that bakery. That way no one notices this sudden, big influx of Mexicans. Gradually they just take over all the jobs. And of course Connie splits the rent they pay, which, I might add, is exorbitant, with the landlord. In this case, Read."

"Not exactly. Some of it goes back to the employment agent. He's got to be paid. And some of it comes to me."

"Yes. To you. 'The wolf.'"

Lee laughed out loud. "You like that name? I like to think of myself as a wolf in sheep's clothing."

"There are a lot of people to be paid in this little scheme. And a lot of mouths that have to be kept shut."

"Oh no," Lee said. "Not really. Connie doesn't know me— only the coyote. And she doesn't know about Morgan. And Read..." Lee laughed again. "He doesn't know about anyone. Nor does he want to."

"But there's still an Achilles' heel in the system, isn't there? Connie is a very sensuous woman." Nick could have left that out, as far as I was concerned. "And women like that aren't going to be celibate—not a woman like Connie. So she takes a lover. Whoops, bad luck for her. He just happens to be an undercover agent for the INS. He's probably already got her made."

"I'm afraid so." I could almost believe the sadness in Lee's voice. "And you know, I really liked Glenn Bohannon. I could've helped him a lot with his business."

"So Glenn is on to Connie, and he's sleeping with her. Probably has access to her house, her mail. And when her instructions come in, in a letter from Aparatos Norteamericanos, he sees her reading them—maybe marking her calendar. So he waits for his first opportunity, and he steals them.''

''That stupid, stupid woman.'' Lee's voice was frosty, his eyes even colder. ''Get this. Bohannon's gone to Cal, see, to tell him who he is and that he's got this investigation going on. Cal, being my friend, well, naturally he calls me. Well, lo and behold, who's Santos sleeping with? Same guy! She calls the coyote all in a lather and tells him the whole story. I add it up, two plus two, she's sleeping with the goddamned INS!

''I really don't like to get involved in this kind of thing, but what choice did I have? Now, the coyote tells me about this nut they grow there in Mexico. And it tastes real good, he says. So he sends some back with the next shipment.''

''And you grind it up, put it in a little shaker and bring it into my kitchen.'' Nick's face was hard, a Greek mask of tragedy. His voice bit into the charged air. ''You framed us for murder—Julia, that is. How could you do that?''

Lee shook his head and looked at me. ''Hated to do it to you, Julia. I just didn't have a choice. You see that, don't you?''

''Yeah,'' Nick spat. ''We see. Just didn't have a choice about Tomás, either.''

''He got in my way—asked too many questions. And Ms. Santos couldn't seem to control him. My driver Buddy saw him in a bar, talking to Bohannon. That's when I knew I had to get rid of him, too.''

''So, you stole my carving knife, with my fingerprints on it. How'd you get hold of it?''

''Simple. The day Julia was arrested I came by for a cup of coffee. You called that cook of yours while I was here. It must have been pretty urgent, 'cause he went tearing out of here and left poor little old Tammy to close all by herself.''

''So you—''

''Waited till she went into the ladies' room, slipped into the kitchen and grabbed the knife. With a napkin, of course. I left before she came out. Oh, don't worry. I left the money for the coffee on the table.''

"So you used the knife on Tomás."

"And bingo! They've got your prints."

"Just like you framed Julia for Glenn's murder."

"Why not? It worked the first time, didn't it? But the killing's almost done now."

Lee stood up and gestured with the gun for Nick to do likewise. "This has been very entertaining. But I think it's time to draw the whole episode to a close. Let's go into the kitchen, shall we?"

THIRTY-TWO

LEE PUSHED ME roughly ahead of him, through the wait-station door, past the grill and into the kitchen. "So who are you going to pin this one on?"

"Oh, it'll be an accident." He twisted my arm behind my back and gently laid the muzzle of the gun against my temple. "You got some tools, Nick?"

"Of course."

"Then go get them. And remember, I've got Julia."

Nick ran back to dry storage, returning in a second with his toolbox. "You can let her go now, Lee."

He jerked up on my arm, forcing me to cry out in pain. "Push the wine cooler away from the wall." Nick did as he was told. "Now, unscrew the back of it. Take the whole thing off."

I felt the pressure ease from my arm as he watched Nick work on the cooler. We were standing with our backs to the grill and wait-station door. Perhaps if I could spin around and head for the door, he wouldn't have time to aim.... How long would it take to dial 911?

"Okay, that's good." Lee walked me over to stand next to Nick, nudged him up against the wall and carefully placed the gun on Nick's temple. "Now, Julia, you get a bucket of water."

"What are you going to do, Lee?"

"You'll see. Accidents are one of my specialties."

I found Otis's mop and bucket and filled it in the food sink, dawdling to give Nick time to think of a way out. I was beyond thought, choked with fear and anger.

"That's enough. I said, that's enough. Bring it over here," Lee ordered.

Maybe I could throw the bucket at him. But the bucket was heavy and would take a second to heave, and a finger on a trigger was too quick. If Nick was going to die, he wasn't going without me. We went into this together, and we'd go out together—married, circles intertwined and never ending. Like the *stefana*.

"Pour it onto the floor, Julia." I got as close to the floor drain as I could.

"Not over there," he shouted angrily. "Right here. All around the cooler. That's right. Just like that."

He shoved Nick over next to me, next to the cooler and smack into the puddle of water. "You know," he said, "you really shouldn't work on electrical equipment unless you know something about it. Water and electricity are a lethal combination."

He leaned over, careful to avoid the water on the tile himself, and jerked the wiring from the back of the cooler. It soughed, sighed, and the compressor shut down. The kitchen was ominously silent, but for the crackling and popping of the live wires he held in his hand.

His smile was macabre—those eyes so peaceful, as though there was nothing wrong with what he was doing. I was riveted and almost didn't notice the quiet movement behind Lee as Spiro came through the wait-station door, stopped, then carefully laid a string of garlic on the steel table. But Nick had seen him too.

"I want to say a prayer first, Lee. Will you let me do that?"

Confusion flickered in his eyes, but only for a second. "What kind of a Christian would I be if I didn't let you say a final prayer? But make it quick."

Nick grabbed my hand, squeezing it gently, and pulled me around him, to the right, next to the wall.

"Hey, stop. What are you doing?"

"It's a tradition in our church, Lee," Nick lied. "The woman stands on the right."

"Okay," he said grudgingly. "But you just lost yourself a little prayer time."

We bowed our heads slightly, just low enough to appear to be praying, but high enough to be aware of peripheral movement. Spiro was coming toward us, moving on cat's paws like a panther, his big hands at the ready. Nick's voice echoed through the kitchen.

"Piase to pistoli, kai ego tha piaso to kalodio. Kai Julia, jerko sto pluggo. Sto tria." We lifted our hands to bless ourselves, fingers to forehead—*"Ena"*—to breast—*"Thio"*—and to shoulder—*"Tria!"* And we lunged.

Spiro's knee went to the small of Lee's back, left arm around his neck, the right flying up under the gun hand. The pistol cracked, sending a shower of plaster down on our heads even as Nick dove for the wires. I spun, slid in the water, falling against the wall. My fingers clawed the tile, slipped and clawed until finally I had the plug in my grasp. I jerked it and turned, just in time to see Nick land in the water, the loose wires high above his head.

Lee rolled on the floor, moaning in pain. "Oh God, I think he's broken my back. That big lummox of yours, he's broken my back."

Spiro grinned, passed the gun to Nick, and loped back into the grill. In a second he was back, dangling the string of garlic from his fingers. He pointed to Lee.

"Ithes? No garlic?" He shook his head. "Bad luck."

Sirens screamed into the parking lot. Taylor was the first into the kitchen, his gun trained directly at Nick's chest. He was followed by Jimmy and his red-haired partner. Sam lumbered in behind. His face was flushed. He pulled a pistol from under his jacket and pointed it at Spiro.

"Been chasing him for half an hour."

Spiro grinned and tipped his hat at Sam. "Hi. Fine."

"Wait, Sam. It's Lee you want. He's confessed the whole thing."

"Bullshit!" A moan came up from the kitchen floor. "They called...called me to come in..."

"And Sheriff Taylor's part of the scheme, too. He's on the take."

"How dare you!"

"I've got it all on tape, Taylor." Nick jerked his head. "Right out there, by the register." The tall, dark shadow of Navarro lingered in the wait-station door. "Agent Navarro, would you get the tape out of the sound system, please?"

He returned in a moment, holding the tape carefully between his thumb and index finger. "This it?"

"You don't believe him, do you, Navarro?"

The agent's voice was icy. "Sheriff Taylor, why didn't your investigator know that Glenn Bohannon worked for me? Glenn told me himself that he reported to you. But when Sam here contacted me, he said you never told him. If it hadn't been for finding Glenn's badge, he wouldn't have known."

"He's lying. Sam knew all about it."

Sam opened his mouth, looked from Spiro to Cal, turned, and silently pointed the gun at his superior. Jimmy's mustache twitched. He glanced at his partner and nervously fingered the legs of his pants. Taylor backed up toward the wait-station door.

"It's a lie."

A shrill scream from Lee. Spiro's foot rested on his shoulder. *"Alethia,"* he said. "Truth."

"He knew. Cal knew. I paid him to keep his mouth shut. About everything." He rolled and moaned. "Oh God, help me, please. He knew..." His eyes rolled back before he passed out.

Taylor spun, dropping his head to charge through the wait-station door. He didn't count on Navarro, who simply swiveled, stuck out his foot and tripped him. The sheriff's gun skidded across the floor as Sam heaved himself over Taylor's prostrate body to block the exit. Nick grabbed the gun, pointed it at the sheriff, and tossed the other one to me. I'd never held a pistol before. It seemed so heavy. I didn't know if I could use it, but if it meant protecting Nick, I was willing to die trying. I trained it on the group of them, still not sure of friend or foe.

I held my breath and waited, knowing what must be spinning through Nick's mind. He clasped his gun with both hands, sighted down the barrel and smiled. "You thought we'd run. You did everything you could to make us run away. I wouldn't have my green card. Julia would be a fugitive, charged with murder, all the evidence pointing right at us. A conspiracy. And when you caught up with us... A pair of murderers on the run, shot by a law enforcement officer in self-defense. Line of duty. Case closed."

Nick released the safety on the gun. "Jimmy's limping. Why is that, Jimmy?" The deputy took a step backward, straight into the barrel of Navarro's gun. Navarro reached around and relieved him of his weapon. Spiro silently edged around the room behind the red-haired deputy.

"Because my dog bit you, eh? When you attacked my wife."

"No! No, I—"

"And how about your partner here? He's pretty quiet, isn't he? Doesn't talk much?" Nick grinned. "Or maybe he can't."

"You son of a bitch," his partner hissed. "You did this to me."

"And you threatened my wife with your filthy pictures, and tried to beat the hell out of me. Was it on Taylor's orders?"

Spiro slipped his left arm around the redhead's neck, squeezing until his face blended with his hair and, under Spiro's strong fingers, the weapon slipped from his hand. Navarro nudged Jimmy with the gun.

"Sheriff Taylor," Jimmy said. "He said we were just gonna scare you into admitting you killed Bohannon."

"And he left town so nobody would associate him with the attacks. Just in case we reported it to Sam, in case you got caught, he'd claim you were acting on your own. Hell, he wasn't even there when it happened! You'd take the fall for it, Jimmy. You and your slimy partner here."

Jimmy glared at Taylor, the truth of it all dawning in his cold eyes. "But I was just acting under orders. Sheriff Taylor, tell him! I was under orders!"

Taylor whined, crawled on his belly and tried to pull himself up on Sam's pant legs. Nick followed him with the gun. He aimed.

"I ought to shoot you," he said. "I ought to put a bullet in you for every hardworking immigrant you've terrorized. And one for every illegal you, and your buddy here, have extorted. Yep, I ought to shoot you. In fact, I think I will."

I held my breath as he took a step forward. Taylor shrieked and clawed at Sam. Navarro watched Nick from behind shrewd eyes but made no move to stop him. Nick stepped toward him again, raised the gun and clenched his teeth.

"Bang," he said.

THE BLUE LIGHTS cast spinning shadows through the dining-room windows, rather like an exotic dancehall, I thought. The ambulance tore out, gravel clattering against the windows, just as it had the morning Glenn died. This time it carried Lee. I poured four cups of fresh coffee and set them out on the family table.

"It's all on here, Sam. Every word." Nick pushed the cassette tape across the table. "And the rest of the evidence is still locked up in my safe. I'll get it for you before you leave."

Sam Lawless was quiet.

"I guess you're going to tell me we shouldn't have taken this into our own hands. But there were people to protect, Sam. Morgan's wife. His brother-in-law. We couldn't risk their lives."

Still, Sam said nothing.

"You see," I chimed in, "we had proof of lots of crime, but still nothing to link with the murderer."

He lifted an eyebrow.

"Okay, I guess you're going to charge us with something. You might as well get on with it. I'll call Warren." I headed for the phone.

"I could, you know. I could charge you with obstructing justice, breaking and entering, and probably a half dozen other crimes." He grinned. "But I won't. I may live to regret it. The attorney for the defense may chew me up and spit me out on the witness stand, but I'm not going to charge you with anything. In fact, far as I know, you've got no documents. But that tape should buy me a couple of search warrants. The truth is, I was trying to figure out how to apologize."

"Then you really did believe we killed Glenn?" Nick's face was a mask of astonishment.

"Well, maybe just a little. But after I talked to Navarro and found out Bohannon was INS and Taylor had known it for a while, and your green card was okay—well, it just didn't add up. What was the motive? Competition? You wouldn't have helped

Bohannon if you'd felt that way. Besides, it didn't make sense that you'd kill him in your own restaurant.

"And another thing, why was Taylor after your hide? He wouldn't hardly let me even interview the Buffaloes." He stopped and grinned before he went on. "Kept pushing me to arrest you and close the case." Sam stopped, took a sip of his coffee.

"I don't like to be pushed."

I SAT in the circular drive and stared at the front of Northridge Convalescent Center, loath to pass through the electric doors. I couldn't say why, exactly, except that I had the nagging feeling that Nick and I had undermined a marriage and a family. The faces of the children—Bradley, Corrinne, and Todd Fox as they had looked in their school pictures—swam in front of my eyes.

But Bobby had the right to know that we had entered his home and found the loan papers, that his brother-in-law had been arrested, and that Sam would probably be coming to question him. I forced myself to climb out of the Honda and walk slowly into the building. At the sign-in desk, my request was met with some confusion, requiring a consultation with a superior and, apparently, a call to the nurses' desk on Bobby's wing. I supposed that since Morgan was no longer calling the plays, the chain of command was muddled. Eventually I was allowed to sign in and go to Bobby's room.

Northridge had not changed. It was still smug and self-satisfied, populated in the main by patients whose needs seemed capricious at best. Perhaps the discovery of how rampant human exploitation was in Delphi had heightened my sense of the absurd. I was still thinking about it all when I entered Bobby's room.

He was sitting in his wheelchair near the window again, just as I had seen him before. But this time he was dressed in street clothes and when he turned, his face cracked into a drooping smile.

"J-j-ul-ulia," he said. That he remembered my name, and could summon it so quickly, was an excellent sign.

"Hello, Bob—" I stopped in the door. Dina stood with her back to me, bending over the bed to pack a stack of folded clothes in an open suitcase. At the sound of my voice, she stood up straight, but did not immediately turn around.

"Oh. I'm sorry..." I stumbled. Bobby waved his hand, as if to say it was all right.

"G-g-go home. No! Go-o-ing home. Now."

"You're leaving Northridge?"

He nodded as Dina turned to face me. She smiled, and I hastily searched her face for some sign of anger and recrimination. A tinge of sadness hovered around her smile and her eyes were bounded by deep, dark rings, but there was no sign of malice in them.

"Yes. I'm taking him home to my house. But we'll be moving shortly, probably to the mountain cabin. At least for a while. I won't be able to keep the house, of course."

"Dina, I didn't...I didn't know how deeply he was involved in it all."

"Would it have made a difference, Julia? Be truthful?" I hesitated only a moment.

"No. But I'm sorry anyway."

Dina waved her hand and turned back to her packing. "Don't be. You know what a sham our marriage had become. And the worst of it all, of course, is that he tried to kill Bobby." She walked around the bed and stood behind her brother's wheelchair, her hands on his shoulders. He reached up and patted her gently with his good hand.

"M-morgan change-d," he drawled. "Got l-l-ost."

"Yes," Dina said, staring out the window. "I lost him a long time ago."

I stayed only long enough to set up a time to begin therapy with Bobby. He had a long way to go to complete recovery, but the loving support of his sister promised more than any doctor might have thought possible.

THE BUFFALOES were back up on A deck. Their numbers were smaller, with certain members conspicuously absent, and they were considerably less boisterous. Like a chorus in a Greek tragedy, they told and retold what they knew of the story. Sonny stopped me as I made the rounds with the coffeepot.

"They're my friends, you know. I can hardly believe they did all that. But maybe they did—that'll be up to a jury to decide. You and Nick did the right thing, Julia."

"I know we did, Sonny. But thanks for saying it. It helps to know there are friends behind us."

His eyes gleamed. "Now, you're gonna sit down here and tell us the whole story, aren't you?"

I glanced out into the parking lot. Warren was alighting from his Jeep. He looked tired. He'd had five full days with his clients, handling arraignments and trying to post bond. Warren had some decisions to make. He couldn't handle all their cases. They were turning on each other like a pack of starved wolves, each angling for a plea bargain, turning state's evidence against the others. And all the indictments were not yet in—there were the employers of aliens still to be rounded up. It seemed doubtful that the Delphi incarceration facilities would even hold them all.

Lee was in the hospital under heavy guard while Morgan and Read warmed cots in the county jail. Sheriff Taylor, Jimmy, and his partner, were several cell blocks down from them, isolated from the other prisoners. I had to hand it to Sam. He moved quickly. Bail for the six was denied.

They picked up Connie Santos as soon as she returned to town. She was riding with Buddy in the semi. Sam's deputy says she was something to behold, in a red silk shirt and jeans. I did not share this information with Nick.

She was charged as an accessory to murder, as well as an assortment of lesser charges relating to her trade in illegal aliens. Buddy's charges were the same. He agreed to turn state's evidence against his boss. There were three illegals in the truck. The INS summarily returned them to their native land.

Tomás, we learned, was working undercover for the Seguridad Nacionale of Mexico, partnered with INS to break a ring of alien smuggling that was hurting both countries. It was the fire in Auburn, Alabama, that had first caught their attention—twenty-five Mexican citizens burned to death in reprisal because some of them had not paid the coyote. It was the ugliest part of a very ugly story. Ramón and Elena identified Tomás' body and returned with it to Mexico. They could not have stayed in the United States, of course, but they didn't seem to want to, anyway. Agent Navarro allowed Spiro and Miss Alma to accompany them to the airport. Their departure was hard on Miss Alma. She had become very fond of this young couple in the last few days. She and Spiro are discussing a vacation in Mexico.

"Here comes Warren," I said. "He can fill you in." I left the coffeepot on the deck and made my way back to the family table, where Nick sat with Billy English. Billy's hand flew across his notebook, a broad grin stretched across his face. The story had been breaking in bits and pieces over the past few days, but no one had been able, as yet, to put it all together. Billy was getting his first exclusive, interviews with Nick and me, and even, after a fashion, with Spiro. He already had the photographs that would accompany a big spread in the *Sun.* He might even get picked up by a wire service. And the *Sun* had asked him to do a series on bigotry in the South. He told me proudly that he had tentatively titled it "Prejudice—How Far Have We Come in Fifty Years?" Billy English was on his way.

"...so I acted like I was praying, but I was really giving Julia and Spiro instructions in Greek—"

"Since when is *'jerko sto pluggo'* Greek?" I said.

Nick laughed. "Well, I had to be sure you understood."

I laid my hand across his cheek. "I always understand you, Nick."

"I hear you got yourself a story, boy." Norm Pearson stood over us, glaring down at Billy. He held a large white box in his hands.

"Yes, sir. Of course, I'll need your advice on it. Can I show you my first draft when I get it finished?"

Norman clapped Billy on the back. "Anytime, my boy. Come to me anytime." He wandered toward A deck.

"Hey, Norm." Tammy pushed her pencil behind her ear and tore a ticket off her pad. "Whatcha got in the box?"

"Hmm? Oh, beignets! New little Cajun cafe opened up right

next door to the *Sun*. Thought we ought to give them a little business." He strode toward the deck. "Hey, fellas. I got beignets for breakfast!"

"Now, I'd like to get the story from Spiro's perspective."

"Yes," I said. "That should be interesting." I went to call him from the kitchen, noting with some pride the new sign above the door. EMPLOYEES ONLY—ABSOLUTELY NO ONE ELSE ADMITTED, it said. I dodged the garlands of garlic flanking the doorway.

"You go on," I said. "I'll fix Tammy's order."

Rhonda slipped a ticket through the window. Sam's diamond flashed on her left ring finger. I watched as she paused a moment, held it under the warming light so it glittered, and smiled to herself. When I returned to the dining room, Spiro's story was cranking out, full throttle, with Nick translating as fast as he could.

"You see, he's from Crete," Nick explained.

"Neh, neh. Apo tin Kriti!" Spiro nodded solemnly, as Billy scratched notes on his pad.

"Hey, Julia!" Mitch was waving an empty coffeepot at me. "How about a little more coffee to go with these French things?"

I grabbed a fresh pot of coffee from the wait-station and a pad of tickets. When I reached the deck, I snagged the box of beignets and handed them to Rhonda.

"Dump them."

I turned back to the Buffaloes, pulled a pen out of my pocket and smiled at their astonished faces.

"Gentlemen, the rules have changed. Coffee is sixty-five cents a cup. Free refills with a meal order only. Now," I said in my sweetest voice. "What can I get y'all for breakfast?"

FREE BOOK OFFER!

Dear Reader,

Thank you for reading this Worldwide Mystery™ title! Please take a few moments to tell us about your reading preferences. When you have finished answering the survey, please mail it to the appropriate address listed below and we'll send you a free mystery novel as a token of our appreciation! Thank you for sharing your opinions!

1. How would you rate this particular mystery book?

   1.1 ❑ Excellent   .4 ❑ Fair

    .2 ❑ Good   .5 ❑ Poor

    .3 ❑ Satisfactory

2. Please indicate your satisfaction with The Mystery Library™ in terms of the editorial content we deliver to you every month:

   2.1 ❑ Very satisfied with editorial choice

    .2 ❑ Somewhat satisfied with editorial choice

    .3 ❑ Somewhat dissatisfied with editorial choice

    .4 ❑ Very dissatisfied with editorial choice

Comments _____

_____(3, 8)

3. What are the most important elements of a mystery fiction book to you?

_____

_____(9, 14)

4. Which of the following types of mystery fiction do you enjoy reading? (check all that apply)

  15 ❑ American Cozy (e.g. Joan Hess)

  16 ❑ British Cozy (e.g. Jill Paton Walsh)

  17 ❑ Noire (e.g. James Ellroy, Loren D. Estleman)

  18 ❑ Hard-boiled (male or female private eye) (e.g. Robert Parker)

  19 ❑ American Police Procedural (e.g. Ed McBain)

  20 ❑ British Police Procedural (e.g. Ian Rankin, P. D. James)

5. Which of the following other types of paperback books have you read in the past 12 months? (check all that apply)

  21 ❑ Espionage/Spy (e.g. Tom Clancy, Robert Ludlum)

  22 ❑ Mainstream Contemporary Fiction (e.g. Patricia Cornwell)

  23 ❑ Occult/Horror (e.g. Stephen King, Anne Rice)

  24 ❑ Popular Women's Fiction (e.g. Danielle Steel, Nora Roberts)

25 ❑ Fantasy (e.g. Terry Brooks)
26 ❑ Science Fiction (e.g. Isaac Asimov)
27 ❑ Series Romance Fiction (e.g. Harlequin Romance®)
28 ❑ Action Adventure paperbacks (e.g. Mack Bolan)
29 ❑ Paperback Biographies
30 ❑ Paperback Humor
31 ❑ Self-help paperbacks

6. How do you usually obtain your mystery paperbacks?
   (check all that apply)
   32 ❑ National chain bookstore (e.g. Waldenbooks, Borders)
   33 ❑ Supermarket
   34 ❑ General or discount merchandise store (e.g. Kmart, Target)
   35 ❑ Specialty mystery bookstore
   36 ❑ Borrow or trade with family members or friends
   37 ❑ By mail
   38 ❑ Secondhand bookstore
   39 ❑ Library
   40 ❑ Other _____(41, 46)

7. How many mystery novels have you read in the past
   6 months?
   Paperback _____ (47, 48)   Hardcover _____ (49, 50)

8. Please indicate your gender:
   51.1 ❑ female   .2 ❑ male

9. Into which of the following age groups do you fall?
   52.1 ❑ Under 18 years   .4 ❑ 35 to 49 years
   .2 ❑ 18 to 24 years   .5 ❑ 50 to 64 years
   .3 ❑ 25 to 34 years   .6 ❑ 65 years or older

*Thank you very much for your cooperation! To receive your free
mystery novel, please print your name and address clearly and
return the survey to the appropriate address listed below.*

Name: _____

Address: _____City: _____

State/Province: _____ Zip/Postal Code: _____

In U.S.: Worldwide Mystery Survey, 3010 Walden Avenue,
P.O. Box 9057, Buffalo, NY 14269-9057
In Canada: Worldwide Mystery Survey, P.O. Box 622,
Fort Erie, Ontario L2A 5X3